THE
SUMMER
I REMEMBERED
EVERYTHING

ALSO BY CATHERINE CON MORSE

The Notes

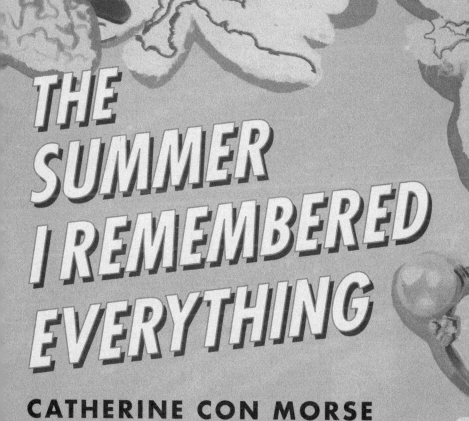

THE SUMMER I REMEMBERED EVERYTHING

CATHERINE CON MORSE

Crown ♛ New York

Crown Books for Young Readers
An imprint of Random House Children's Books
A division of Penguin Random House LLC
1745 Broadway, New York, NY 10019
penguinrandomhouse.com
rhcbooks.com

Library of Congress Cataloging-in-Publication Data is available upon request.
ISBN 978-0-593-71142-2 (trade)—ISBN 978-0-593-71144-6 (ebook)

The text of this book is set in 11.2-point Warnock Pro.

Manufactured in the United States of America
10 9 8 7 6 5 4 3 2 1

The authorized representative in the EU for product safety and compliance is
Penguin Random House Ireland, Morrison Chambers, 32 Nassau Street,
Dublin D02 YH68, Ireland, https://eu-contact.penguin.ie.

Random House Children's Books supports the First Amendment and
celebrates the right to read.

To Pete, my gardener.
And to Libby, our wild-haired girl.

Roses . . . appear delicate but have adapted to most climates. They can be made to bloom all through the year until winter. The more they are cut back, the faster they grow, and the stronger they are.

—ALEXANDER CHEE

CHAPTER 1

IT'S THE FIRST DAY of summer vacation and I'm on my hands and knees in the bathroom scrubbing mildew off the tub. If only my older sister, Tessa, didn't use so many products. There would be no gobs of her hair in the drain, no peppermint body bar melting on the soap dish, no brown-sugar face scrub all over the rim. The worst part is the quiet. No Mitski, no true crime podcast, nothing to distract me from the smell of Clorox and the occasional stray toenail clipping on our pale green bath mat.

Actually, the worst part is I have to do the toilet next.

It all started when my report card arrived.

"Psychology?" Tessa said. "How do you get a C in psychology? It's, like, the study of your*self*."

Nothing bad ever seems to happen to Tessa. A bad day for

her is like a normal one for me. But that just means I'm going to have the more interesting personality. I already do.

"Well," I said. "Maybe I'm still getting to know myself."

"Do you *want* to be a walking cliché?" Tessa said.

Dad sighed. "That's enough," he said to her. To me, he said, "You're grounded. Three weeks." He stood at the bottom of the stairs while I hovered near the middle, halfway to my room.

I couldn't wait to slam the door like white kids do in the movies.

"What the crap?" I said. Not because I didn't deserve it, but because my parents had never grounded anyone before. I was surprised Dad even knew how to ground me. In my experience, anyway, immigrant parents don't ground; they're so strict already. I pictured Andy Huang, who lived down the street, getting grounded and almost laughed.

"I'll tell you what is crap," Dad said, his accent becoming a little more prominent, like it did when he got frustrated. *Is* sounded like *ees*, and he rolled the *r* in *crap*—which would have been hilarious if he wasn't yelling at me. He shook my report card in the air. "*This* is. Getting a C in this easy class!"

Under my breath, I mumbled, "It was a C *plus.* In *Honors* Psych."

Dad started taking the stairs toward me. "Emily Chen-Sanchez, I'm not finished yet!" he said. "And don't go into your room. Your room is too fun to be a punishment."

Mom poked her head out of their room, where she'd been resting.

". . . no respect," I heard Tessa saying from downstairs.

I rolled my eyes. "Shut your face, Tessa!" I shouted.

To my mother, I said sorry. I was saying sorry to my mother a lot this summer, and it was still the end of May, which isn't even technically summer yet.

"Where should she go, then?" Mom said to Dad. I couldn't tell if she was being serious or making fun of the whole situation. My parents do that sometimes. They share a sense of humor that Tessa and I don't get.

"El baño," Dad said.

Mom laughed, like this was the funniest thing she'd ever heard.

My parents speak three languages between the two of them, and their first languages—Spanish for Dad and Mandarin for Mom—always make an appearance when they're agitated. No wonder the Spanish phrases I know are ones like *saca la basura.*

"Seriously?" I said.

Dad gestured toward the door, waiting for me to walk right into the bathroom that I share with Tessa.

He said I had to stay there for at least an hour, until I was ready to talk—*calmly*—about what had happened and the plan I would take to rectify the situation. Dad works in marketing. I'm not exactly sure what he does all day, but I know he manages a bunch of people who all use words like *rectify.*

"And give me your phone," he said.

So into the bathroom I went. But by the time Dad came to check on me, I was painting my toenails a fire-engine red and had a soothing/moisturizing/replenishing mask on my face. That was what did it. Dad handed me the yellow cleaning gloves and a sponge and said, "Scrub."

⁓⁓⁓

That night, I want to take dinner into my room, but my parents won't hear of it. That's another thing I don't get about them: how we can be all mad at each other, but they still want to have dinner at the table together. It's like a subtle form of torture.

Naturally, Tessa is talking about yet another internship that she applied for. Something about working in the emergency room, which is what Tessa's been wanting to do since she was like seven.

I try not to listen. There's only so much achievement talk you can take from someone whose room is right next to yours. Someone whose high school CV is as long as a term paper—not to mention someone who actually *has* a CV in high school. Someone who delivered a TED Talk at age fifteen about the importance of good mental health among adolescents and, at age seventeen, wears her hair in a neat bob like our mom's, partly because it's more professional and partly because it's efficient. Tessa is all about efficiency.

Instead of listening, I help myself to more potatoes and load them up with butter.

"Don't eat so many potatoes," Mom says, interrupting Tessa. "You need some green vegetables."

"Have more pork," Dad says. "You need protein for swimming."

"Do you really need butter?" Tessa says. Yes, she interrupts even herself in order to nag me. She makes a point of stabbing her butterless potato and putting it into her mouth while eyeing my buttered one.

Even when all you're doing is eating, you can count on my family to comment on your every move.

It's when I'm feeling things super intensely that I start to have ideas for my next drawing. And it's happening now. I'm so pissed at all three of them that I get this great sketch going in my mind: Mom, Dad, and Tessa as a family of cockatiels, sitting at a tiny dinner table in a birdcage, while I, larger than life as some other bird, stand outside looking in. I could title it something like *When Will It Be My Turn?* or *Never Fitting in That Cage* or simply *Outside the Family.* Maybe it's too on the nose, or too *Ugly Duckling,* but you get the gist.

When I have an idea for a drawing, it's like a fly buzzing around in a jar, just desperate to get out. I feel so much better once I've written it down in my Notes app, or better yet—if I'm able to—I start sketching it out in pencil right away, even if it's just on the top corner of the page I'm using to take notes in class.

Since I can't start anything during dinner, I repeat *birds, birds, birds* in my head so it sticks.

Even on regular, non-grounded weekends when I don't leave the house much, I can at least escape into my art. I put on my headphones and my art shirt (an old T-shirt) and suddenly it's like I'm not at home at all—I'm in a real studio with exposed brick, good lighting, and other artists working around me, in somewhere like Brooklyn, where people create cool things all day.

But recently my parents have been making a stink about how much time I spend drawing. Mom doesn't love how the chalk pastels stain my hands and nails—she wants me to use gloves, but it wouldn't be the same—and Dad thinks that my wanting to apply to art school is just a phase. So sometimes I take my supplies to a coffee shop. That's the nice thing about pastels. You don't need a whole lot to get set up; it's not like watercolor, where you've got a bunch of brushes and paints and water and a palette.

"God, you're *so* weird," Tessa says, and I realize I must have zoned out for a bit.

Mom says, "What was that—'Brr brr brr'?"

Dad just laughs.

That's when it hits me: This is how it is going to be every night for the rest of the summer, and I won't be able to bear it. Three weeks may not sound like much, but it's nearly a third of the summer. I need to get out of this house.

I've never had a job before, unless you count babysitting jobs here and there. I applied everywhere last summer—Marble Slab Creamery, Barnes & Noble, Publix—but they all said I didn't have enough experience. How are you supposed to have experience if you can't *get* experience in the first place? And what kind of experience do you really need? I can scoop as well as anyone, and you bet I can put things into bags. Not that those jobs really interest me much. Who wants to work in a place with fluorescent lighting, where the most interesting thing you do is try to figure out if an herb is parsley or cilantro? What I'd really like is a job in a beautiful space, like in a museum or a swanky hotel, or the type of place where you wear cute shoes and take an elevator to your office. But I don't need a fancy job. A gig doing faux calligraphy for greeting cards or drawing caricatures outdoors at eight bucks a pop would do. Honestly, I would even work in one of those paint-and-sip places, if they'd have me.

Though, as you can imagine, there aren't many places like that in Green Valley, South Carolina, and besides, I'm not sure that I could work there if I'm not legally allowed to sip.

That night, in my room, I start scrolling for jobs on RiversEdgeRoundUp.com, our neighborhood's online newsletter. I'm not only doing it to get out of the house. It would also be good on my résumé for college (that is, if I don't get into art school) because with mediocre grades like mine, it'll be good to have some real-world experience to back them up.

I scroll through the site, and it turns out everyone in River's Edge needs help with something: there are ads for pet sitters and babysitters and house sitters, and plenty of ads for yard work—if you can stand working in the scorching heat and humidity. Dad won't let me get a job like that, though. He'd say something like, *We came to this country and worked our whole lives so you can always have a nice clean job inside.*

Of course, the inside job should preferably be in business or medicine or law.

I ignore all the ads for sitters and tutors because I want a job where I can spend the whole day away from our house, not just a couple of hours. That way, I can still leave home while being grounded. I'm almost to the end of the ads page when I see it, a job that is perfect for me:

Lady nearing ripe old age—but not quite ripe yet—seeks a youthful companion to help with sundry things around the house. Looking for a certain je ne sais quoi. Will know it when she sees it.

The lady didn't have an email address; you were to call the number. Payment would be discussed in person.

I close my bedroom door and dial the number.

The phone rings twice, and then a cheerful voice says, "Granucci residence!" She doesn't sound old. But then maybe she just has a strong voice. She takes her time on the "nu" in *Granucci* and the "res" in *residence,* so that it's like a little song.

I tell her my name and why I'm calling.

"Emily. Chen. Sanchez," she repeats slowly, as if sounding it out, or practicing. I don't blame her. It's not like it's hard to pronounce, but people get hung up on the double last name and the repetition of the *ch* sound, not to mention the three cultures in one name. "And do you like to be called Emily?" she says. "Or something else?"

"Emily's fine," I say. Everyone calls me Emily except Dad, who calls me Rillo (pronounced *ree-yoh*), short for *amarillo,* because his favorite color is yellow and he thought *Emily* sounded close to it. Except I'm not exactly sunshine and daffodils.

"Do you have any experience in taking care of the elderly?" Mrs. Granucci asks.

"A little," I say, thinking of my ama, who I sometimes took walks with around the park when we visited her in Los Angeles. "Well, not really. Nothing paid, if that's what you're asking." It drives Mom up a wall when I say something and then directly contradict myself in the same breath. But what can I say? Everyone is full of contradictions.

"I'm still in high school," I explain, in case Mrs. Granucci can't hear it in my voice.

"Young," she says. "I like that. Have you had other summer jobs?"

When I tell her I haven't, she says, "That's a good thing. All people want is experience these days, and they end up getting robots and overeager smile machines doing the work for them."

"That's what I always say."

Mrs. Granucci tells me to come by tomorrow at ten, that she wants to get a look at me, ask me some questions. "Will you walk here? Or drive?" *Drive* sounds like "drahve."

"I'll ride my bike over."

"Even better," she says. She pauses, then adds, "I don't want to see you all gussied up. I want to see what you're like on a *normal* day."

That night, I plan my outfit, lay the options on my bed. I want to wear shorts, but it's still an interview, after all. Mrs. Granucci said not to try too hard, so I won't wear a dress. I decide on my favorite jeans and a nice top. The jeans are pale blue and frayed on the bottom because I cut them that way, with a hole in the knee—a stylish hole. Tessa offers me one of her blazers, but it's not that kind of job, and besides, I'm not about to let her think I need any favors from her.

⁓ℓℓℓ⁓

When I come downstairs the next morning, Mom, Tessa, and Dad all turn toward me, the exact same expression on their faces. There are a few things that my parents moralize: doing your best at school is one of them, and getting up early is another. I have friends who sleep till noon—which is exactly what I would like to be doing—but in my family that is a strict no-no. You have to wake up by nine, and even that is frowned upon, even that is pushing it. Nine is my parents' idea of sleeping in.

Dad is sitting at the kitchen table, stroking his thick mustache while on his iPad, having gone to the gym, showered, and taken care of a variety of household chores before I've even poured myself a bowl of cereal. And this is Saturday. Dad hasn't been too keen on my looking for a job at all. His parents owned a store in Panama, so Dad grew up working there after school, and that's partly why he doesn't want *me* to work. (*Why do you need a job? You have everything you need at home. You're lucky you don't have to work like I did!*) Dad asks me to give him all of Mrs. Granucci's information before I set out—her street address, email, and phone number—even though I'm only going to be out for an hour or less.

"She doesn't have email?" he says when I tell him. "Something about that rubs me the wrong way."

Everything rubs you the wrong way, is what I want to say. But I just say, "She's old."

"Age doesn't matter. Your grandparents have email."

"And if you're not back in like thirty minutes, she'll be getting a call, an email, and Dad showing up on her front step," Tessa quips.

"Go upstairs and blow-dry your hair," Mom says, "so it has a nice style. And don't you want to put some color on before you go to that woman's house?"

"At least some lipstick," says Tessa. "Otherwise, it's like you don't care."

That's kind of the idea, is what I think. Girls who look like they care too much just seem desperate. But I guess that's the thing about the South: looking like you care too much means you care just the right amount.

"My hair *does* have a style," I say. "I just don't know what style it's going to be."

∼ℓℓℓ∽

I set out on my bike. I've made it around the corner of our street when I see Matt Ziegler vigorously spraying the weeds in his front yard. He told me all about that weed killer: it's made of vinegar, salt, and dish soap because, as he explained, acid and sodium chloride work together to kill plants. His back is turned to me, but I know that T-shirt well: it has *Science Will Save Us* on the front and a big ketchup stain near the bottom. He's wearing denim cutoffs, because he is the only guy in

11

the eleventh grade who can pull off jorts, Birkenstock sandals that he wears all year long (with socks when it's cold), and dark green gardening gloves he's had forever. He has his Great Smoky Mountains National Park cap on, but I can see his hair peeking out beneath it and I swear it's already getting lighter. Matt and I have lived six houses down from each other since the fourth grade. We made it through middle school carpools, Ms. Watkin's Honors World History, and seven years of River's Edge swim team—both of us hating the butterfly with a passion. In fact, we're usually good friends, maybe even best friends. Just not right now. I consider turning around, but I don't want to be late for my interview. I lift my butt off the seat and pedal extra hard and fast by the Ziegler house. I hear Matt go, "Hey! Em? Em!" but I pretend not to hear. Then I feel bad, so I just yell, "Let's talk later!" without turning around, and hope he heard me.

River's Edge is full of hills, so I'm huffing and puffing before I'm halfway to Mrs. Granucci's house. She lives at the very edge of the neighborhood, at the end of Rock Road, where the houses are different. I watch the mailboxes: 302, 304, 306, 308. She's in 310, and even before I see it I know what 310 is: the Spanish house. That's what we always called it. It's the most unique house in the whole neighborhood, massive and made of white stucco, with a brick-red tile roof like one of those houses in Southern California. When I get there, I can't bike up the driveway—it's that steep—so I lean my bike against a weeping willow. I'm sweating in my jeans as I walk up. At least I've got that classy hole in them for ventilation. The front porch has a couple of white wicker chairs and a veritable greenhouse of big plants, all lush and overflowing their pots. I ring the bell.

The door opens, and what I notice first is the blast of cold air that escapes and touches my skin, like walking past a grocery store with automatic doors. A woman appears in the doorway. She's almost a whole head shorter than me, which makes me feel like a giant, but that doesn't stop her from standing super straight and tall and looking me in the eyes with her chin pointed up.

Is this what tall guys feel like when girls have to look up to kiss them?

The woman looks sturdy, in a bright floral dress and the type of metallic sandals with a block heel that all the Southern ladies are wearing this summer. Her hair is full and thick, and she wears it cut just above her shoulders, big and wavy, in an unnatural orange-red shade that's clearly dyed. She has on lots of mascara, peach blush, lipstick the color of poppies. On her ears are enormous blue jewel earrings, the kind I always try on in thrift stores but never buy.

That hair, though. I feel like you could make a slammin' typography in that hair.

In the ad, Mrs. Granucci described herself as nearing "ripe old age," so I pictured helping someone stumble around her house with a walker, asking me to bring her more tea or to read aloud from the Old Testament while she dozed off—like Jo did for Aunt March in *Little Women*. But it's clear that I won't be doing any of that here.

She smiles and holds her arms out to me as if for a hug, but instead places her hands on my shoulders. She has a strong grip. "Emily," she says, drawing out my name warmly with recognition, as if I'm her niece that she hasn't seen in a long time. She looks me up and down, from my hair—which manages to be both frizzy from humidity and flat from my helmet—to my sandals. Then, tentatively, she adds, "Chen? Sanchez," as if to make sure she's got things right.

"You got it," I say. "Nice to meet you, Mrs. Granucci."

She extends her arm into the gleaming foyer, which has high ceilings and is full of natural light. A tall white vase full of probably expensive blue flowers sits on an end table with a mirror above it.

"Come in to my humble abode," she says, even though the place doesn't look that humble to me. "Can I offer you anything to drink? Lemonade?"

"Sure, thanks."

Stepping in, I fight the impulse to slip off my sandals, which is what we always do at home. Mrs. Granucci's wearing hers inside her own house, so I figure I should keep mine on—although I could never understand why white people leave their shoes on. I asked Matt about it once, and he said it's because they're just too lazy to take them off only to have to put them back on again, and sometimes, it's a vanity thing.

That part, I get. Shoes really can make the outfit.

We make our way into the living room. The windows are adorned with white lace curtains like we're in a cottage by the sea, and the walls are lined with books—old books with gilded lettering on thick spines. I wonder if she actually reads any of them, or if they're purely decorative. Below our feet is an Oriental rug of rich reds and blues. Even the wallpaper is dramatic: dark blue with white flowers and little white birds. There are two still life oil paintings and one watercolor landscape on the wall. On the glass coffee table—on white agate coasters with gold trim—are two tall glasses of lemonade with ice cubes that are perfectly square.

"Sit, please," says Mrs. Granucci.

So I take a seat on the plush white couch, settling myself into a faux fur cushion, and Mrs. Granucci sits across from me in an armchair with a floral-themed notepad—the pages so covered with pictures of flowers that there's hardly space for writing anything. You certainly couldn't make a vertical grocery list, for instance. But that's how Southern women are: they're always making grocery lists on notepads with, like, *Faith can move mountains!* or *I am fearfully and wonderfully made!* written at the bottom of the pages.

Mrs. Granucci picks up a pair of horn-rimmed glasses from the coffee table and puts them on. "Well," she says. "Aren't you pretty."

I look at her, startled. No one ever calls me pretty. I tan easily and have lots of freckles, and I have dark brown hair that's so long it almost covers my boobs. Tessa is petite with a sweet, heart-shaped face like Mom, but I'm tall and lanky like Dad. Dad and I both have "cheekbones that can cut glass"—that's what I heard Meghan Morehart telling people in the bathroom at school once, anyway. But it's Tessa who gets all the second glances when our family goes out. I think it's partly due to how she always has a pleasant face on, even when she's hating your guts. The rest of us get stared at, too, just because we look so different from other people in Green Valley. You don't usually see a Latino man and an Asian woman and their mixed kids walking around in our town. Once, a man even approached Tessa and asked if she was the actress from *Crouching Tiger, Hidden Dragon.* "Which one?" is what she asked him.

But I figure Mrs. Granucci is the type who feels the need to assure every girl that she's pretty right away. That's what old-school Southern people do sometimes, as if your looks— and what they think of them—are the most important thing about you.

"Thank you," I say.

"You *are,*" Mrs. Granucci insists, even though I've already thanked her. "You know," she adds, "I believe I've seen you around."

I don't know what to say to that. This is a comment I get often. People "see me around" because, well, I stick out. Maybe she's seen me, but if I've seen her, I can't remember. I take a sip of the lemonade. It's sour as all get-out, and I try not to make a face.

Mrs. Granucci is still examining me, my face and my hair, and I know the question that's coming next.

"Your family," she says. "Where do they come from?"

People are always asking me that—*Where are you from?* It's the most annoying question on the face of the earth be-cause there's no point in asking it. What are they going to do with that information? I could correct them, saying, *You're trying to ask me what my ethnicity is.* But why is it my responsibility to educate them on what they're asking? I appreciate that at least Mrs. Granucci has the sense to ask where my *family* is from.

"Dad's from Panama and Mom's from Taiwan." And because I know the usual follow-up question, I add, "They met in grad school at Carolina. Dad was doing his MBA and Mom was doing her PhD." I shrug. "We're just your typical tri-country family."

That makes Mrs. Granucci laugh, a big booming *ha!* "You're feisty," she says, and then jots something down (where she can) on her floral notepad in looping, careful script.

Already, I can see myself enjoying it here very much. The air-conditioning is blasting through the house, keeping it as cold as a movie theater, where you have to bring a sweater. My parents like to open the windows and just use fans until we absolutely can't stand it anymore, so I love central AC. Matt calls me an air-conditioning junkie.

"Evelyn, you're what grade in school?" Mrs. Granucci regards me over the top of her glasses.

"Emily," I say quickly, then add, "Going into eleventh."

She smiles at me. "Whoops. Emily. You will soon discover that your glamorous employer is senile. You, on the other hand, are tall and strong. What's your secret?"

I cross my legs. "Mom made us drink a lot of milk. And I'm on the River's Edge swim team." I give a fist pump. "Go, River Rangers," I say half-heartedly.

"Aha. *That's* why you've got such a great figure. Other girls would kill for that!"

I certainly haven't heard *that* before, either. I have almost no curves, and sometimes I can't help feeling like there's too much of me, lengthwise. Oftentimes long-sleeved shirts stop before they should, leaving my wrists high and dry.

"Favorite stroke?" Mrs. Granucci asks.

"Breaststroke."

She raises her eyebrows at that.

I shrug. "What can I say, I like taking my time. Butterfly is my least favorite. It burns my core and makes me feel sloppy, like I'm just scooping water out of the way."

Mrs. Granucci jots something else down, then asks, "And what is your favorite subject in school?"

That, I can also answer with no hesitation. "Art. It's always been art."

She smiles. "Now *that's* something you don't hear every day. What do you love about it?"

The truth is, I can't remember *not* loving it. All kids color and draw at some point—it's a standard kid activity, like jumping on a trampoline or riding a bike, except with zero chance of injury. But for me, it was more than just something to do on a rainy day. It was how I could be wherever I wanted to be, whenever I wanted.

"Once I start drawing something, it's like everything else just fades away, you know? I can do it for hours and it only feels like I've been at it for like twenty minutes."

I don't know how else to describe it. *Fun* isn't the right

word—it's not scrolling Instagram with Heather while eating cookies. It takes effort.

"It must be nice to have a class you truly enjoy, that feels like a break," says Mrs. Granucci.

"Yeah, but the new art teacher, Ms. Henderson, she doesn't inspire me," I tell her. "All she does is teach technique. She's not curious about what we're trying to do, what we're trying to say or express. It's like, I'm sorry, I don't want to paint a banana. I want my art to tell a story."

That's when I tell her about the summer art camp I went to in eighth grade, where I discovered chalk pastels.

Mrs. Granucci clasps her hands together. Her eyes have lit up even more, if that's possible. She sits back in her chair, inviting me to continue.

"They're like . . . okay, picture the chalk you used as a kid, but times a thousand. Sidewalk chalk is almost see-through and it washes off, right? Pastels are the real deal. Each one is a little brick, like a Lego. A block of vivid, highly pigmented color. And they're messy, but that's what I like about them. I like making new colors with my hands."

She nods. "That was a fantastic explanation. And I would love to see some of your work sometime—only if you feel comfortable with that, of course."

"You would?"

Honestly, I don't really let anyone look at my work except Matt and Heather. I haven't shown my parents anything since freshman year, after Dad saw a drawing I did of Tessa with plants growing out of her head, and he asked me if I was trying to depict that she was smoking weed. Heather is super into my work, because she has to be. It's just part of the code of our friendship. She's loyal that way; she'd support me even if my new hobby was underwater basket weaving. But Matt looks at my work because he gets it. When he looks at my drawings, he really *looks*. It's like he's truly seeing me, like he really knows me. And sometimes, I'll admit it, that can be a little frightening.

"Absolutely," Mrs. Granucci says, nodding vigorously. She gestures to the wall behind me. "As you can see, I'm a bit of an art collector myself."

I turn around and look at the watercolor painting, which is a sunlit snowy day in the woods somewhere, but she continues. "We'll talk about my art another time. Let me ask you this: Why do you want this job? You probably have better things to do than watch an old woman inside all day."

I take a breath, unsure of how honest I'll be. Then I just blurt out, "I'm grounded. And I need a break from my parents and sister for at least part of the week."

Mrs. Granucci sits back in her chair. "Grounded? Whatever for?" She clicks her pen and regards me.

"Some stupid school thing."

She raises her eyebrows again but doesn't inquire further. "So my house is the escape hatch, then."

"No. I mean, yes, in a way. I mean—"

"Oh, it's all very fine, dear. We're all running away from *something* these days." Then she leans toward me like we're at a slumber party and she's about to tell me her crush. "Do you like to bake?"

I've only ever made cakes from boxed cake mix, or cookies by cutting disks off a frozen log of Toll House dough. Or even more often, I just eat the dough. "I love dessert. But my mom, she never really bakes anything. And so I haven't really, either." I don't tell her that my grandmother, out in California, uses her oven as storage because she never bakes a thing.

For a split second I'm sure Mrs. Granucci won't hire me. Then she says, "As you may have noticed, I keep this house very cool. And part of that is because I bake. Butter needs to be cold—for pie."

I nod. I'm a fast learner. If she wants pie, I'll make pie.

Then she smiles mischievously. "Another thing is, I have a piece of art coming in that requires a cooler temp. Plus, I run hot. And yes, it costs a little more to keep the house this cool, but when you get to be my age, what's a little more money to keep the temperature exactly as one likes? I won't be around much longer anyway. Ha!" This seems pretty morbid for a Saturday morning, but at this last word she claps, throws her head back, and laughs.

It seems wrong to laugh, but I also feel awkward just watching her, so I manage a chuckle. And what piece of art is arriving that needs to be cold? An ice sculpture?

"What else will I be doing when I come over besides baking?" I ask. "If I get the job, I mean."

"Oh, keeping me company. And helping me with some things, reminding me of things . . ." She taps her forehead with one manicured fingernail. Her nails are long and gleaming, painted the color of a Creamsicle.

"Okay, can do," I say. Frankly, it sounds perfect: an entire job where my sole duty would be to spend time with my own personal old person.

Then she puts her notepad down on the couch.

"What I need most, Emily, is for you to *remember.*"

As she's saying this, she leans forward, reaches out, and presses her fingers gently against either side of my head.

I don't move. It seems important that I not move.

"I want you to hang on to things up there, in your brain," she says. "Your young, sharp, simply *wonderful* brain."

This close, I can smell the lemonade on her breath and whatever cream she uses on her hands, which doesn't smell like anything in particular. Just lotion. On my temples, which I hope aren't too sweaty, her fingers are cool.

"Yes, ma'am," I say.

She drops her hands. "You'll know this house so well that everything will become a routine. Tick, tick, tick, an imaginary checklist up there saying what you need to do. But more importantly, I want you to remember what I tell you. About my life."

I nod. I don't know why, but my heart is beating fast and loud. I wonder if she can see it through my thin blouse. It's so hot out, and I'm not—as my best friend Heather puts it— "blessed in the chest," so I'm not even wearing a bra.

"You'll let yourself in on Friday nights and lock the door behind you—both doors. You'll make sure the stove and oven and appliances are all turned off. Then you'll sleep in the guest bedroom. That way we can spend Saturday together, and some Sundays when I need you."

"Can do," I say. It seems almost too simple, and with the perk of being able to spend the weekend in her gorgeous house, too good to be true. Dad trained us to check and double-check. He unplugs most things before we go to bed, making sure that all the doors are locked, testing the knobs himself even though we can see that they're locked. He checks the oven and stove twice, sometimes even three times. I know that if my parents find out what I'll be doing at Mrs. Granucci's, they'll remark on how I'm more willing to take care of this lady's house than ours.

I mean, they wouldn't be wrong. It's a beautiful house.

"Then you'll start this Friday," says Mrs. Granucci. *Frahdee*. "In the evening. Let yourself in—I'll show you how in a minute—and just make yourself at home. I'm a heavy sleeper but an early riser." She grins. "It's because of my meds."

It seems like that's supposed to be a joke, so I smile, too, even though we probably shouldn't take her meds lightly.

"Oh, so that's it? I got the job?"

She takes her glasses off. "Do you want the job or not? Yes, that's it."

I glance over at her floral notepad, where she hasn't written much at all.

I'll find the key inside the key safe in front of the door, she says. She gets up and shows it to me. It looks like a tiny house for a garden fairy, but when you turn it upside down there's a secret latch you can push and the key pops out. I pick it up and practice taking the key out of it. It feels heavy, expensive, not like the green plastic frog key safe my parents have, which

Dad insists on keeping hidden inside a bush—even though the whole point of it is to hide the key.

"When you come in," says Mrs. Granucci, "you'll find a pair of shoes to wear. I'll leave them in a bag right here."

I follow her to the front closet, where she brings down a cloth bag. From the bag, she takes out the most beautiful pair of shoes I have ever seen. They are bright blue leather with a pointy toe and a low block heel, and they're fabulous. My parents would say it's dirty to wear someone else's shoes, and maybe it is, but these look like they've hardly been worn at all, and besides, it's basically the same idea as a vintage shop. At the sight of them, my feet are twitching inside my sandals, like they can't wait to get them on.

"These are an eight," says Mrs. Granucci. "I like for my companion to be as classy as I am." She sees me eyeing them, and then, as if they're a reward that I can't have till later, she slides them back into the bag.

"Now, these"—she gestures to my thrift-shop jeans that my parents think are from the mall—"these are nice. Original."

"They are?" I look at the frayed hems, the hole, and the patch that I sewed on.

She nods. "I think we're going to have a lot of fun working together."

CHAPTER 2

IT'S BRUTALLY HOT OUT after being in Mrs. Granucci's ice-box of a house, the sun higher in the sky, but I don't even care. Not only do I have a summer job, a *comfortable, easy* summer job at that, but I'm going to be paid to wear nice shoes. If Heather had been there, she would be all, "Okay, what just happened!" My legs are pedaling, but really I'm sitting on that couch after baking a cake, then eating said cake, then being paid to eat said cake. It couldn't be better.

I decide not to tell my parents about how Mrs. Granucci basically asked me to be her human journal. Something tells me this would freak them out, and the freak-out would lead to questioning, and the questioning would lead to them saying I shouldn't work for her. I've been through this sort of thing enough times to know what'll happen. There was that one time when Tessa came down to breakfast wearing a pom-pom in her hair for spirit week, and Dad asked—I kid you not—if there was any possibility that the stick from the pom-pom would poke somebody in the eye. Or worse, poke Tessa herself in the neck and cause her untimely demise.

There's no one like my dad to have such a penchant for predicting highly unlikely disasters.

I won't tell Dad that she put her hands on my face, either, and I definitely won't tell about the shoes. Dad is the biggest germaphobe: He carries several different kinds of hand sanitizer on his person. He never opens public doors with his bare hands. He's skeptical of cloth napkins in restaurants. I've seen the man eat french fries with a fork and knife. And when it comes to other people's preowned clothes and shoes, forget about it. Dad is convinced that, even if we wash it in hot water, we could contract a rare skin disease from a 1970s madras button-down.

When I get home, my shirt is stuck to my back and sweat is dripping into my eyes. The lack of AC isn't helping, either, although everyone else in my family seems to be doing just fine—none of them having pedaled uphill in the heat. There's also the fact that I am an especially sweaty person. I'm always drying my hands off while drawing. I've tried everything: shaving my armpits regularly, using extra-extra-strength aluminum hard-core antiperspirant. I even used topical medication for a brief time, but it made my hands all dry and itchy. Yet if Tessa runs three miles (which she does, with surprising regularity, because *of course* she runs for fun), she can get away with using one of those all-natural deodorants made of baking soda and rosemary.

But next weekend, things will be different. Mrs. Granucci's

place is as cold as a refrigerator. And I love sticking my head in the refrigerator.

I fill a tall glass of ice water, dunk my finger in it, and swirl the ice cubes around to cool it down faster. Mom is standing there chopping broccoli.

"Don't put your hand in there," she says, on cue, about my finger in the water. I knew she would say that. I do it anyway.

"I got the job!" I announce.

"Okay," she says, as if I just told her I would be having a burger for lunch.

I try not to take this personally. I saw Mom's Rate My Professors ratings once. Sometimes a kid googles their mom, you know, just to see how the public perceives her. It turns out the public is very divided—they either love or hate her. One review read, "Professor Chen-Sanchez is the best! So deadpan, so great. I've never been as challenged. This woman kicks ass and she knows it." But another read, "Do *not* take her. She will wring you dry. Homework is *very* hard, projects impossible, exams automatic failure. She is evil incarnate!"

It's true: Mom does fail a few kids every term, usually in Intro to Comp Sci. "They didn't do their work," is how she puts it. So I guess I can see why my bad grade made both my parents so mad—and I'm not even in a hard college class like my mom's.

All I know is that I wouldn't want to have her as *my* professor.

Working at Mrs. Granucci's is not the most impressive job in the world to get, I'll give Mom that, especially since it sounds like all I'm doing is whatever Mrs. Granucci needs around the house—which is probably more than what I do in my own house. Is there something slightly hypocritical about this? Maybe. But everyone knows that the most mundane things—grocery shopping or doing laundry or watching TV— all feel different when you're doing them with someone who doesn't live with you.

"Tell us about it during lunch," Mom says. "Come make the rice."

ℓℓℓ

About a month ago, Mom went to the doctor for a checkup, and the doc found a three-and-a-half-centimeter lump on her thyroid. Mom said it felt like there was an olive in her neck—a jumbo-sized one.

"A tumor," Dad had said, but the way he said it made it sound like *two more.*

We all did our best not to freak out. Apparently there are bad tumors and not-bad ones.

Then they did an ultrasound on Mom's thyroid, but somehow that didn't give them enough information. So they did a CT scan, and that still wasn't clear. Recently they did a biopsy and we're supposed to be hearing back about that pretty soon. It's wild how slow things move. You find out something like that and you feel shitty, and then you just wait, and wait, for the doctor to look inside and tell you more information and what they're going to do about it. Now we're waiting for the biopsy results before they possibly schedule surgery to take the tumor out. Maybe her thyroid, too. Apparently a human can function without a thyroid, which I didn't know a couple of months ago. It's the butterfly-shaped gland in your neck that regulates mood, so I'm kind of hoping that Mom gets to keep hers, for obvious reasons.

Usually I'd be super annoyed with Mom, but ever since the diagnosis I try to tread carefully, pick my battles. It doesn't seem right to fight with someone who could possibly have one of the bad tumors.

௸

Rice is an art in the Chen-Sanchez household. First of all there's the rice itself: hefty, fifteen-pound sacks of the Japanese brand Kokuho Rose, quality jasmine rice. The bags are white with a hot-pink trim. Every month we make the drive across town to Great Panda Market. I wish it wasn't called that. I wish the Asian places around here didn't have such uncool names, just begging you to make fun of them, like Golden Chopsticks or Tales from the Orient. Great Panda Market is two floors. I have no idea who actually buys things on the first floor, which is full of dusty knickknacks, old lamps, heavy Buddhas, face creams from Korea—but not the hip K beauty that everyone wants. The basement is where we go to stock up on bok choy and dried squid and sesame oil. And Yan Yan, you can't forget the Yan Yan. It's like Pocky but better: the sticks are bigger and you can dip them straight into the chocolate. The very last thing we grab is the rice, laid gently in the car like a baby.

Then there's the making of it: I scoop out two cups of rice

and rinse the grains with water in the pot of the rice cooker until the water runs clear. Then I add clean water—it's enough when I lay my hand, palm flat, against the rice, and the water dances up along the middle joints of my fingers. We use the rice for everything, not just Chinese food. We make Panamanian food, too, like arroz con pollo and arroz con leche.

During dinner, Dad's phone rings, but he just lets it ring. My parents have rules like that. No phones during dinner because dinner is sacred family time. Every now and then I can see Tessa's hand flinch when her phone vibrates on the kitchen counter, as if she's got fifty-four text message notifications waiting for her. She's in at least three different group text threads. I don't see how they have so much to talk about.

"I'm going to be interning at the hospital," Tessa announces as I scoop rice onto my plate. She shakes her hair as she says this, like someone in a movie, waiting for us to compliment her. Then she lets out a little squeal. For years, it has been Tessa's dream to be on the EMT team at school, and then to become a paramedic, and then to go to med school and be Dr. Chen-Sanchez, working in the emergency room. Her boyfriend, Steve, is on a similar track—he wants to be a hand surgeon.

I honestly couldn't think of a worse job. All that stress and bodily fluid.

"Excelente, Tessa," says Dad.

"That's wonderful news," says Mom. "Hěn hǎo."

"That's great!" I say, fake smiling as I take another bite of rice.

And seriously, great. Way to share before I do. If someone says excellent or very good about Tessa one more time, I swear I'll—

"And, Emily, you got a job at this lady's house?" Mom says.

"Yep!" I say. "I got the job as Mrs. Granucci's companion."

Mom says, "Very good," and Dad nods his agreement, and Tessa says, "Cool!" But they don't seem particularly impressed or excited.

"And what will you be doing there?" says Mom.

"Well, anything she needs from me, I guess. Like . . ." That's when I realize that Mrs. Granucci didn't say very much at all about what we would be doing, apart from the safety measures in the house (which would take, what, five minutes, tops?) and remembering her life story. "Like being her conversation partner and making sure she doesn't fall when she's walking," I hazard to say.

"She sounds desperate," says Tessa. "She wants someone around to keep her company. It's sad, honestly! And you know, studies show that the elderly are often ignored, and they feel invisible. So I think it's great that you're going to be taking care of a lonely old woman."

That's also what makes Tessa annoying as hell. She thinks she knows everything about people, like she's so perceptive.

"She doesn't seem lonely to me," I say. "And you weren't even there. Anyway, I start Friday night and will be there all day Saturday. And some Sundays. At the Spanish house."

"It's on the weekends?" Mom says, at the same time that Dad says, "She wants you to spend the night there?"

31

"Wasn't the whole point to be occupied on weekdays?" says Tessa.

"What's the difference? It's summer anyway."

"Well," Tessa says, "it's different for *me* because on the weekdays I'll be at the hospital, and on Saturdays I volunteer at the library. But I guess you're right, your weekdays and weekends are pretty similar, except for swim team."

"Anyway," I say, "I'll help her with computer stuff, and learn patience or whatever. I think it'll be good on my résumé."

"You're gonna be her IT support?" says Tessa. "Couldn't she find a comp sci major to help her out? I can't believe you're getting paid for that."

"You're just jealous. You'll probably be cleaning up vomit and updating people's medical records. I can't believe you're *not* getting paid for that."

"I am getting paid!"

"Yeah, but it's so little that it's basically nothing."

Dad frowns at me. "Something about this new job rubs me the wrong way. Call us, you know, if anything weird happens while you're over there."

"Like if she falls down or something?"

"Well, that, too," Dad says. "I meant more like if she asks you to do anything that seems off."

"Like *what*?" I say.

Mom says, "Don't worry about it. You know how Dad is always just very skeptical of everyone."

Dad tries to act like he's cool and calm, and all my friends like that he's friendly and has a loud laugh, but on the inside he's so anxious that I'm pretty sure ours is the only house in River's Edge that has an alarm system. Something is *always* rubbing him the wrong way about something or other.

"Do you really need to go work there?" he continues. "You can use the time to study for the SAT, or to practice driving."

"I *know*," I say. There's nothing worse than having your dad tell you what to do when you already know what to do. When in fact, you are full of self-loathing about that very thing already. I've been through driver's ed, and I have my permit. I just don't like driving.

"But what will you *do* there all day?" Tessa asks for the millionth time.

"More than you do in your whole life," I snap.

That doesn't make any sense and I know that, but see how easy it is to get annoyed at Tessa?

Even now, she just laughs it off and says, "Oookay?"

Is that what it's like to be that confident? I wouldn't know.

Then dinner's over, thank God, and as I take my plate over to the sink, Mom says, "Remember, you're grounded. No talking to Heather, and no talking to Matt."

Inadvertently, I stiffen. Don't parents know anything? Heather is away on a combo study abroad/mission trip in London, which doesn't sound much like a mission trip if you ask me.

And Matt, well. Matt and I haven't talked in two weeks, four days, and, let's see, about seven hours, not that I'm counting.

llo

Matt and I haven't talked since The Incident.

It happened at Jayson Applebee's end-of-the-school-year party: Jayson had told his parents he was having friends over to make dinner and watch a movie. Did they believe him or—because they're chill ex-hippie parents—did they know what was up and trusted him to manage his own party? I'm still not sure. The important thing is that they weren't at home, home being their mansion/farmhouse with an actual corn maze on the property. When we arrived, people were helping themselves to ice cream from a soft-serve machine and making floats out of root beer and PBR. Zoey Kebabian was writing everyone's names on Solo cups because she is that type of person.

I had spent most of March and April listening to Matt go on about Zoey Kebabian. She was the whole reason why we were at the party at all. Zoey is one of those people who participate exceedingly well in class—so much so that sometimes I thought she should be teaching Anatomy and Physiology, and not Ms. Callaghan. When she did her presentation on neurotransmitters for the Student Lecture Series, even I had to admit she was really hot in her glasses and blazer, like a sexy scientist in a movie. On top of which, she's Armenian, which is just plain cool.

Matt was all nerves—he wouldn't stop talking from the minute his dad dropped us off—and he refused to drink. I wasn't about to pressure him. I mean, this is someone who has repeatedly told me that every drink you have increases your chance of getting breast cancer by 7 percent. He hasn't had a drop in his life. The guy won't even drink caffeine unless he considers it an absolute necessity, which is almost never.

The plan was for Matt and me to go up to Zoey together, and then I would make myself scarce while Matt talked with Zoey, which would culminate in Matt asking Zoey if she wanted to hang out sometime.

I had a plan for myself as well. I didn't want to date anyone; I just wanted to have my first kiss. It didn't matter whether it was special or not. It didn't need to be long, or even particularly enjoyable. I just needed it to happen so that I could be an upperclassman with that rite of passage behind me, like getting my driver's license (which I have yet to get, but that's beside the point). So my plan was to leave Matt with Zoey and then kiss Pratik Desai—who had utterly transformed himself with contact lenses and a guitar solo over spring break—in the corn maze. That way, I'd still be in a public place if anything went awry, but not in full view of everyone that people would start yelling at us to get a room.

We had gotten to the point in the party when I was talking with Pratik and watching Matt out of the corner of my eye. Zoey had refilled his Solo cup with lemonade, and he was sipping it gratefully—gulping it, actually.

They were talking about science. I could tell because Matt was gesticulating wildly and then doing that thing he does where he looks for a pen because he is just itching to sketch out a molecule or a line graph or whatever it is scientists draw. Then Zoey put her hand on his arm for a second, and she was smiling, and then Matt said something else and she laughed again. Oh my gosh, were they actually flirting with each other? But the next thing I knew, a bunch of girls showed up, she touched Matt's arm again, and then she smiled at him in such a sympathetic way it made me want to punch her.

Matt glanced over at me, eyes all wide. Then he started laughing, laughing so uncontrollably hard, and at first, this didn't surprise me too much because Matt *is* the type to burst into laughter when he's in a state of shock. But his eyes were glassy, like he also might cry any minute.

"So . . . ," I said to Matt, leaving Pratik at the PBR float station.

"She said she'd think about it and get back to me."

"Okay," I said. "Thinking about it isn't no."

He gave me a look, like *I wasn't born yesterday.* "It's not no, but it's pretty damn close to it."

"Are you okay?" I asked.

"I need to sit down." He was about to just plop down *on the ground*—which, for tall people like us, can be a feat—when I steered him over to a tree stump.

That's when Matt dropped his head onto my shoulder and sighed, and I caught a whiff of his breath.

It was boozy as all get-out.

Of course. Of course Zoey Kebabian gave him the spiked lemonade. And of course Matt thought it tasted weird ("weirdly bitter," he'd said, figuring it was "rich-people lemonade, kombucha lemonade, or some other bougie lemon beverage.") And of course he kept drinking it because that's what you do when the girl you think is the love of your life keeps pouring your beverage at a party.

He was *sauced.*

I made him drink two cups of water. So much water that he groaned. As we walked, I could hear it sloshing around in his stomach.

I know. Gross.

We both looked out at the corn maze, which was so dark that I questioned having my first kiss there. It didn't seem so romantic anymore.

"Easy," I said, guiding Matt over to a bench. I was wondering if we should go home.

That was when Matt put his head on my shoulder, I mean *really* on my shoulder. I could feel his sweaty cheek against my sweatier neck.

"Whoa," I said, nudging his head up with my hands. "You got this, you can sit up."

"You smell good," he said.

That, I knew, was the lemonade talking, because as I mentioned, my deodorant does nothing.

"*You* smell like booze," I said.

For a beat, we just sat with each other. Then he started to slump over a bit. Shit. I was going to have to somehow sober him up before Mr. Ziegler came to get us again.

I barely knew what was happening next. I saw Matt's head coming and ducked, but he grabbed my hands and planted one on me, landing closer to the side of my mouth than on my lips. All I could think was his mouth was all sticky, and I caught the smell of chocolate ice cream under the booze, yet somehow it felt, nice? Or would it feel nice if basically anyone was kissing me? But at the same time, it felt completely and utterly weird? For a few seconds, my stomach felt like it did before I have to do a presentation in class. Butterflies, I guess, but more intense, like bumblebees or something. But maybe that makes sense because I'm the type of person who can't even stand it when my own *mom* hugs me for too long, much less when my best friend from childhood goes in for one.

My hand flew up to the spot where his mouth had been. Yep, sticky.

"Matt!" I said, because I couldn't think of anything else to say.

"Sorry, I'm sorry," he said, and when our eyes met he looked so embarrassed. "I am so, like, out of my mind right now. Also, geez, you're not kidding when you say you have sweaty hands. They're practically *dripping*."

Well, that made me want to punch him.

Then, from near the bonfire, someone screamed, "Cops!" and everyone scattered. Only the designated drivers sat around the bonfire, casually holding their marshmallow sticks toward it.

Matt grabbed my hand—so sticky! so sweaty!—and we ran to the barn, which was pitch-black inside and smelled like both hay and cats. We could hear other people whispering, rustling, trying to hold in laughter. Could hear responsible Pratik Desai (so he wouldn't have been able to be my first kiss, anyway) and Max Edelman talking to the cops, saying that it must have been a house farther down the street. All the while, we crouched in the loft between bales of hay.

Matt put his face very close to mine, and it was taking all my self-control to not push him away or tell him to get lost.

"Em," he whispered. "I'm really, really sorry."

I patted his arm, nearly swatting him, by which I meant to convey that now was really not a good time to revisit the conversation.

But he did not take this hint. "That was not cool of me at all. Like I said, I'm just kind of all over the place right now. And now, now you can understand why I never drink at all."

"Just forget about it." Then I added, "That one doesn't count. It does *not* count as my first kiss."

"That makes sense. It was a mistake."

Beside me, I could hear the rustle of some . . . *things* in the hay. Mice? Were there mice scuttling around in this barn? Most likely. I am not very familiar with barn situations, being a suburban kid myself.

Then Matt said, "I have to take a whiz so badly. You've never had to break the seal this bad."

"Shhh," I whispered.

But he didn't shut up. "I'm good at holding my pee a long time, too. You know that. From swim team. But my bladder is begging for relief."

I told him once again to be quiet, and wondered if the cops were going to do a search of the barn. Then I started counting, which is something I do sometimes when I'm waiting.

I'd gotten up to five hundred, when right next to me there was the sound of—well, of a fly being unzipped, and then peeing. That unmistakable hiss. I couldn't really see anything or anyone in there, but the sound was coming from Matt's direction.

I wish I was the only one who heard it. But I wasn't.

This is a friend I've hiked with, so I'm no stranger to the sound of him taking a whiz. Did he, afterward, zip up his jeans and try to act like nothing had happened? Yes, yes, he did.

I don't know how people knew it was him, but they did. They'd heard the sound, and somehow when we had all emerged from the barn again, they knew it was him.

"Oh come *on*, Ziegler, couldn't you wait just five more minutes?" they said, after the cops left. "You could have moved another five feet away, at least."

Matt started lying his ass off, but the boy can't lie.

So I said, "Come on, lay off him," which only made things worse.

"Is your girlfriend going to defend you now?" Jayson Applebee said. He has a face like a Boy Scout, but he knows how to hit you where it hurts.

That I have not talked with Matt since makes it seem like I was judging him just as badly as everyone else was, but the fact that he peed in a barn isn't even the worst part. Not to me, anyway.

Even though, let's face it, that was pretty bad.

Once swim team practices started, people would come up

to him and yell "Matt the Pisser tried to kiss her!" because high schoolers are the worst people on the planet. If someone like Jayson Applebee had done that, everyone would think it was hilarious in a different way; they'd be high-fiving him. People respect Matt, but he just doesn't have that kind of social capital.

He's left me a million voicemails at this point—he's the only one of my peers who actually does that. The voicemails are his usual conversation starters, like did I know that Iceland was the first country to have a democratically elected female president? And did I know that cottage cheese sales have increased by over 15 percent this year? And did I know that people have been using cinnamon since like 2800 BCE?

The most recent one, though, just starts with, "Real mature, Em. I already said I was sorry. And I need to tell you something."

I know I'm being a jerk. I feel horrible about it. But the discomfort I feel now doesn't come close to how weird it could be when we do talk again. Which, we will, of course we will. I should reach out, say that it really wasn't a big deal, that we can go back to being friends. But he kissed me—or at any rate tried—thereby changing our friendship forever. The thing is, I wanted a first kiss, but the one from Matt scared me. I know I should be more mature than this. But I need time to prepare. I'm putting things off, procrastinating reaching out to him so that we can stay in this limbo where we are still friends and nothing has changed. If we hang out, will he try to do it again? Do I want him to, even a tiny minuscule little bit? I don't want to think about that. So many times I've typed out a full text to him, only to delete it seconds later. Because if and when things get weird between us, and our friendship changes—or, God forbid, *ends*—what am I supposed to do then?

CHAPTER 3

AFTER DINNER ON THE following Friday night, I receive a text:

> Hi E, it's Mrs. Granucci. Key will be in key safe as I showed you. Let yourself in and you are welcome to anything in the kitchen. Make sure all appliances = off (unplug small appliances such as coffee maker, etc.) Check stove and oven = off. All doors locked and bolted. Lights off both indoors and out. See you in the morning.

I can't help wondering if she's calling me E because we're being casual, or because she forgot my name. She did call me Evelyn at the interview, after all. Her text has nothing I didn't know already (including that the text is from, well, her) but I figure it doesn't hurt to have the reminder just the same.

Once I get to Mrs. Granucci's place, I stop for a second and look at the house, just soaking up the feeling of being here.

It's regal on its little hill, like an estate, bathed in a warm yellow glow from the porch lights. I walk my bike up and bring it around to the backyard. We live in a neighborhood where people are more likely to return a wallet than steal a bike, but still. If Dad were here, he'd tell me to put it in the garage, and Mrs. Granucci herself seems to take safety very seriously.

Everything is just as I'd been picturing: cool, dark, and silent. With Mrs. Granucci soundly asleep, it's like I'm all alone in the house, a feeling I love. I switch on a Victorian lamp with a fringe shade. My stomach's growling: swimming and biking make me constantly ravenous. In the kitchen, I open the refrigerator.

Usually people keep ketchup and jam in their fridge doors, but Mrs. Granucci's are packed with jars and jars of pickles: long fat dills and small sweet disks and spicy relish and gherkins. Not just cucumbers, either. There are pickled carrots sliced into coins, red onions in hot pink semicircles, even mushrooms of different shapes and sizes. I help myself to the gherkins, which must be homemade, since the jar has nothing except the date and *Gherkins* written on it. I crunch on them over the sink. My parents would say it was too late for a snack before bed; they would say pickles have no nutritional value; they would ask why I was eating them like that instead of putting them on a plate. "At least eat them with something, a piece of bread." So I thoroughly enjoy my tiny act of breadless rebellion. Then I make sure the stove is turned off, the oven, too. I double-check the front door, the back door, the side door that leads to a little garden. I unplug things.

I pause for a second at the photos in the living room.

There's a family photo that's got to be from the eighties, and I love Mrs. Granucci's big hair, even bigger than it is now, and her frosted blue eye shadow. Love her son's tube socks with stripes at the top, her husband's huge square-framed glasses.

I go into the room I'm staying in, beside the living room. It has its own bathroom, like a hotel suite. I brush my teeth and wash my makeup off. The only things resembling towels are these little white cloths with lace trim. I inspect them, wondering, not wanting to mess them up. That's when I notice that they're all monogrammed: *LHG*.

Geez. Mrs. Granucci is Southern as shit.

I bring an issue of *Better Homes & Gardens* from the bathroom into bed with me, just because I can. In the guest room, I feel so grown-up. It's a far cry from my own bedroom, covered in posters and colored Christmas lights, home to a money plant that Matt got me last year that I have yet to kill. This room, on the other hand, is as good as the ones in my magazine, with its single white bed with fluffy white pillows and a big brass full-length mirror, a midcentury modern chest of drawers. I have this itch all of a sudden to take a photo and send it to Heather—that's what I would do if I were on an actual trip somewhere, staying in an Airbnb (and I can't help but feel like that now), but I think better of it.

After I've sniffed all the perfume-soaked ads and skimmed through yet another celebrity house they've designed themselves with a custom espresso maker that is self-cleaning, I close my eyes and try to think through my latest drawing. Even if I'm not able to put pencil to paper, it kind of feels like it counts for *some*thing. Plus, @eatsleepdraw, one of my favorite

Instagram artists, says that we make art when we sleep, that when we wake up in the morning we're able to see things differently, get unstuck. I started sketching a couple of nights ago, and as usual everything took much longer than I thought it would. I shouldn't be surprised by that anymore. Getting ideas is easy; I'm full of ideas. It's not that hard to write down "family as birds." Matt calls my idea list my recycling bin: a place where I drop things off and pick them up again, sometimes in a new form. The tough part is execution: Do the cockatiels resemble my family members, and if so, how? What do cockatiels actually look like? How big is the birdcage in relation to me-as-a-bird? What kind of bird do I choose for myself so I don't come across like I think I'm better than them? Then there's all that logistical, even mathematical stuff that people don't realize artists need to do: Decide placement. Measure out each element on the page to know how much space each will take up. Make sure the birdcage is drawn correctly to scale. Figure out how to depict the birdcage so it doesn't obscure the birds.

Now my brain is really on a roll, and I figure I won't sleep if I don't write at least some of this down. I take out my phone (even though Matt would say that's the opposite of helping myself sleep) and type into my Notes app until I'm so sleepy I risk dropping my device on my face.

ℓℓℓ

In the morning, I'm awake and alert well before my alarm. The _pad pad pad_ of slippers against the tile is the first sound

I hear, and it's a sound I'm familiar with because both my parents wear slippers around when it's not summer—and even sometimes when it is. Mom always says it's better to wake up as soon as your hosts do, if not earlier. But I'm not really a guest, I'm an employee. Probably, in that case, there's even more reason to wake up early. I make the bed as quickly as I can and step out of the room.

Mrs. Granucci is wearing a floral nightgown and fuzzy pink slippers. Her hair is no different from how it was when we met; she must have slept with rollers in, or maybe she's been up a while. Her smile is huge and her eyes bright. Not even my parents seem that excited to see me in the morning, I guess because I'm not very excited to see them, either—or anyone for that matter.

"Emily!" Mrs. Granucci says, as if we've run into each other at the grocery store. "You're up. Are you a morning person? An early riser?"

"Not at all," I admit. "How did you sleep?"

"Oh, me? I always sleep like a rock."

"Really?" My grandmother—who is probably around Mrs. Granucci's age—perpetually has trouble sleeping, it seems.

"I'll tell you a secret." She leans her face toward me the slightest bit, then says in a stage whisper: "It's the meds!" She gestures to her banana-shaped pill box beside the sugar bowl on the counter.

What kind of meds are they? I almost ask. But I figure it's better not to pry, at least not on the first day of my new job.

"Before we eat breakfast, I do need to show you something very important." I follow her through the living room. I wonder if she's going to remind me about the shoes, which I can't wait to wear. But then she opens the front door and we both step out into the morning. It's hardly seven but it's already an oven out. On the front porch, Mrs. Granucci squats down with some effort—by the time I think to offer to help, she's already on her way back up—and holds out the fairy house key safe. Again.

"The spare key is in here, and it will always be in here," she says.

I'm about to say, *I know, that's how I got in.* But something holds me back. I don't want to sound disrespectful or smart-alecky. Or is this some sort of test? Is she showing it to me again and am I supposed to tell her I remember every exact detail about the spare key?

But then she says, "I need to make sure you understand, Emily. It will always be in here, and you need to always put it back in here."

Well, whatever. She's old, and old people forget things sometimes. Heck, even I forget things sometimes. I don't want to embarrass her, so I say, "Got it. Spare key, always in key safe; key safe, always in same spot." I hold out my hand. "Here, I got it."

I lay it carefully on the ground.

Then Mrs. Granucci claps her hands together, and her face seems to take on a completely different expression, not nearly as troubled now that she knows I'm capable of remembering the key. "With that out of the way, let's make ourselves something fabulous."

"Oh, you don't need to go through any trouble. I usually just have cereal."

"Cereal?" Mrs. Granucci's eyes widen. "No wonder you're as thin as a pencil!" She looks me up and down. It seems Mrs. Granucci is often going to look me up and down. "And I'm not going to go through any trouble—*you're* the one who's going to make this. Now, would you like coffee or tea?"

At home I still had juice or milk, like a little kid, but Mrs. Granucci makes her coffee extra strong and pours it over ice with milk and sugar and cinnamon. This was another thing that my parents would not like to see me drink, and it was all the more delicious for it.

"My favorite is eggs Benny. The thing about these eggs," she tells me, "is they're high-risk and high reward. If you're not precise, you can end up with eggs that are a little undercooked or overcooked, or turn out lopsided, a lot of white in one spot. The sauce can be a runny yellow mess. And nobody wants that. But make the sauce perfectly, and you have a glossy pool of sunshine that tastes like . . . like . . ."

I'm watching Mrs. Granucci carefully, patiently. Something tells me I shouldn't jump in and volunteer words for what she's trying to say. I'm waiting for her to say it tastes like, well, lemon and eggs, but she says:

"Like the first day of sunshine after three miserable rainy ones."

I would very much like to make a sauce that tastes like that.

She lowers her voice, even though we're the only ones in

the house. "So, E, please pay very close attention. If you learn to do this small thing perfectly, then you'll do well with the other, more important things that will become part of your life here."

It reminds me of how she spoke to me on the day we first met. *My life here? It's just a summer job.* But I don't say that, of course. What worries me more is that I'm not really the type who does much of anything "perfectly." That's Tessa's jam. I tend to be more of an "okay, good enough" type of gal. But I resolve, right then, to try. If it's that important to her, I'll do my best to do it perfectly.

"Yes, ma'am," I say, taking two eggs from the carton.

"We used to have these on special days," Mrs. Granucci continues. "Christmas morning, birthdays. Ed—that's my husband—made them. One of the few times I'd let him into this kitchen. In fact, he'd shoo me away and handle the whole production!" She shakes her head. "But these days I usually join my son, Robbie, for the holidays, and his family of course has their own new traditions now." Then she smiles at me. "Which, of course, they should!"

She opens a drawer full of kitchen utensils and takes out a pin with a plastic pearl at the top. She has me take an egg in one hand and a pin in the other, and puncture the top of the egg, ever so carefully. Once the water is simmering on the stove, I lower the egg into it. "Then count to ten, and take it out with a slotted spoon."

I do as I'm told. She tells me that this gives the egg a higher chance of keeping its structural integrity before it gets poached. Then it's time to make the sauce.

"Watch for color," she says as I whisk the egg yolks with the lemon juice and water. "I know you can do that—you're an artist! They need to be, as Julia says, 'thick and pale,' so they'll be prepared 'for what is to come.'"

I wouldn't call myself that, an artist. I guess I technically am one, since I make art. But it's not like anyone pays me to do it. Still, hearing Mrs. Granucci call me that makes me feel good, like art is something to take seriously. Under her watch, I whisk till my arm is sore, watching the yolks go from dàntà to Irish butter. Then I'm taking the saucepan off the heat, then putting it on the heat, and back off again, making sure the temperature is just right.

But the emulsion isn't blending the way it should. Mrs. Granucci says, "What's going on? Tell me exactly what happened that caused this."

This is something Matt would enjoy. It reminds me of some of the chemistry experiments we got to do last year— only more interesting and with a better reward.

"The emulsion broke. Maybe because I wasn't whisking continuously," I say. "Or, I was, but it still fell apart somehow."

"Precisely. This ought to save it!" Mrs. Granucci adds the tiniest drop of water, then takes the sauce in hand and whisks it super fast.

Once the sauce is saved and the English muffins are toasted, I slide one poached egg onto each. One lands nicely on the muffin, but the other hangs off by a bit, and I—not a particularly delicate person—use my fingers to nudge it back on. That sends some of the yolk spilling out onto the plate. A pool of sunshine that is slowly congealing into a pool of yuck.

"Shoot," I say. "I'm not good at this."

"Nuh-uh-uh," says Mrs. Granucci. "Zip it! I will have none of that type of talk on the job. It's your first time doing it. You're going to get the hang of this. Tell yourself that and move on. Because you know what, your brain hears what your mouth says.

"Now, before the sauce, prep the finishing touches—very important. Like adding jewelry and makeup to an outfit. Or shoes. Because we eat with our eyes, don't we? Snip these chives at a diagonal—very finely—and sprinkle just the right amount on top."

"What's just the right amount?"

"You'll know it when you see it."

So I do as she says, and again I use my eyes, trying to see the dish the way I would an outfit, or a drawing.

Then I grind pepper over the top, and sprinkle smoked paprika for both aesthetics and flavor. It's like a piece of art—it needs a couple of contrasting colors to really pop.

"Lovely," says Mrs. Granucci. "Not quite perfect, yet, but you can try again next weekend. Thank you very much."

That's when Mrs. Granucci gets a faraway look in her eyes. She picks up both plates and makes as if to carry them to the kitchen table. Then she stops, halfway there. When she turns to me again, it's as if she's suddenly remembering I'm there at all.

"Well!" she says. "Are you hungry or not? Now we feast."

lll

After I do the dishes, Mrs. G suggests we go for a walk, before it gets too hot.

I've got my hand on the door when she says, "No hat? Emily, if there's one piece of advice I can give you, it's that you've got to protect your skin."

That's the one piece of advice you have for me? I think. But I keep my mouth shut. I learned from Matt—who slathers sunscreen on himself like he's frosting a cake—that white folk burn so much more easily than my family. But I keep my mouth shut about that, too.

As she hands me a floppy hat, she says, "Oh my goodness, now I can't find my keys. I always put them right here. . . ."

Then Mrs. Granucci closes her eyes and says, "Sweet baby Jesus, can you please use your fabulous God magic to help us find them!"

I've lived in the South my whole life, but I can't say I've heard a prayer quite like that. It seems to work, because minutes later, she jangles them in the air, saying, "Praise God Almighty!"

Then Mrs. G leans into the mirror, which is tarnished and cracked at the sides. "I love this thing," she says. "It's old but beautiful, like me! And my God, do I love lipstick. One swipe can change your life. It's very important."

Then we're off, each with an ice-cold bottle of water that starts to sweat the minute we're outside. And all I can think is I hope I don't run into anyone I know. I look more ridiculous than usual in this hat.

Mrs. G mentioned she was close to eighty, but she walks

fast, and the entire walk she speaks to me directly, crisply. She employs three-syllable words for things that she loves: *marvelous, terrific, fantastic, outstanding.* I'm guessing she's lived in River's Edge awhile, and yet she still finds plenty that is fabulous: The way the massive, sprawling oaks lean over the street. Two plump squirrels chasing each other. The squeal of little girls in pink swimsuits as they run through a sprinkler on a front lawn. The smell of honeysuckle.

"Ooh, my, would you smell that! Nothing like nature's summer perfume to make your walk just heavenly!"

"Sure," I say, but I'm not so sure. If I'm feeling hot, then Mrs. Granucci has got to be sweltering—but she doesn't complain, just smiles through the sweating and dabs at her brow with a handkerchief. We stop under one of the oak trees to sip our water.

At least I'll be around if she gets heatstroke or whatever. If I don't get it myself first.

"Lordy," she says. She pushes her hat off her head, fluffs her hair, then puts the hat back on again. "These hats sure do make your hair sweaty, fast."

As we walk, she tells me about everything she's involved in: She volunteers on the River's Edge Community Board; she's a Friend of the Green Valley Public Library; she sponsors the music department at the Greenwood School for the Performing Arts, which means some students receive a Granucci Scholarship. "It ain't much," she says, "but every bit helps!" She sings in the church choir—"It may not sound like it, but I can *blend.*"

It feels like the whole neighborhood is out for a walk. People say hi to me whenever I'm on my bike or walking, and I say it right back whether I know them or not—it's just part of Southern People Code—but for Mrs. Granucci it's a whole 'nother level of this. They all know her name, and not only that, but everything going on in her life as well.

"Hi, Leila! How are your rosebushes doing?"

"Morning, Ms. Leila."

"See you in choir tomorrow."

So many people know her that it makes me wonder why it took *me* so long to meet her.

The neighbors glance at me with a certain smile that I know very well. They keep grinning, but their eyes are questioning: *Who's this?*

At one point Mrs. Granucci hands me her tote bag—only for a second, but still—and that's when I can't help feeling like the non-white hired help.

If I were blond, with perfect skin and a big perky smile, the ladies would be all over me. They might even ask about my parents, who they'd know from tennis or golf, or church. I know this because I've seen it in action before. Trust me. Green Valley is the type of place where people have lived for generations.

But Mrs. Granucci at least makes things better when she says, "This is Emily, my companion!" It's nice when people introduce you by your name rather than your title first. And the other old white people say, "Nice to meet you, Emily," because of course people are going to be nice when *she's* the one introducing me. But when my whole family is out for a walk, things are different. People say hi and move on. They don't ask questions. Or worse, they ask dumb questions like, *Where are you from?* The worst ones try to guess. *Are you Filipino? Vietnamese? Thai?*

Thank you for guessing all the Asian countries, I ought to say. *I wasn't aware there were so many!*

It's people like that who make me want to leave South Carolina—and all the states that touch it—forever.

When we're back home, Mrs. Granucci says it's time for lunch. She has me "fix us a couple plates" while she takes a seat with her feet propped up. Then we both sit at the table together, and then Mrs. Granucci asks if I'd mind if she says "a small prayer."

"Not at all," I say. My own family doesn't say grace before meals, but it's fine by me if she does.

"Lord Jesus, thank you for your life and your death. Thank you for your love for us. Thank you for this abundant, glorious food and for the hands that made it. Please bless those hands. Amen."

The prayer seems like overkill, especially when it's just ham sandwiches and pickle spears, salt-and-vinegar chips, and lemonade. I want to make a joke about blessing my hands but can't think fast enough.

After lunch, Mrs. Granucci says she needs to show me her china, and I'm confused until she strides into the dining room, where the china cabinet is.

"Now these here are my everyday plates. But for special

days, I do have this absolutely lovely china." She leans toward me and whispers, "It's Royal Copenhagen. My mother-in-law gave this set to us on my wedding day."

I raise my eyebrows and say, "Ooh," and try to act impressed. But to be honest, I don't see that much difference between the fine china and her everyday plates, which have little pink flowers on them. They're both just white plates. The fine china has gilded edges.

"And now these," Mrs. Granucci says, opening another drawer, "are the Wedgewood. These are for *super* special days. Holidays and the like. Or, if we're having quite a big function, like Thanksgiving or a shower"—it takes me a beat to realize she's talking about a bridal shower or a baby shower—"you might need to use both sets, and that's fine."

"Oh?" I say. "So I'm going to be . . . serving food on these?"

"Well, Emily, I'm showing you everything just in case."

Just in case of what? I'm wondering, but she's already moving on to the other pieces in the china cabinet. I have to admit I don't see the point of plates that are only for display and not for eating—but to each her own, I guess.

My own parents don't have "wedding china," as far as I know. That, I'm learning, is just one of the differences between Mrs. Granucci's family and us.

Then the phone rings, and Mrs. Granucci rushes to answer it. I'm startled. I don't know anyone else in River's Edge who still has a landline. When she answers, it's clear that it's someone she knows well, and it sounds like it could take a while, so I decide to wander over and look at her art.

Call me a creep, but I love wandering around other people's houses. You learn so much more about them that way. I find myself back in the living room, staring at her paintings up close.

There's a still life of lemons in a bowl, and a pitcher behind it with pussy willows leaning out of it. It's acrylic, and there's something so pleasing about the way everything was placed together: the pebbly bright surface of the lemon beside the smooth, gleaming pitcher and the fuzzy buds of the plants. Someone decided to put those specific objects together. The pitcher is somehow both delicate and sturdy. But what strikes me most is that the lemon is more lemon-y than any lemon I've ever seen in real life. It's downright gorgeous. Maybe that's what's so great about still lifes; that they make you see things differently, find ordinary things beautiful.

"Well, you're certainly entranced," Mrs. Granucci says beside me, and I almost jump half a mile.

She grins. "You were staring at the thing for *minutes*! I've been standing here, watching you gape at it."

Now I don't feel as creepy about looking at her stuff.

"Someone took months, maybe years, to make it, so I figure I might as well take *minutes* to look," I say.

"A great point. People ought to slow down."

"Oh yeah. People go way too fast in museums. If you went to a restaurant you wouldn't try to order everything on the menu, so why do people make it their mission to see everything in an art museum?"

"I couldn't have said it better myself," she says.

For the first time all day, I think of Tessa and her hospital work. Sometimes I feel like my life is so unimportant by comparison. So not useful. I say as much. Tessa was learning how to save lives, while meanwhile I was—

"Well, *excuse* me! Useful, my ass!" Mrs. Granucci snorts. "*I* for one think that it's these earthly pleasures—God forgive me—that make life worth living! Paintings and music and delicious food. Not to mention, you're caring for an old lady. *That's* certainly important work, watching over a life. If that's not important, I don't know what is!"

Looking after Mrs. Granucci—if that's what I was doing— didn't seem all that difficult or even necessary, if I was being honest. It's not like I was looking after a baby. In fact, she didn't seem to really *need* me. It was more like I was around to keep her company while she did what she liked. But that was fine with me. Made my job way easier.

"Now, listen, Emily, you should know that at four o'clock sharp, I have a drink of vermouth. Just one drink, and then you'll wash this little blue glass by hand."

When I ask her what vermouth is, exactly, she tells me to do my own research.

"Well, it seems like it's used mostly for cooking," I say, after a brief search on my phone.

"Yes, here in the US, that's true. But my family is Italian, and this is the Italian way: a little something sweet to sip before dinner. Call me when you're twenty-one and we'll have some! Or maybe even a bit before then." She winks.

I take the amber bottle from the top of the pantry, and she

shows me how to pour just the right amount into her glass, then I bring it to her as she settles into the couch.

"What will you do tomorrow?" I ask.

"Go to church, Lord willing!" she said. "Maggie Costello comes by and I give her a ride. And yourself?"

"Well, we're Catholic," I say. "Because, you know, Dad's from Latin America and I guess Mom ran into some Catholic missionaries in Taiwan or something." The way I say it is almost an apology. I don't want to say it that way, but it is impossible not to living in the Bible Belt. Every week someone tells me we are going to hell for being Catholic. On top of which, we are dangerously on the verge of becoming Christmas-and-Easter-only Catholics.

Mrs. Granucci's eyes widen. "I love Catholics! Well, I *technically* am Catholic myself." She crosses herself right then, as if to prove it to me. "Besides, I do looove me some Communion. Sometimes I even double-dip and go to 8:00 a.m. Mass, and then over to the Baptist church."

"But why do you need to go to both?"

"Friends. A girl's gotta have friends to survive. Even loner artists like yourself." Mrs. Granucci puts her hand on my shoulder. "Speaking of which, you can just call me Leila. Or, if that's too daring for you, call me Mrs. G."

CHAPTER 4

WHEN I GO BACK home that evening, Tessa's painting her nails with her feet propped up on *my* magazines. This shouldn't bother me as much as it does—and it wouldn't, if she were Heather instead of Tessa, doing the exact same thing. Isn't it crazy how the littlest thing can cause the Gila monster to take over the nice person you were outside the house? I used to blame it on PMS, but obviously, even though PMS happens *a lot* (too frequently, if you ask me) it's not happening daily. Key difference.

"Get your feet off my mags," is the first thing I say when I come in.

"Nice to see you, too," says Tessa, not looking up. She's painting her toenails a shade of mint-chocolate-chip pale green that I actually really like. A shade that is definitely more my personality than hers, and I'm *so* pissed at her all of a sudden.

I take a deep breath. It's just nail polish, I tell myself. The thing is—and I know this about myself because Heather and Matt have dissected it with me—I always need to set myself apart from Tessa. I can't compete with her, so I need to be different. For that reason I don't paint my nails any of the conservative colors that she does. Yes, it's a small thing, but at least it's something. But now here she is, using *my* color.

Dad comes into the room then. "Rillo! How was your time at that lady's house?"

"Mrs. Granucci's," I say. In my head, I correct myself: *Mrs. G's.* "It was good. We had really good food—" I begin, but then it seems insensitive to share about that when we're mostly eating soft foods because Mom's throat hurts due to her thyroid condition.

"What kind of food did you have? It's not all casseroles and fried things, is it?"

For some reason, my parents' idea of white people's food is always casseroles and fried things.

Before I can answer, Dad says, "And what did you do all day there?"

He emphasizes "all day."

"I cooked—" I begin. Tessa raises her eyebrows, as if implying that I'm not the greatest cook. I ignore her. "I learned, you know, how she runs her house. We went for a walk. She has a lot of art and nice furniture that needs taking care of." Okay, so I haven't done anything for her art or furniture yet, but I likely will. And I figure it sounds impressive; it'll sound good on a résumé for art school.

But Dad says, "We didn't raise you to be a housekeeper."

"That's not what I'm doing!"

Dad looks hurt. "We hardly get to see you, and all you're doing is taking care of this lady's house?"

"You have me all week!" I huff.

When I've been gone for twenty-four hours, my parents act like I've been gone for years. And when we're "finally"—as they put it—reunited, they don't even seem that happy to see me.

Besides, studies show that having too much free time is just as harmful as having too little. What I don't understand is why my parents want me around when it's not like we're spending any quality time with each other. We're not having interesting conversations or doing an activity together. If I were home, I'd be holed up in my room drawing anyway. So what's the point?

"Remember how Tessa spent her summers when she was your age?" Dad says. Tessa was "my age" last year, but whatever. "She was at the library every morning when they opened."

Only home for five minutes and I was already being nagged and compared. Why do I feel like people outside my house always listen to me better? Besides, it was different for Tessa. Steve would pick her up with Frappuccinos in hand. If I had a free ride from a boyfriend and free Starbucks, I'd go to the library more often too.

From the couch, Tessa wiggles her toes and caps the polish. At least she knows—sometimes—to stay quiet instead of making things worse.

Dad gets on the computer in the living room, no doubt doomscrolling, no doubt about to tell me what fresh disaster is about to befall us. It seems everything gets recalled and could cause you to become ill, or die: romaine lettuce, eye drops, phone chargers. Dad wasn't always like this. Well, he was, but it came with a healthy dose of humor as well. I can't help thinking that Mom's thyroid jumbo olive has made things worse, made him feel that terrible things are around every corner.

"So, this old lady has you come over to take a walk with her, but if she's able to walk by herself, why does she need you around?"

I sigh. "Dad—" I begin.

"I just don't want her to take advantage of you. She's an old woman and I still don't understand what you do over there."

"No one's taking advantage of anyone. She's paying me, fair and square."

He speaks evenly and slowly, as if I won't understand what he's saying otherwise. "I *understand* that she's paying you, but even a paid job can have an employer taking advantage. And she's so much older than you, hija. All I'm asking is that you're careful."

"Okay," I say.

"Go spend time with Mom. She misses you."

Sometimes I think Dad makes things up just to mess with me, or to send me on epic guilt trips. It doesn't work on me as well as Tessa. Like, I don't really think my mom said that she misses me. She probably literally said, "Where's Emily?"

and Dad spun it into this thing that means I need to go and sit with her.

Mom's in the kitchen, smashing garlic with the back of a knife. I stand next to her and start unpeeling them, clove by clove. It's satisfying how easily the skin comes off.

"Oh, thank you so much, Emily," she says. "Do you think you cook more at that lady's house than you do here?"

See? This is why Heather calls her a tiger mom with claws wrapped in velvet. Does Mom miss me? Or does she just like to give me a hard time?

Then Tessa comes in and starts lining up all the spices, taking out pots and pans, as if trying to show me that she knows her stuff, and it doesn't matter that I'm helping—she's boss in the kitchen.

"My girls," Mom says. She takes each of us by the arm and pulls us toward her. "It is just so wonderful having you home with me this summer."

My sweaty shoulder is almost touching Tessa's. She seems to notice it, too—she tightens just the slightest bit, and so do I.

Have you ever been simultaneously in awe of someone and also completely jealous of them and annoyed with them? That's how I feel toward my sister. I've never wanted someone else's approval so much—and at the same time I find her infuriating. I've never admired someone so much, and at the same time I wish she'd live a little.

It wasn't always like this, with Tessa. Don't ask me what happened, it was all so gradual. She got popular in high school, I wanted to do my own thing, and from there we grew apart until we basically only put up with each other because we live under the same roof. But I used to want to be just like her. Everything she did was cool. When she was in third grade and I was in second, she won the science fair with a contraption that would turn the pages while you were reading. I mean, have you heard of anything more delightfully nerdy? Even now, I want to be that kid's friend. I didn't know what resentment was then. All I knew was how to adore, how to try to be a little more like her. But I found that I couldn't. Be like her, I mean. She was always going to be better at that kind of stuff: detail-oriented school assignments with strict deadlines and a clear structure. Some days it felt like the only thing I was better at than her was making art.

Well, and getting dressed. Tessa has style, don't get me wrong. I'm just more original.

This is how Tessa's mind works: she tells herself to do something and then she does it. I tell myself to do something, and then I turn around and do exactly the opposite. The task just sits there, waiting and waiting in the back of my mind, until it disappears into a song that I've put on repeat, and listening to it and then reading about the band is much better than starting my geometry homework. My brain is like those times when you take out your phone just to check the weather, and thirty minutes later you're deep into the Wikipedia entry on tacos.

Sometimes I wonder if that's just how I'm made. If I need to be told *not* to do something if I'm going to get anything done. Maybe that's even why I draw so frequently.

You'd think that something like Mom's possible illness would bring Tessa and me closer together, but it only seems to have brought out the worst. We're both helpless in this situation. There's nothing we can do that will change anything—as much as Tessa likes to act like there is.

The thing is, I look up to Tessa, a lot, even now. It may not seem like it, but I do.

"It's good you're home," Tessa says. "So you can do the veggies." Under her breath she adds, "You can at least do *something* around here."

God. I look up to her until she says something like that.

The girl could cook a five-course meal in the time it takes me to put a salad together. It's not like she needs my help. I almost say something like, *Garlic is technically a vegetable, so I've already done something,* but it's clear she's in a mood.

She practically throws the vegetables onto the counter, where they land with a dull thud. Steam is rising from the rice cooker, and next to it there's some mail addressed to Tessa, all from colleges, and a few envelopes that are probably bills, all of them opened but left there, to be dealt with later. Next to that, the carrots and bok choy are in their plastic produce bags, shimmering with condensation.

And all I can think is, *Still life with bok choy.*

While Tessa starts making rice, I peel a couple of carrots and toss the scraps, then slice them into coins. I take the bok choy out next and start arranging things on the cutting board.

I'm trying to create the sense that, even though these are all objects, there is life in the scene. Someone—or multiple someones—has been here with them, has just touched them. Everything's kind of messy and unfinished. The flaps of the envelopes are open, the timer on the rice cooker counting down the minutes. No, they're not the most beautiful objects, but it's not about that—not necessarily anyway. Once I saw a still life with toilet paper—rolls and rolls of it rendered in acrylic with the late afternoon sunlight slanting in through the bathroom window—and it was weirdly beautiful. I love that someone thought to do that at all.

When Tessa turns around to check on my progress, I'm taking photo after photo of the bok choy, the carrots, the rice cooker, and the mail. "Can we keep things moving?" she says, not even bothering to call me a weirdo.

After dinner, I go to my room to draw.

That's what keeps me going most days. I like it because when I'm drawing, blending colors with my fingers and searching for just the right shade of green, my brain doesn't wander and my hands don't itch for my phone. And okay, I know I said earlier that I don't want to paint a banana, but after seeing that lemon at Mrs. G's, I mean really seeing it, I think I get it a little more now. I grab my phone, select the photograph I like best, and challenge myself to a still life. I spend two hours with just my pencil, making sure things are exactly how I want them. You can erase pastels, but I don't usually. I make sure I get things right with my pencil first, because I like the feeling of there's no going back.

The following weekend, Mrs. G has me on breakfast duty while she gets ready. It's pancakes this time, made with cake flour and bread flour and a healthy pinch of baking powder so they're ultra-fluffy—really putting the *cake* in *pancake*. So that's what I'm working on when I hear a rustling outside, near the front of the house. I put the whisk down, dripping batter onto the counter, half wondering if I just imagined it. But no, there it is again. It sounds a lot like someone trying to open the door.

Suddenly I picture all of Dad's worst nightmares coming true. All his fears of abduction and burglary and someone demanding we give them all our money . . . or else. And of course they would come to the Granucci house—Mrs. G has paintings, she has jewelry, she has shoes that are worth a lot.

And unlike my overprepared, overly cautious dad, she has no alarm system. It's my duty, of course, to protect her house.

I press myself flat against the wall and shuffle toward the door, step by silent step, holding my breath, and keeping one eye on the door.

But this is River's Edge, and it's broad daylight, and the door is locked and bolted because that's what I did last night. I walk right up to the window and peek through.

It's a boy around my age, and he's impeccably groomed. In eighty-degree weather, he's wearing all black from head to toe, the sleeves of his button-down shirt rolled up at the forearms. His hair is wavy and dark and he's wearing sunglasses. The second thing I notice is that—and this is the super-weird part— he's holding another person upright: a man with floppy hair.

"Uh, Mrs. G?" I call over my shoulder. I try to keep my voice down so that it's not exactly shouting. I don't want to freak her out or anything.

But now the boy is rapping at the door, clearly struggling under the weight of this other man. "Mrs. G!" I yell.

And she comes running. You've never seen a woman in her late seventies run this fast. It occurs to me that next time—hopefully there will be no next time—I ought not to startle her. I could give her a heart attack, literally.

But once she sees who's at the door, she stops dead still in her tracks, and then she throws her head back and laughs.

"Bless me, Ezra! I completely forgot you were coming today," Mrs. G says as she opens the door. "And with George!"

Ezra's panting a little from having carried . . . George . . . from the car to the house. "Where should I put this, Aunt Leila?" he asks.

"Let's put him in the living room, and he'll welcome our guests and scare all the squirrels away, ha! And," she adds, her voice growing serious, "he'll scare away any intruders. Actual intruders, that is."

Ezra carries George into the living room, propping him up gingerly against a wall.

"You took long enough," he says to me. "This could've melted."

"*This* . . . being?"

Mrs. G is aghast. "Do you mean to tell me that people your age don't recognize a wax figure of George Harrison when you see one?"

We all regard George for a second. He looks so real; his skin even has little imperfections. His hair is glossy and long and falls to his shoulders—like Jesus, I can't help thinking. His eyes are intense, under big bushy brows, and he's wearing a paisley shirt. He's frowning.

When I look over at Ezra, his expression isn't that much different from George's. Except that, if I'm being honest, Mrs. Granucci's nephew is smoking hot, with dimples and intense hazel eyes.

Damn.

Mrs. G and I follow Ezra to the kitchen, where he fills a glass with ice water and drinks the whole thing without stopping.

Mrs. G puts her hand on Ezra's shoulder. "And you! Why are you dressed like an undertaker on this gorgeous day? You must be stifling in those jeans."

"I've got a gig later with the trio."

"At the museum?"

"The retirement center. Where I'll see several of your peers."

Mrs. G smacks him on the arm. "Well," she says, "I know they'll love it." Turning to me, she says, "As you've likely surmised, Emily, this very rude young man is my nephew."

Ezra sticks out his hand and we shake, as if we're at a business meeting and not just two teenagers meeting at his aunt's house. His grip is strong and his hand is big and cool from holding the glass. I can't remember the last time I shook hands with someone my age. Possibly never.

Matt likes giving people a fist bump when he meets them, and although I've always thought that to be the pinnacle of dorkdom, at least it feels warmer than this handshake.

"I'm her *great*-nephew," Ezra says. He gestures to Mrs. G. "She's my grandma's sister, which makes her my great-aunt."

"He's the greatest," Mrs. G says.

"I am," he says.

Mrs. G lightly punches him in the arm. "I'm going to put on a summer sweater. You two talk. I'll be right back." And with that, Mrs. G goes upstairs and leaves me alone with her strange nephew.

Excuse me, her *great*-nephew.

Ezra and I regard each other. Heather says I have a severe look sometimes—she says it scares people—but Ezra has a true stare.

I hoist myself up onto one of the stools.

He leans against the kitchen island, his sunglasses hanging from his shirt collar. I should get in the habit of carrying mine around. It would help so much with biking. I'm always squinting into the sun instead, riding with my eyes half-closed, really "asking for it," as my mother would say.

"So, what do you do around here? Housekeeping?" he says.

I scoff. It's just a joke—and I guess it's meant to be funny, because the kitchen is a mess—but it still strikes a nerve. "I'm her companion. Or, as she sometimes calls me, her *personal assistant.*"

He puts his hands up. "Came out wrong." Then his eyes fall on my shoes, the heels, and he says, "Pretty dressed up for an in-home job, don't you think?"

"You're one to talk," I say, eyeing his all-black outfit. "Do you ever try for just a smidge of variety?"

"Black is what musicians wear. Anyway, that's what they teach us at school."

"Where do you go?"

"Greenwood School for the Performing Arts," he says. "You know. In downtown Green Valley?" He makes air quotes around *downtown,* as if it doesn't deserve that designation.

I slip off the stool and open the refrigerator, pretend I need something in there. "I've heard of it," I say. Then I get back to the pancake batter. I keep my voice light so he won't think I'm impressed. And the truth is, I'm annoyed, because he set me up to ask him where he goes to school so he could brag.

"Well, I'm not, like, a snob or anything. If that's what you're thinking."

"Is it true? What they say."

"What, the sex and drugs?"

"That everyone's super smart and you're always studying or practicing all the time, but okay, that too."

"What does 'smart' even mean anyway?" he says.

Geez. Is this the type of thing they talk about at that school?

I get the stove heating, and he reaches up into a cupboard for a bowl.

"You tell me," I say. I almost add "smartass," which is what my mother calls me sometimes after she has a drink. "So what do you go there for? Don't you have to, like, choose a major or something?"

"Cello."

"Cello, yourself," I say, as if saying hello.

This seems to irritate him, which pleases me. "I'm really good at cello!" he says. "Besides, it's the sexiest instrument, and not just because it goes between your legs."

I make a face. "Humble, much?"

He nudges the bowl toward me. "Since you're my aunt's assistant, maybe you could assist her by putting some ice cream in there for her nephew?"

I roll my eyes. Even Matt, who likes everyone, would call this guy a piece of work.

Ezra just grins, then fetches the ice cream and scoops it for himself. Okay. So maybe he's aware of his own bullshit, which makes it a little less bad. Or, is this his version of flirting with me?

Then he says, "Whoa. What does she have you doing that makes your fingers all . . . colorful like that?"

I look down at my hands. The pads of my fingers, the outside of my pinkies, and even some of my nails are stained dark green from the other night, trying to find the right shades for the bok choy drawing. It's weird, how pastels wash out of your clothes easily enough, but stay on your skin. "Oh. This is from drawing. I do stuff with chalk pastels."

"You do 'stuff'? You mean you're an artist, too, like me." He regards me differently then—with more interest, maybe, and more respect. "Maybe *you* should apply to Greenwood."

I read about it once, but there were too many things to give up: going to school with Heather and Matt, for one. "No thanks," I say. "I don't prefer to live at school."

"Are you good?" Ezra says. "At drawing, I mean."

"I guess I'm good?" I say. Who walks around saying they're good at something? I guess Ezra does.

"If you're doing it regularly enough that your hands are like . . . that, then you must be," he says, nodding at my stains appreciatively.

He goes to the coffee maker and pours the rest of it over his ice cream.

Then I hear the sound of Mrs. G padding down the stairs again. "Do you really need that much caffeine before you play?" she says as she comes back in. "Oh, and Emily, we *must* go hear them sometime. They play absolutely beautifully!"

"I can take caffeine," says Ezra. "We've played together a million times and it's easy, crowd-pleasing shit."

She smacks his shoulder. "I wish you'd told me! In fact, if I'd known you were playing today, I'd have put it in my calendar!"

"Would you have, though? You forgot I was coming today with Mr. George Harrison over there."

It's clear he's just teasing her, but for a second, Mrs. G's face falls. "I don't know what happened," she begins. "I'm so stupid sometimes, can't remember a thing."

"I'm joking," Ezra says quickly. "Don't worry about it, Aunt Leila. I'm sorry, I should've reminded you." So, the pretentious dud has a heart after all. He glances down at his coffee-covered ice cream puddle. "Check this out. I think I made a poor man's affogato?"

I can see how he is her nephew. They both like fancy things.

75

Before he leaves, he and Mrs. G hug for a while. "It's such a treat having you around in the summer," she says.

He nods at me. "Emily," he says.

"Ezra," I say. What are we, characters in a Jane Austen novel? But the way he said my name was kind of nice.

Mrs. G sees him out, and then calls from the living room: "After breakfast, Emily, I'll teach you how exactly you're going to take care of George."

～ℓℓℓ～

Monday through Friday is swim practice, but that's only in the morning. On some weeknights we have swim meets, but most of the time, the rest of the summer day stretches on, waiting to be filled. Some people would kill for this amount of free time, but I'm sort of terrified of being bored. Every summer for the past few years I tell myself it'll be the last summer, that I'll quit or at least just be a lifeguard. The thing is, though, I think I'd get bored being a lifeguard. The times when you have to put your skills to the test are thankfully few and far between. Maybe that's why I keep going to practice even though I'm over it—at least it's something to do. Plus, Mom always says that swimming makes me strong.

Coach is Rachel Jackson, and her family is one of two Black families in our neighborhood. We met a few years ago and it wasn't even swim-related. She was running in a lavender sports bra and color-block leggings—looking really good, if you ask me—and I was on my bike, my hair a sweaty mess, when she waved at me and said, "Let's talk."

She stood there with her hands on her hips, not even winded, saying that her family had just moved from Atlanta because her dad had been promoted to vice president of his company and "blah blah blah" (her words, not mine), and she couldn't believe her family had moved to this all-white neighborhood where the only non-white people she saw were the Amazon truck drivers and—she hated this, goddam she hated this so much—the cleaning woman at 806 Meadowforest Lane.

"What's it like?" she asked. "How do you stand it?"

At that precise moment, I kid you not, a little old white lady slowed down her car when she saw us: two girls of color having a conversation on the side of the road in River's Edge.

I said, "You find your people, I guess. You learn who to put up with and who's just full of bullshit."

She nodded, all serious. "I'm pretty good at calling people out on their BS."

"People are always telling me they saw my mom giving someone a pedicure at VIP Nails, or asking if my dad owns the Mexican restaurant on Highway 14."

She nodded. "Someone's always thinking I'm delivering things. People like you and me," she said, "we have to stick together."

But after that, she went to the private Christian school her parents had picked and the next year was off to college, and we both got busy and didn't run into each other much. Then I went to swim practice and guess who was coaching me?

Swim practice is what makes my mornings an emotional roller coaster. Usually I spend the hour before it with a pit of dread in my stomach, but once I get there, I don't mind it so much because I don't have to feel, don't have to think. The minute you're in the water it's go go go, and the minute you're out of the water, you stand there dripping in your one-piece, waiting behind the others, with only enough resting time to check out who painted their toenails or has hair under their armpits, and there's hardly the energy to do that. Mostly you catch your breath before the next set. At least you're all suffering together. Everyone is sort of unrecognizable in their goggles and caps.

We're swimming the warm-up, which is a 400-meter freestyle, when I see Matt swimming in the lane beside me as I take a breath. And every time I breathe, he's a little farther behind. I'm not the greatest swimmer, but that boy is helpless in the water. I've tried to tell him before and coaches have tried to tell him, too. And sometimes his technique changes for a few minutes, but then he goes right back to flailing along. I think the only time he got something other than fifth or sixth place was when we were swimming against Honey Creek, who are honestly just not a great team, and he got a fourth-place ribbon. Oh, and there was that one time he came in second because there were only two people swimming his event.

Matt does swim team because he has this extreme sense of duty. His parents both swam in college and now his older brother does, and his little brother swims on the guppy team—so of course Matt does it. Some people have soccer moms, but Matt's parents are the ones selling candy or timing us at swim meets. They're also the ones who came up with the River's Edge composting initiative, so he's always on my case about getting our compost set up. It's important that he's involved in the neighborhood *somehow.*

Coach doesn't like for us to be talking between sets, and yet, as we're all waiting for instructions for the kick drills, Matt whispers, "Em! Hey, Em."

Well, I don't want to embarrass the guy in front of everyone, after what he's been through. I give a half-hearted wave, try to say with my face that we'll talk another time.

Then we're all in the water again, going at the speed of manatees, and Coach Jackson is yelling at me to keep my core engaged and make white water.

After practice, what I usually do is throw my towel around my neck and bike home sopping wet—partly because it feels good to be in the sun when you're still soaked, and partly to avoid talking with anyone after practice. I like Coach, but I'm not going to seem like a suck-up staying afterward to talk with her. My other conversation partner would be Matt, but when I take a look around for him, he's nowhere to be seen. He must be on babysitting duty. I check my phone. Sure enough, Matt has texted. *Mom left me with Russell again, call me when you see this!* So I'm making my way to the bike rack when I hear a high-pitched female voice call:

"Emily!"

I turn around. It's Zoey Kebabian. Did I see her at practice? Probably. She had a swim cap and goggles on and I likely just skimmed over her face without thinking about it.

When she smiles, her teeth are perfectly square and

straight, and so white. I should ask her what kind of toothpaste she uses. Or maybe they just appear that white because she's so tan.

"Hi!" she says, all bouncy and nice.

I say hi back. Inadvertently I search for Matt again.

"Your summer going well?" Zoey asks, as if we're good friends, even though we're barely acquaintances.

"Yeah, overall."

"I love summer. It's like everything lightens up for everyone over the summer, doesn't it? People become more carefree, and just, happier."

I couldn't disagree with her more; in fact I read an article about how some people get seasonal depression in the summer because they're so cranky from the heat. It makes people grumpy. Sometimes I think there's too much pressure on summer, pressure to do all the things you can't during the year, pressure to transform yourself into someone new before school begins. And you can't exercise outside as much because it's so hot, and maybe you're not sleeping as much because you're so hot. Workloads lighten, and even though people say they're happier when they're not working, maybe people need structure to stay sane. That's why drawing is so great for me. Time flies by when I'm doing it, and there's always something to figure out, some new thing I need to discover. Yet I, for one, am always relieved when the first day of true fall rolls around—that first crisp morning when you need to put on a sweater.

"It's nice to have no school," I say. It's also nice to have more time to draw, but I don't need to tell Zoey that. "How's *your* summer going so far?"

"Yeah, it's going really well, you know? And, like, with my new relationship . . . ," she says, trailing off.

"Oh yeah?" I say. "You're dating someone . . . new?" This is odd, this entire exchange so far. That Zoey would want to talk to me at all is something, but that she'd want to tell me about her dating life is even stranger.

She smiles again, big, but this time it's like I've made her uncomfortable, somehow. "You're just joking, right?" she says.

All I can think is that her hair is naturally great. It's a little damp, but it's long and dark and curly, not wild curly but more like civilized waves, as if she styled it. Except she didn't, because there's no way she got up before seven to do that and then put it under a swim cap. And yet she's so genuinely nice, I can't even hate her.

"Sorry, I must be missing something," I say. I wonder if it's something I should have learned from social media. I try to remember who Zoey has dated before, if anyone. Our school is so big it's hard to keep track. For a split second, I feel bad for Matt that she's seeing someone else.

She makes a face. "Matt didn't tell you?"

I study her for a second. "Matt?" I parrot back.

"Oh my god, I'm so sorry! I should have let him be the one to tell you!"

"Oh—I . . ." It's sinking in now, and I'm not sure what to think of it. Mostly, I'm shocked. Maybe he was going to tell me that Friday evening when I was making my way to Mrs. G's and ignored him. Or maybe he was going to, what, announce it as we were waiting in line for drills? That would've been awkward, but I wouldn't have put it past him. Now I know why he wanted me to call him so urgently.

"Yeah," I say, "I think he wanted to tell me, but we keep missing each other. I started a new job, and I've been grounded."

All I can think is, wow. Matt got the girl, a really *cute, smart, nice* girl at that. I've often thought that more girls ought to like Matt—the same way I think more guys ought to be into Heather—but still, I wasn't expecting this. I guess when she said she'd think about it, she really thought about it.

"Well," I say. "Cool. I'm happy for you guys."

That's the right thing to say. It's not what I'm feeling, but how often do I say out loud what I'm really feeling? The thing is, I'm not sure *what* I'm feeling. Mostly surprised. Back when Heather briefly dated Jared Watkins, I felt annoyed, because it meant we had less time together. And weirdly I felt kind of hurt, because suddenly it was my job to listen to her go on about how great he was, and it was like I'd been replaced. Is that what I'm feeling now?

Zoey's smiling, I mean really smiling, ear to ear, and her happiness is so palpable it almost makes me mad, even though I know that's not rational.

"Can I ask you about something, though?" She leans toward me.

Here it comes: She's (already) discovered something unpalatable about Matt. The way he can spout statistics about how food waste is a major contributor to climate change, or how he fancies himself a meteorologist because he knows the names of different clouds, or how he sometimes loses his temper in an embarrassing way when doing anything that involves academic competition—and it starts out seeming like he's joking but then you realize he's not. Or that he can watch video after video about, say, sheepshearing, and then he'll make you watch said videos and even when you can't see what the big deal is, you keep watching because he is so impressed and delighted by the thing.

And in spite of everything, I'm ready to defend Matt, because yes it's annoying, but it's *my* annoying friend's habit, and even I have to admit sheepshearing is pretty damn cool.

So I'm waiting for one of these, but instead Zoey says, "You've been friends for so long, and, like . . ." She lets her voice trail off.

"What?" I say.

"I just, I wanted to make sure that, like . . ." She smiles again, and I can see that it's not the smile of trying to ingratiate myself to her but a smile of unease. "Sorry, it's hard to talk about," she says. Then she lets it all out in a steady stream of words: "You don't *like* like him, do you? Because he told me, like, what went down, but it sounds, like, you know, the lemonade got to him, and it sounds like you guys haven't talked in a while, so I just wanted to make sure, like . . ." She stops, but I don't need to hear any more. I get what she's implying, and no. No no no, I am not about to be someone's pity case. *She's* checking on *me* to make sure that *I* don't like *Matt*?

That is all kinds of messed up.

At the same time, I don't feel so great about it, and it's hard to put my finger on why. Shouldn't I be so psyched for Matt? I make myself smile back at Zoey. "Matt and I have been friends for a long time," I say. "You don't need to worry about me at all."

CHAPTER 5

"NOW *I* AM THINKING of the greatest idea," Mrs. G says the following Saturday morning. "We should take ourselves somewhere *fabulous* for brunch."

"Okay, where do you want to go?"

"Either Sandy's Sunny-Side or the White Moose." *White* sounds like "watt."

"Where's the White Moose?" I ask.

"You haven't been to the White Moose?" Mrs. G says. "Oh *my*. They have the most delicious coconut almond lemon squares!"

Lemon squares don't sound like brunch, first of all, and second, I'm not much for lemon desserts—what's the point? Just give me the chocolate already. But okay, I'll try anything once.

I plug the White Moose into Google Maps, and then it hits me. I haven't been there because it's on the west side of Green Valley. My family went there once to eat at a restaurant. Afterward, walking down the street to get to our car, Mom starting crossing—she always has this habit of walking way ahead of us—when all of a sudden, a car, windows down, four sketchy white dudes in it, came careening around the corner.

Dad yelled, "Angie!" and yanked her out of the way.

I heard one of those dudes mutter "Dumb Chinese" as the car sped off.

And yeah, maybe we don't need to avoid an entire area of town because that happened, but there was a vibe to it, you know? Like we didn't belong there. Not that we belong on the east side of Green Valley, either, or even in our own neighborhood—but at least no one's tried to hit my mom with their car in those places.

But, okay, with Mrs. G, I'll risk it. It's easier when you're one different-looking person walking around with a white person than it is to walk around with your own family who are *all* really different.

Am I worried that I'm about to be driven by an almost-eighty-year-old woman? Honestly, no, because I think it's even worse being driven by Heather sometimes—and amazingly she hasn't gotten into a wreck yet. Besides, Mrs. G takes herself pretty much everywhere. She takes herself to church, and to the grocery store (when Ezra doesn't bring her groceries), and to water aerobics class on Wednesday mornings. We get into her gray Lexus, which is extra shiny and has cream-colored leather seats.

She's a little slow on the turns sometimes, and driving through River's Edge, she is definitely in the middle of the road once or twice, but generally I think she does really well for her age. And I can tell she's absolutely loving it, her big pale pink sunglasses on, pearl earrings glinting in the sun. We zip out of the neighborhood—and I mean zip. Gleefully she shows me how quickly she can accelerate. We go from being at a standstill to forty in just a few seconds.

"I love this car," she says. "I did lots of research on it. Sure, Robbie helped a little, but at the end of the day it was me who chose it. Don't tell me women don't know how to choose cars!"

Seeing Mrs. G driving so easily—and so happily—makes me ache to drive. But I hate everything about it: practicing with Dad (although he tries to stay calm, his presence in the car already makes me more nervous), having to constantly be on the alert for other cars, and just how, like, even if you're doing everything right, someone could come out of left field and hit you. After every single practice session, I can't help feeling so relieved the moment we pull into the garage without a scratch.

Matt shook his head when I told him this. "Em. Driving is *so* easy these days, so easy. Why are you making up problems about other drivers that haven't even happened yet? Even my grandma can drive, and she's like ninety. But also, you can only control what you can control . . . and in most cases it's surprisingly a lot. You can brake, and you can honk. . . . You seriously need to chill about it."

But that's why I'm determined, once I've left high school, to move somewhere where you don't need a car to get around. If I had the choice, I'd honestly even have Tessa chauffeur me around everywhere. At least while she's watching the traffic all I have to do is sit there and zone out while I'm taken from point A to point B.

Being in the car with Mrs. G, I'm impressed.

"And . . . here we are!" she exclaims.

We go in and I can see immediately why Mrs. G likes it. It's not just a brunch place; it's a thrift shop. The ceilings have crown molding. The floors are black-and-white tile. Inside, Mrs. G gushes over every little thing, holding up a navy-blue velvet dress, a seven-dollar lamp with a floral shade, tiny tea-cups. At the entrance of the café area, waiting for a table, is a large group of older women. They've all got the same haircut, their hair various shades of white and gray, and they start to take up the four-seaters and two-seaters around us.

We finally sit down, and that's when I see none other than Matt, walking a stack of dirty cups and saucers toward what I assume is the kitchen of the White Moose.

I'm surprised, but I shouldn't be. He told me months ago he applied to work at some cool café on the west side. And besides, Matt has always liked old things. His family plays records on an actual turntable when I come over.

Next thing I know, he's at our table.

"Good afternoon, ladies," he says, a big grin on his face. He sets our waters down. "My name is Matt and I'll be taking care of you today."

Mrs. G says "Good afternoon!" back.

"No way," I say.

"What can I get for you? Perhaps some of our scrumptious world-famous Grandma Mabel's cookies?"

He's so good at this job, it's like he's doing an imperson-ation of a waiter.

Mrs. G is delighted. She clasps her hands together and says, "Oh my *goodness*. We must try one of those. Don't they sound spectacular?"

"I don't know," I say, "because his adjectives didn't actually describe the cookies."

Matt says, "I said 'Grandma Mabel.' The nostalgia should entice you. It's a tried-and-true consumer marketing strategy."

"*My* grandma never made cookies," I point out. "Asians don't bake."

Matt smirks. "Oh, sure. Except for that red bean cake your mom makes for Lunar New Year. And what about moon-cakes? And those enormous bags of pastries you bring back from Atlanta?"

Mrs. G sits back and looks at both of us. "You two know each other?"

"Since the fourth grade," Matt says.

"How nice!" Mrs. G says. "I'll have the ginger lemonade and the White Moose omelet special. And we'll share one of those cookies, please."

"Excellent choice," Matt says. "And for you, Em?"

"Iced coffee. Please."

"Decaf?"

"Regular."

Matt makes a big show of checking his watch. "Isn't it a little late for that? The half-life of caffeine is—"

"Oh come on," I say. "I need my late-morning jolt, so just pour the caffeine already."

"Of course," Matt says. "The customer is always right. I just don't want you to be up late scrolling."

"Such service," says Mrs. G. "Caring for our health and everything!"

"Oh, it's my pleasure," says Matt, really hamming up this waiter-ly presence.

I order a sausage, egg, and cheese with hash browns on a croissant.

"Classic," Matt says. "Be back soon with your drinks. Your food will be out shortly."

"What a lovely young man," says Mrs. G.

"Not always as lovely as he seems," I mumble.

"Speak up! You wouldn't talk like that to your mama, would you?"

Unfortunately, that is exactly how I talk to my mama, more often than not. "Sorry," I say. "I didn't say anything important."

Mrs. G purses her lips, no doubt about to tell me some Southern Lady Code about how I need to say everything as if it's important or something like that. But then she lowers her voice and leans over the table toward me. "Did this young man do something horrible? We can leave, if that's the case. Or request a different server."

I shake my head. "Oh, I appreciate that, but it's nothing. He . . ." I'm not sure how to describe what Matt did without sharing the whole story. But if I did tell Mrs. G the story, she might even be pleased. I could imagine her saying, *Well, at least someone tried to kiss you!* "Honestly, he didn't really do anything much."

Mrs. G nods. "Listen, Emily, when you get to be my age—or

really, as you get to be older and older than you are now—you let fewer people in. And fewer people let *you* in. That's just how it is. We don't go to school or join swim teams. It gets harder to make friends. But we are happier around others—that's true even for self-proclaimed misanthropes like yourself. What I'm saying is, if what he did is forgivable, it wouldn't hurt to patch things up."

I nod. "I'll think about it," I say.

"Good. I still miss my best friend from high school, Sheila Mather. A wonderful girl. I wish we hadn't lost touch."

"Couldn't you try to find her online?"

Mrs. G waves this away. "Oh, she wouldn't want to hear from me. But just remember, good friends aren't easy to come by."

Matt drops off our drinks, and I take a sip of the iced coffee. "This is definitely half-caf."

"Excuse me?" says Mrs. G.

"Matt does this thing where he makes it half regular and half decaf." I shake my head. "He's not a real coffee drinker. He doesn't understand how that completely changes the taste."

"Well, this lemonade is delightful. And I'm shocked that you haven't been here before. It's not just for old cronies like me, you know!"

I take a breath, wondering if I should tell her about Mom. It's always a toss-up and it usually lands on tails—deciding whether to tell a white person about a racist encounter. Do I risk making things totally uncomfortable for the sake of vulnerability?

Mrs. G tries my coffee and says she can't tell that it's half-caf but is impressed I can, and then Matt brings our food. That's when I decide to tell Mrs. G. She listens, taking thoughtful, dainty bites of her omelet, and then shakes her head sympathetically. "That's terrible, terrible," she says. It would be great if she stopped there, but then she adds, "I love Asians, myself. They're hardworking, they're smart, and they're resilient."

That bit, I didn't see coming, and I'm not sure how to correct her.

It's when people say things like that that I want to punch them in the face.

But I don't punch Mrs. G. I just say, "And I love old white people," keeping my face as deadpan as possible. "They're so cute, and sweet, and gentle."

Mrs. G looks at me like she doesn't know what to think. Then she nods. "Point taken. I'm sorry. I should not have said that."

"Point forgiven."

Honestly, it wasn't even that bad of a comment, coming from someone as old as Mrs. G. It's not like she called me "oriental" or anything.

Mrs. G says, "I should know not to stereotype. My own family moved to the States during a time when people didn't take too kindly to Italians. We were a big Italian family packed into a brownstone in Brooklyn. All six of us." She says this proudly.

"Your last name is Granucci, though. So did you marry another Italian or did you not change your last name?" Then, when her eyebrows go up, I find myself blushing and saying, "Sorry, that was rude."

Mom says I have absolutely no filter, that my mouth is going to get me in trouble someday. She says this as if someday is a ways away, as if I haven't already gotten into plenty of trouble already. Tessa, on the other hand, becomes someone else around teachers. She says that's the normal thing to do. But I think why not just be mostly yourself most of the time? It seems like less energy that way. It sounds exhausting to me to do otherwise.

But Mrs. G just smiles and says, "I thought you'd never ask!"

Mrs. G shows me a photo of Ed Granucci on her phone.

"Very handsome," I say. And I'm not just saying that. He looks like a refined bookstore grandpa in a cardigan and nice sneakers and square-shaped glasses. His hair is all white, but there's plenty of it, like Steve Martin, and his smile is wide and his eyes are bright. I mean, for an older dude, that is one nice-looking man.

"And even more handsome on the inside," says Mrs. G. "When you were in conversation with him, he gave you his entire attention. Even before these damn things"—Mrs. G holds up her phone—"that wasn't easy to come by. They say you shouldn't put all that pressure on your spouse, for them to be your best friend, but with Ed, it wasn't something we thought about—it was easy. We had so many years of friendship behind us, anyway! We were always curious about what the other person was thinking, was feeling. And we weren't afraid to call each other out, tell each other like it is. I still talk to him every day. He knows all about you."

"Hope he thinks I'm an okay companion."

"He's glad I have a feisty young person around. Keeps me young!"

"How did you meet?" I ask.

"Oh, you know, back then everyone met everyone in high school or just, around the neighborhood."

"So you were high school sweethearts?"

"Heavens, no. We dated other people, but we ran in the same crowd."

I drain my half-caf drink, and Mrs. G and I clean our plates.

When Matt returns, we both get our wallets.

"Shoo!" Mrs. G says, waving mine away. "You're my very special personal assistant. There's no way I'm letting you pay for my treats."

"Oh?" Matt looks from Mrs. G to me. "A pretty sweet gig you've gotten yourself, Em."

We get up to wander around the shop, picking up old jewelry and vintage home goods and vinyl records. Heather will love it here, when she's back.

"Need help finding anything?" Matt says, though I'm pretty sure he's supposed to be waiting tables.

"How about a fully caffeinated beverage?" I say. "I'm going to write you a bad Yelp review."

"Ah, but my service was impeccable! And who are the people going to believe? Me, the friendly waiter who they absolutely adore, or you, a stubborn customer who can't prove I made her drink half-caf?"

"When were you going to tell me about Zoey?" I ask. See? There it is again. No filter. I could be nicer about it.

"When were you going to return my calls?"

Okay, fair.

"I just wish I hadn't heard it from her," I admit.

"Yeah, that part I'm bummed about, too. I wanted to be the one to share my good news."

"I'm happy for you." Ugh. Why do I keep saying that when I don't really mean it? "It's . . . it's great that you're together."

Matt grins. "Thanks. Maybe the three of us could hang sometime."

"That would be fun," I say, though suddenly I'm feeling this stab of jealousy. Like, what, Zoey's replacing Heather now? "The three of us" always meant the three of *us*.

Then his face turns serious. "Em," he says, "I'm not exactly sure what happened—I mean, I guess a lot of things happened, right? At the party," he adds quickly, as if I need that. "But we can just both forget about it, right? And put it behind us? Especially since, well, now Zoey and I are a thing." Matt checks the tables. From one of them, a couple with two kids eyes him impatiently.

"Yeah," I force myself to say. "We can forget about it."

I just need some time for this new thing to sink in. It'll be weird, won't it, that he's dating someone and I'm not. But I guess it doesn't have to be. Nothing has to change. He can date Zoey, and he and I can still be friends. I can forget the sweaty ice cream kiss. He was drunk anyway.

Right?

And besides, as Mrs. G has reminded me, good old friends are hard to come by.

Later that day, Mrs. G tells me that George Harrison is the underrated Beatle.

"What about Ringo?" I ask.

"Pfft. People go wild for drummers," she says, as if that explained everything.

I spend Saturday afternoon taking care of George. Combing his fake hair, making sure it falls just so on his forehead, dusting his face—especially his nose, since that is where dust will settle—and adjusting his tie if it needs straightening. Mrs. G says I have an eye for detail. I swap the tie he was wearing for another with a bolder pattern, using YouTube to help me tie it. Then I ever-so-carefully change his jacket.

That's when I hear Mrs. G talking to someone on speakerphone.

"Ah . . . oh, we had a delightful lunch," she says. "Sandwiches. Chicken salad with cranberries and walnuts. What wasn't delightful, though, was how the bread kept scraping the roof of my mouth."

I freeze. We didn't have delightful chicken salad sandwiches. We didn't even have chicken. I have to admit I'm kind of impressed that she made up the whole thing about cranberries and walnuts, and the bread being too hard. Or maybe—and this makes me breathe with relief—maybe she ate this recently and it's stronger in her memory than our brunch. Maybe it was an honest mistake. Maybe she's not trying to cover up that she can't remember what we had for brunch.

Could I ask her about it? I don't want to embarrass her.

And maybe it's not a big deal. Lots of people can't remember what they ate hours ago, but they'll remember the best fried chicken they had years ago.

"Love you, too, Robbie," Mrs. G says. "Oh, I've got to go, there's Ezra at the door."

I hear them in a flurry of greetings and hugs.

"Emmmmmily," Mrs. G sings. "Meet us in the laundry room."

"Coming!" I say, zipping up the jacket on George halfway.

In the laundry room, Mrs. G grimaces. "You'll have to see an old lady's underthings! I'm so sorry, Emily. But I'm not embarrassed, I'm too old for that."

"Got it," I say. "No problem." It's fine, I can wash my hands after. Mom would have a cow if she knew I was doing someone else's laundry when I really could be doing my own more often at home, but she doesn't have to know about this.

Ezra holds up a tank top made of some sort of expensive fabric like cashmere that makes zero sense to me—because why would you wear a *tank top* made of warm fabric? I guess if you're Mrs. G, and you keep your house and your car super cold all the time, you can wear these sweater sets in pastel colors.

Ezra's already at work sorting through her clothes. "So what brought you here, really?" he says. "You just needed a summer job?"

"Yeah, and what's wrong with that?" I ask. How is it that I'm sort of annoyed by him, but at the same time, I find it super sweet that he's helping to do his great-aunt's laundry?

"I mean, I don't know what your friends are like, but most

of mine end up working at, like, a coffee shop or grocery store—"

"Oh, so not all of them are classical music snobs who are constantly playing gigs?"

To my surprise, this makes Ezra chuckle, showing me that dimple on the left side of his mouth. A curl of his hair falls across his forehead and he shoves it back in place.

"I mean it's unusual, right? To be someone's companion, in their house," he says.

"She was trying to escape!" Mrs. G winks.

No. Oh, no, I'm not telling this boy who goes to a selective high school about—

"Grounded because of a school thing, is that right?" says Mrs. G. "School is overrated!"

"In college," Ezra says, "you can do what you're good at, and that's what really matters."

I huff. "Try telling that to my parents," I mutter.

The good news is, I'm going to be un-grounded by the time the weekend rolls around. Although I have to wonder how much difference it's going to make, since Heather is away and Matt . . . is with Zoey now. It's still weird to think of him having a girlfriend.

I am looking forward to talking to Heth, though.

"It was psychology class. I got a C plus," I explain. Saying it out loud, I feel the same wave of shame and guilt as the day I was grounded for it.

"Why, Emily!" Mrs. G exclaims.

"I know," I say. "I've already been through several talking-tos about it, so spare me. I'm not living up to my potential, I can do so much better, I should probably go to a child psych center and get checked for some sort of executive functioning issue and blah blah blah."

But Mrs. G is shaking her head. "No! On the contrary, I thought it was going to be far worse! I thought that you were in real trouble."

"*Real* trouble?"

"Oh, who knows! A school conduct rule or what have you. But nothing so little as a *grade*. What you're talking about sounds to me like completely normal teenage behavior."

When Mrs. G says the word *grade*, it seems to take away so much of the weight of what it is. I wish I could hear that word the way she says it all the time.

"Of course, that said, you should still do your best. But you know, I didn't even *go* to college," Mrs. G says, almost as if she's bragging about it. "And I turned out okay! We only had enough to send me to Carolina for one year, and that was it for me! I still got to learn so many things, just not in a formal school setting." Mrs. G folds her hands as if to say *and there you have it*, a neat and easy solution all wrapped up in a bow.

I smile. At least even if she does get preachy, she knows when to stop.

"Well," she says, gesturing to the laundry, "I'll let you handle this while I take care of some things in the kitchen."

Ezra leaves then, too, something about how he knows I can take it from here. I try to make a game of folding, timing myself to see if I can get the whole load folded in under ten minutes. Then I hear the sound of a cello in the living room. I know nothing about classical music, but it sounds heavenly: rich and mellow and soothing. I poke my head into the living room. Ezra's playing with his eyes closed, head moving to the beat every now and then, dark hair flopping. He's completely wrapped up in the beauty he's creating, and it's—okay, I'll admit it—really hot. Maybe that's what I look like when I'm making art—I wouldn't know. I sure hope so.

～ℓℓℓ～

On the day I got my exam back, Mr. DeVaney said, "I *know* you can learn this material. I *know* you're smart." I waited for him to say, *because your sister was in my class and she aced it.* That's what all the teachers say, but Mr. DeVaney didn't mention Tessa at all.

People are always calling me that, smart and talented. But I have to wonder if it's because we're Asian. Sometimes I wish I could just be blond, for that reason. No one ever assumes you're smart if you're blond, and then you can prove them wrong. Instead, I feel like I spend so much time trying to prove that I'm not that special.

I looked down at my exam. The F at the top was big, red, and circled, as if it needed all that.

"Emily," he said, "I know your family's going through a hard time. If you were just having an off day, you can take it again at the end of the summer, and I'll change the grade to a new one."

The truth is, I wasn't having an off day. My vibe had been

off all year, and I'm pretty sure Mr. DeVaney knew this; he was just trying to give me an out. Right before the exam, while my classmates were cramming their heads full of last-minute facts about cognition and collectivism, I was in the library flipping through old issues of *Teen Vogue*, trying to get inspired for my next drawing. I *can* work hard, but sometimes it feels like school doesn't really matter. It didn't shock me anymore how lazy I could be, so I wasn't surprised that I ended up with a C in Honors Psych. Mr. DeVaney says not to call myself lazy, that "your brain hears what your mouth says." And I guess he's right. I *can* be productive. I *can* focus. I can spend hours down in the art room at school working on a drawing, trying to get the color exactly right, with no one to distract me. The thing is, sometimes you don't really know what color is right until you see it. Only you can know, and no one else can tell you that. It's not something that my parents or Tessa understand.

Matt says he knows I can do better in school, that I slink by as a mostly B student because I'm afraid of success, of what will happen if I start doing well. But that, as my friend, it's not his job to tell me what to do with my attitude toward school, so he's happy to give me a kick in the pants whenever I want it. But if I don't want it, he won't. Besides, if I'm saving that time and energy to draw, then that's fine, as long as it really is going toward the art—because he's convinced I can get myself a big fat scholarship to one of the art schools. I'm not sure he knows how very competitive those are. But he's happy to "light a fire under my butt," as he says. I've wondered about maybe asking him to help me finish projects so I can get my portfolio in tip-top shape. That's my main problem: not finishing what I start. Always feeling like I can do more. As @eatsleepdraw says, "You will feel it leave you" when you're done, truly done, with a piece of art. And I have to admit it's been a while since I had that feeling. Even the stuff I showed in the school art show last spring didn't feel completely finished.

I'm thinking through all of this, sorting and folding Mrs. G's laundry, when I hear a high-pitched wail from the kitchen. Then the three distinct syllables of my name:

"Em-i-ly!" Mrs. G cries. The cello music comes to a halt.

My heart drops. I run into the kitchen, expecting disaster. But nothing's on fire, nothing seems to be broken, and she's not hurt or anything.

I start to ask Mrs. G what's wrong when I see it: suds, trickling from the bottom of the dishwasher and all over the kitchen floor.

"I'm an idiot," Mrs. G is saying. "I used the wrong soap! I used the regular dishwashing soap *in* the dishwasher!"

"It's okay, it's okay," I say. I turn off the dishwasher and do my best to step around the foaming suds.

"I'm so stupid, Emily," she says. "I wasn't thinking straight."

"People have definitely made this mistake before. At least the floor will be shiny and squeaky clean." I try to smile.

"What would I do without you?" she asks. Her voice isn't spunky and bright like usual. Instead, she sounds—I hate to admit this to myself—a little pathetic. She puts a hand to her forehead.

Ezra appears and springs into action, grabbing cups to scoop up the soap.

"It's just frustrating is what it is!" Mrs. G says. "Well, when you get to be my age and you have sticky notes up there, none of them stick anymore!"

Ezra manages a laugh and puts his hand on her shoulder. It's kind of . . . nice? I guess? How he can be sort of grouchy and skeptical one minute, but knows how to perform when he's needed. I guess that's what makes him a good musician. And a good nephew.

"It *is* frustrating," I say. "But it's the first time this has happened, and I can always just remind you how to do it, or even do it for you going forward."

"That's right. Well, that's why I hired you." Unexpectedly, Mrs. G's eyes get a little glassy.

"You go relax," I say. "It's really not a big deal—Ezra and I can clean this up."

"Emily's right," Ezra says. "We got this, Aunt Leila."

After Mrs. G leaves, he says, "It feels like we're in *Stranger Things.* Deadly white foam is creeping from this appliance."

"You know," I say, "we didn't actually have chicken salad sandwiches for lunch."

He looks at me blankly. "What are you talking about?"

I take a deep breath. "This afternoon, I heard her on the phone with Robbie, and he asked what she had for lunch, and she said sandwiches. That wasn't true. I think she forgot what we had. I just thought you should know."

Ezra shrugs. "I forget what I eat all the time."

He drops a handful of kitchen towels on the floor.

"Yeah, but . . ." There was lunch, and now this. What if things get worse? "Still, maybe I'll just load the dishwasher from now on," I say. "I might even hide the dish soap somewhere."

Shoot. Why do I sound so much like Dad? Mrs. G isn't a child, but my impulse to protect her sure feels like she is.

"Oh come on," Ezra says. "It was just a mistake, a one-time thing. She's not going to drink it, or anything."

"You never know," I say. "Didn't I just tell you she made up what she had for lunch?"

"One time!"

He huffs. Still, he grabs the dishwashing soap and puts it high up, in the cabinets above the refrigerator, where Mrs. G definitely won't be able to reach it.

"You can get that," he says. "You're tall."

⁓ℓℓℓ⁓

Later, after Ezra leaves, I pour Mrs. G her vermouth in the little blue glass, and a lemonade over lots of ice for myself.

Outside, there's a rare breeze for once, and we sit for a while on the porch. I've never felt so Southern.

Mrs. G says, "Emily, what would I do without you?" and it feels nice to be needed that way. "You know what? You should ask me for a letter of recommendation. For college. I would be happy to write a letter praising your many merits."

I can't say that any teacher has ever told me *that* before.

CHAPTER 6

ON MONDAY MORNING TWO things happen: I am officially un-grounded, and we're going to learn more about Mom's biopsy at the doctor. Tessa, as usual, makes a huge fuss taking care of Mom before we leave the house. She makes Mom's tea and sets a timer for it to steep, unloads and reloads the dishwasher, keeps asking Mom if she has all the necessary paperwork.

Geez. Leave something for the rest of us to do.

Dad has us leave the house forty-five minutes ahead of time even though the hospital's only fifteen minutes away, and even though it's always been at least a ten-minute wait when we arrive. In the car, we're all quiet until Dad says, "Rillo, how long do you plan to keep working for this Granary lady? For the rest of the summer?"

So even when it's supposed to be all about Mom, it always comes back to me, and it never comes back in a good way.

I seriously can't tell if Dad is botching her name on purpose or if he's forgotten it again. I give him the benefit of the doubt; I'm always calling her Mrs. G anyway.

"Granucci," I say.

"Granucci," he repeats. "Granucci." He rolls the *r*, so it sounds like a type of pasta. *I'll have the Granucci Bolognese with cheese, please.*

"I plan to," I say. "I mean, it's a summer job, so it does last all summer."

From the back seat, I see Dad furrow his eyebrows in the rearview mirror. "Why? It's a waste of time. You go there and you can't study anything. You can't even help us take care of Mom."

My whole body tenses. I don't want to have this argument right now, at seven in the morning, when I am barely awake.

The thing is that at this point, there's hardly anything we can do to "take care of Mom." That's part of why thyroid cancer's a bitch. On some level, we all know this, and we're coping with it in our different ways. Like we're all trying to be extra nice to Mom and eat the same things she's eating, because anything's better than admitting we're pretty much helpless until the doc removes Mom's thyroid.

"Jorge," Mom says, patting Dad on the shoulder. "Just let it go."

In the waiting room, there are all sorts of people, most of them on the older side. They sit in wheelchairs or lean on their spouses for support. They have various styles of white and gray hair and some of them are wearing caps or scarves to cover their lack of hair. I've thought before that Mom doesn't look like she has cancer—at least not yet. And that does comfort me somewhat. In fact, I don't get how she *can* have it.

She's not even fifty yet. Every morning she drinks green tea. She does yoga. She doesn't look like someone who is sick. She keeps her hair in this impeccably neat bob, always wears sparkly earrings, takes great care of her skin so it glows, the whole thing.

We sit and we wait.

Well, three of us sit—Dad paces in front of us, as if that's going to make time move faster or make Mom feel better.

Mom, for her part, somehow manages to be the most chill of all of us. She sits there reading and underlining parts in her book that she especially likes; she circles words she wants to look up later.

Tessa is on her Notes app, jotting down questions to ask the doc. She's already gone up to the front desk twice and barraged them with questions. Every now and then she gives Mom a pat on the arm.

And me, I'm reading about the pros and cons of gel eyeliner versus liquid while secretly giving the side-eye to everyone around me, and thinking a million other things, like, *how?* How did Matt end up with Zoey after all, and so fast? What happened (or didn't) at the party?

What if she hurts him?

Or, worse, what if she doesn't, and they date forever? Like even after graduation?

I should be happy for Matt. Isn't this the end of our problems? But if that's true, why do I feel so weird about this?

Then I feel bad that I'm thinking about Matt at all when I should be thinking about Mom. But then wouldn't Matt himself absolve me of that by saying that it doesn't actually *do* anything to constantly be worried about Mom? That in fact, keeping up your mental health by allowing yourself to enjoy thinking about other things would make you a happier, and therefore better, caregiver?

Then a nurse appears and says "Angela Chen-Sanchez?" and all four of us are up, Tessa helping Mom to stand (even though she can definitely do it on her own).

The receptionist considers us, skeptically. "Y'all *all* going in?"

When people say "all" after *y'all,* it kills me.

"Yes," Dad says, "we all want to go together."

"This is an informational appointment. You don't all need to be there." Her eyes sweep over all four of us again. "It can get crowded in there."

"These are our two daughters and they're home for the summer, so we'd all like to go in."

Of course, we live at home the rest of the year, too—it's just that we'll be in school, like any normal kids. But Dad has a way of finessing words to get what he wants.

The receptionist gives a big sigh and acts like this is a huge exception she's making just for us. We file into the elevator and head upstairs.

The doc is Dr. Jessica Kim. She's competent, Korean, and calm. Seriously, walking into her office is like walking into a meditation room or a yoga class but with someone who needs to make sure you know exactly what you're doing and how you're going to practice yoga at home. I like how she takes her time, like she's not in a rush to get to her next patient.

I once asked Mom why all the other Asians we know in town either own a store or restaurant or are doctors, and she said, "You tell me."

She can be infuriating that way sometimes.

At least we're in the best place we can be. It's comforting to walk into the completely sterile, fluorescent-lit building, knowing that you're surrounded by (hopefully) competent medical professionals whose job it is to heal you.

Dr. Kim greets each of us by name. I can't help thinking she's hashtag beauty goals: smooth skin, eyes that slant up in a gorgeous way, like a cat's. Her hair is somehow effortlessly voluminous and I have to wonder if she perms it. I know, I shouldn't be thinking about what my mom's thyroid surgeon looks like, but there just aren't that many hashtag-beauty-goal-type people around here. When you live in a town where no one looks like you, sometimes you're not sure how to feel about your face.

"So," Dr. Kim says, spreading both her hands open. "I wish I could give you actual news. At this point, however, the biopsy is still inconclusive, but this tumor, well, it is suspicious-looking. We're going to have to do surgery. Until we get in there, we really won't know."

"So she'll have a cut . . . in her *neck*?" Dad says.

We can hear the fear in his voice. And leave it to Dad to make things sound dramatic, but even I have to admit that sounds pretty bad. It's scary thinking about a knife to the neck.

"An incision across the front part of her neck, that's right," says Dr. Kim. "I can assure you, Mr. Sanchez, we have an excellent team here. The best in the state. What we'll do is remove the tumor, and then just a part of the thyroid, the left butterfly wing, if it helps to think of it that way." She points to it on a diagram of the thyroid on the wall. "We'll take a look at it, and then we'll talk again."

"And she'll have a scar . . . obviously," says Tessa.

"Yes, but we're going to do our best to make it as subtle as possible," Dr. Kim says. "After a while, you won't even be able to see it. You can use vitamin E to help it fade."

Mom nods, completely stoic, trusting.

Dr. Kim went to Harvard Medical School. How she ended up in Green Valley I really don't know. When they first found her, Dad repeatedly mentioned her credentials (Princeton, Harvard, a residency at Wake Forest, and a fellowship at UChicago), rattling off the schools like she was his own daughter when he was talking about her to other people.

It's funny how I sometimes get the feeling that Dr. Kim is an older cousin who my parents constantly compare me to.

All I can think is, a scar on your neck is not something you can cover up, like a scar on your belly or even your legs. Your neck is just . . . there, unless you wear a scarf or something, and it's not like many people walk around Green Valley in scarves.

Maybe Mom will be less vain after this, I think.

And then I immediately hate myself for thinking that. I'm always thinking things and then regretting them immediately. The good thing is, feelings are just feelings—that's what Mr. DeVaney is always saying. You can't hate yourself for them. You can just let them pass by.

I'm still working on that part.

"It shouldn't take long," says Dr. Kim. "She won't need to be in the hospital overnight. You can all wait here while it's happening."

Somehow, Dr. Kim manages to both come across super proficient and give off a slight air of Southern hospitality. She wears pearl studs and she speaks in this measured way. She's patient with Dad's many, many concerns and questions. She must see worried people every day, must be used to placating them. I can only hope to have that kind of calm—it would be good to learn to be like that around Mrs. G if she has another dishwasher disaster, or worse.

"We're going to take really good care of her," says Dr. Kim.

Surgery is scheduled a couple of weeks from now. Into the elevator we all go, once again.

All I can see is Mom walking around with no hair. She's the one always telling us to enjoy our hair because it's so dark and thick and won't always be that way, and yet now she's going to be the one who should've enjoyed hers—instead of obsessing over every white or gray hair. That's just my wandering brain, though. Dr. Kim didn't say anything about chemo.

According to the American Cancer Society website, 98 percent of people with thyroid cancer are completely cured after five years.

But what about the other 2 percent?

⟞⟍

At home, the day is divided into meals. We've already had breakfast and it's too late for lunch. Dad already took the day off work, so he could be home in case of bad news. But maybe this is worse. No news yet, just more waiting. We all try to make ourselves busy. Tessa calls Steve to update him and receive whatever medical advice he has, then unloads the dishwasher (again). Mom pages through a new textbook she'll be teaching from in the fall, and Dad reads the news on his iPad. I thumb through all the London photos Heather's posted on Instagram, then text Matt several paragraphs about Mom, Mrs. G, and Ezra—we need to make up for lost time. After that, I hole up in my room with my latest sketch, the one with the birds.

Only now it feels wrong to be working on it. Almost self-pitying. What I should be drawing is Mom, in a garden with weeds growing all around her, and all of us helpless to do anything about it. But I don't feel like starting something new, and none of my recycling bin scraps feel right at this moment, either.

Drawing is supposed to be my escape, or at the very least my way to process things. Now it just feels like it's making me dwell even more on my real life.

I grab my phone again because it's what I always reach for even though, as Matt says, it doesn't actually make me feel better, but at least it's a tiny escape in a box, an easier way to distract myself than thinking of an idea to draw. No text from Matt yet. He's not addicted to his phone the way I am.

Or maybe he's with Zoey and won't see my text for hours. Before Zoey, he probably would have come over right after we got back from the hospital. Or we would have ridden our bikes around together after dinner, not talking, just riding around when it was finally cool enough to do so.

Ugh, I hate Zoey Kebabian.

I put on my headphones, then just start blending colors, really getting my hands in there. There's not really a purpose to it, it's just whatever colors I think the music *is.* Whatever colors the music makes me see. I read about this thing once, synesthesia, and I tried to make myself have it, by forcing myself to assign colors whenever I heard sounds. Obviously, that didn't work, and I got really tired, fast. But now I cover the whole page in all shades of purple: eggplant and lavender and maroon. And it seems to calm me down, except for one thought that flares up and makes me super mad for about ten awful seconds: Why does Mrs. Granucci get to be almost eighty with no cancer while Mom is only forty-eight with cancer?

ℓℓℓ

At swim practice I have this one problem, among many: I can never seem to get my goggles right. They're either way too tight, leaving red rings around my eyes for several minutes afterward, or they fill up with water. The days that they actually fit perfectly are few and far between. You'd think that once I adjust them to the right spot, they'd be fine, but that's not how this works. They have a mind of their own as I'm swimming.

Anyway, the next morning during warm-up is when it happens. I'm swimming breaststroke at an okay pace when my left lens starts to fill up with water. It doesn't usually happen so early in practice. Usually I just deal—I keep going and then adjust when I get to the end of the lane. But today I'm in a mood. I fling the goggles off and say "Goddammit!" and stand up in my lane. Not far behind me, Ava McClintock's head bobs up out of the water for a breath and then back down, and up and down again. Then she just swims around me. It's just as well. I would swim around myself, too, under the circumstances.

This really isn't a good look. And yes, I'm stressed, but other teenagers go through way worse.

Like, for example, Jonathan Weller's sister actually has cancer her*self* and she still went to classes. What a badass.

Or, in memoirs I've read, people's parents can be much, much worse than mine. Mine aren't even memoir-worthy. In the grand scheme of things, they're not so bad. I just wish we knew more.

Not that it's at all helpful to compare like this. The "suffering Olympics," or whatever.

Still, I'm pissed.

Coach calls out, "Chen-'chez! You're blocking the lane. Either keep moving or get out of the pool."

I exit.

"Let's talk," Coach says.

I have to wonder if it's something the coaches discussed: That the one female POC coach would be the one to handle Emily Chen-Sanchez. "She can be a handful," I can imagine Trey, another coach, saying. "She's got a temper."

Well, I've seen Coach Jackson talk to a bunch of the girls, so maybe it's not a race thing. Or maybe it is. If it is, I'm okay with it, because it's nice having a female POC coach.

"Sit," Coach says. "Take a breather. Let me see your goggles."

I hand them over and she adjusts them, then hands them back to me to try on. Somehow she has gotten them exactly right, like an optometrist for swimmers.

"You can get your anger out in sports, especially in non-contact ones like swimming. That part is okay with me. But I need to see it in your stroke, in how hard you're working, in how much you're pushing yourself. Don't take it out on your goggles. It's like someone getting mad at a computer. We've all been there, but it doesn't do any good, does it? These goggles don't give a shit about you. Your body, though, you can control."

I give her a "yes ma'am" and then get back in the water. Hearing another teenager tell me I can control my body—don't judge, but I'm skeptical.

Still, it helps. With every pull, I push myself to exhaustion, try to numb the scary thoughts, try to be grateful for this set time when my only task is to pull myself through the water. Even though there are lots of people around me, I feel alone—but in a good way. In the water, there's no Tessa to outdo me; there's no Dad to hover around me. There's no Mom to be worried about. Ironically, it's hard to feel sorry for yourself when you're short of breath and every part of your body hurts.

While I'm waiting in the water for the next set (fly kick

with the kickboards—the worst, in my opinion), Matt says, "You okay?" and I say, "Thanks, yeah," and we keep swimming.

After practice, he comes over and asks again if I'm okay.

I guess if I had a friend whose mom possibly had cancer, I wouldn't know what to ask, either.

"I'm really sorry," he says. "It sucks." That's also what he said via text yesterday, finally. But it does feel good, having a good friend who knows why you feel shitty, even if there's not much they can do about it.

Several feet away, I can see Zoey gently patting her hair dry with a T-shirt. I've read about that before, that it's better for your hair than a towel, but I didn't think people actually did that.

"But at least, like, the odds are good, right?" Matt continues. "My uncle, he had lung cancer and only had like a 40 percent chance of surviving, and he's been cancer-free for years. And, you know, it could be nothing, right? Won't you feel like you wasted energy if you obsess and worry like this, and then it turns out to be nothing?"

Matt has often told me I'm the most anxious laid-back person he knows. I present as chill, he says, but on the inside I'm always on the verge of freaking out.

I just take a deep breath and say we don't have to talk about it anymore.

He nods. "What are you up to now? I'm heading over to Ayer Gardens to get a friend for Skippy."

"Skippy?"

"My bonsai tree? Wait, have you seriously not met Skippy before?"

"I don't think I've 'met' your bonsai tree, no," I say, making air quotes.

"Well, I was disappointed at first, because he looked really different from the picture online, but he's really grown on me. His roots sort of look like legs? He's a sweet little thing."

"Your plant is a *he*?"

Matt puts his hands up. "Em, a plant dad does know these things."

For some reason I think of Ezra. He doesn't seem like the type who would want to get his hands all dirty. Although he does water Mrs. G's houseplants from time to time.

Zoey shows up then and claps a hand on Matt's shoulder. "It's adorable, right? I've never met a guy who's as into plants as this one."

"Yep," I say. "Adorable."

Zoey smiles big and says, "I'm going to get some creeping phlox and they'll be sooo pretty hanging from our front porch! Every flower arrangement should have a spiller, like some delphiniums or at least some ivy or vines. Don't you think?"

"Um," I say, "no strong opinion." I'm not sure what creeping phlox is, but it doesn't sound good.

Also, I had no idea Zoey was into gardening, too.

Zoey punches Matt lightly in the arm. "And maybe we'll get this guy some new gardening gloves, finally."

"Heck no! Those are my lucky gloves," Matt says, at the same time that I say, "Why does he need new gloves?"

Matt smiles at me. "Em gets it," he says. "So do you want to come with us?"

Normally I'd like to. The word *us* annoys me even more.

I used to tag along with Matt—usually in the spring as he made his plans for the summer—learning about propagating succulents and where to plant milkweed for monarchs and the benefits of planting at least two types of raspberries. I wasn't going to use any of it, but it's nice seeing your friend be so passionate about something, not to mention it was just a good excuse to walk around outside smelling all those growing things.

But now Zoey is here, and either way you spin it, it just won't be as fun. Either they're walking around hand in hand and I'm a third wheel; or I try to keep things as they were with Matt, and Zoey asks me again if I like him; or I end up talking with Matt more than Zoey, or Zoey more than Matt, and either of those situations would feel awkward as all get out.

Then something genius occurs to me.

"I can't," I say. "I actually—I have a date, actually."

I don't know why I say it. I thought about playing the cancer card as a way to get out of it, but that just seems wrong, and I don't need Zoey Kebabian feeling sorry for me.

Matt's eyes widen. "You have a *date*?" he says, like it's unfathomable. "May I ask with *whom*?" Then, before I can say anything, he says, "With that lady's nephew? The cello guy who's sort of pretentious?"

Oh, dang. It seems as good as anything. It's not even exactly a lie, right? I mean, Ezra and I *do* spend a lot of time together, and I think he *is* sort of flirting with me. "He's not so bad, once you get to know him."

Zoey throws her arms around my neck, which honestly

feels like a lot, since I don't know her that well, even if she *is* dating my best friend. "That's so great, Emily!" she says.

Matt's face contorts itself into a smile as well. "That is great!" he echoes.

"We better get going," Zoey says, and Matt agrees. "I hope you have fun with Mr. Cello," he says. Then we're saying bye, and they're walking off hand in hand.

I should feel good about myself, but now that I've basically lied to my best friend and he's happy for me, I feel even worse.

CHAPTER 7

AT HOME THAT EVENING, we set the table for five. Steve, Tessa's boyfriend, is joining us for dinner. He wants to come over and give Tessa his support "during this difficult time."

There are some girls at school who love their older siblings' significant others, but I'm not one of them. Don't get me wrong, Steve's perfectly respectable. He has his whole life planned: go to medical school (ideally with Tessa), become a doctor (hand surgery), and then marry Tessa (he's courting her already). This is how they date: he arrives at the door, he talks to my parents, and then he and Tessa go to dinner. It's like he can't think of other ways that they might spend time together. He's on the cross-country team, which is side-cool—you're not trying too hard for the spotlight like football or basketball—so I guess he has that going for him. Mom and Dad adore Steve, but in my opinion, Tessa could do better.

Steve shows up at the door and he even rings the bell, as if he hasn't been here before.

At this point, Heather and Matt just let themselves in

through the garage, the way we usually come in, because I've told them they can (and because what's the point of ringing the bell so formally anyway?).

When Tessa answers the door, Steve has a bouquet of flowers in hand (yes, he's eaten here several times, and he shows up with something every time). My entire family has their beats down pat. Tessa throws her arms around him. Mom shows up and says, "This is too much, you didn't need to bring anything!"

Of course, the day that he doesn't bring something is going to be the one where she says, "Did you notice Steve came to dinner empty-handed?"

"Āyí, nǐ hǎo ma?" Steve asks Mom, because he somehow always needs to sneak in a little Mandarin, really showing us up. Of course, Mom beams. She absolutely loves it.

This is how textbook-perfect Steve is for Tessa and our parents: he speaks Mandarin at home with his parents, *and* he's taking AP Spanish.

"Esteban!" Dad says, and they shake hands, have a whole brief conversation en español.

During dinner, Steve cuts his steak with great care, trimming off the fat, pushing it to the side like this is some kind of science dissection, for God's sake.

Tessa tells us all about work, although it's not like I want to hear about what happens in a hospital, when we've just been to the hospital, *and* while we're trying to eat. Much of it is pretty boring, though, like preparing patients for exams and communicating with doctors.

Mom scoops more rice onto Steve's plate. You've got to be

careful; that's what she'll do if she notices any white space on your dish. Fills it and then expects you to eat it. And then has no problem telling you you've gained weight the next time you see her.

All of Chinese culture is a careful dance of saying no, over and over again, when you really mean yes. That's why every single time Steve comes over, Mom offers him food to take home, and he says, "Ayaahhhh, it's too much, Āyí, bùyào, bùyào," and she keeps filling Tupperware containers, and sometimes he leaves them behind.

One time, she even shoved one into his car before he left.

As we eat, Dad gives Steve all the info we have so far about Mom's possible condition, and asks what he thinks. The guy isn't even in med school yet, and still my parents think he knows everything.

"Well, the C-word is a scary word," says Steve, "but a cancer diagnosis can mean all kinds of things these days. Cancer research has come a really long way. Even in the past five years—you'd be surprised. And, as I'm sure you learned this morning, thyroid cancer—it's weird to say it—but it's almost like the 'good' kind, right? If you're going to have it, that's the kind you want."

Dad nods, both impressed and comforted, then asks Steve where he's applying to college, even though it's summer and he really doesn't need to have his list finalized. Steve rattles off something like twelve schools, looking embarrassed as he does so. All the Ivies and a few Ivy wannabes, like Middlebury and Wesleyan.

"So many!" Dad exclaims.

Steve puts his palms up. "Just casting a wide net in case no school will take me."

Barf. Give me a break.

"I bet you're all psyched for Tessa's presentation at the end of the summer," he continues. "It'll be excellent, I'm sure!"

Tessa just waves it away. "Oh, it's nothing. Just something we have to do as part of this internship." But I can tell from the way her eyes light up that it is most certainly not nothing. "I'm doing a research project on how we can improve emergency rooms," she explains to us. "The hard part is figuring out what to focus on, and then how to present it all so it's both interesting and accessible for non-medical people."

"I'm sure you'll do well," Dad says.

Steve then turns the conversation to me, which would be nice of him if I didn't have to follow Tessa. "Hanging with Ziegler a lot this summer? That is one smart kid."

Ugh, even the way he talks about Matt is annoying—calling him by his last name as if they know each other well.

"Well," I say, "Matt has a girlfriend now, so I haven't seen him much."

I don't know why I even bother explaining this. All three of my family members look at me in surprise.

"Really?" Dad says, at the same time that Mom says, "That's nice," and Tessa says, "Guess that throws a wrench into your plans."

I just give her a look. She's been teasing that Matt and I are secretly an item since the first day we met.

Steve has enough conversational grace to ask what I've been up to, and I tell him about swimming and about Mrs. G.

"A companion to an elderly woman, huh?" he says, sounding genuinely impressed. "That's good work if you can get it. Lots of hospitals need people like that. And you've got a good personality for it."

"Does she?" Tessa says.

"Sure she does," says Steve. "She doesn't take any BS from anybody. And old people appreciate that. They've been around forever, right? They can smell disingenuousness better than anyone."

That's definitely true of Mrs. G. Leave it to Steve to drop a word like *disingenuousness* at the dinner table. Still, it's probably one of the nicest things anyone's ever said to me at this table, or maybe in this entire house for that matter.

I glance over at Tessa and give her a nice big smile. She just nods at Steve like he's the best thing on the planet.

By the time dinner's over, it's too late to call Heather. It kind of sucks having your bestie in such a different time zone. I send her a message saying as much, and ask if we can catch up tomorrow or later in the week.

Emmmm!!! she types, and it's like I can hear her saying it in her usual high-pitched, way-too-excited way. *How* are *you? How is your mom? How is Tessa? How is Matt? Send me latest drawings!!! Tell me everything!*

Heather's parents are born-again believers who won't let

her do anything, which is (A) why it sometimes feels like she's about to scream herself out of her own body and (B) why we get along so well. We have an understanding.

When I ask her how London is, she just writes, *London full of beotches who all know each other, hard to get into group, mission stuff rewarding though, missing you and Matty.*

And I feel for her—it must be hard being so far away and not liking the people around you. At the same time, I have to admit I'm secretly a little glad. At least my best friend in a glamorous European capital misses me while I'm suffering through my not-very-glamorous American summer.

ele

The following weekend is a real scorcher. Even after dark, the air is thick and humid. Mrs. G had told me I didn't need to be there Friday; I could come Saturday morning, and of course Mom and Dad were overjoyed even though we didn't do anything except eat together. After dinner, Tessa is all over Mom, asking her if she needs anything, packing up all the leftovers.

Then Tessa takes the entire produce drawer from the fridge. "Em, can you come help me tear kale?"

"We just had vegetables at dinner," I say.

Of course Dad freaks about how we just cooked and then cleaned the kitchen, and what is she doing taking things out of the fridge again, and Tessa says she has it under control and will *only* be using a cutting board, a knife, a colander, the blender, and a glass. She wants to make a green smoothie that she read about on some website about holistic cancer treatments. I tear kale off the stems and she blends it up with blueberries and lemon juice and ginger.

"Isn't this the sort of thing that *prevents* cancer?" I ask, because I'm pretty sure I know how immune systems work. Tessa tells me to shut up, and she and Mom each drink a glass while we rewatch an episode of *Ted Lasso,* which is the only thing we can all agree on these days.

After all of that, I start to head upstairs. Nobody else ever comes into my room when I'm drawing, which is great, because it's important that I feel alone when I do it.

"Oh come on," Tessa says, "it's Friday night."

"Does it really matter that it's Friday, though? We literally do this every night." Are we going to have this same argument again and again this summer or for the rest of our lives until we both go to college?

Tessa huffs and argues more. I don't get it. Clearly, she's not enjoying being around me and yet she still wants me around. As she's still talking, I just take off—which makes her even more mad—because there's only so long I can go back and forth about an argument that doesn't really make sense. Even Mom and Dad just let it go.

The next day, I text Mrs. G around seven-thirty to give her a heads-up that I'm coming. She doesn't respond, but I figure it's because it's early.

"Text us an update," Dad says while I'm shoveling eggs into my mouth. "Just want to make sure you're safe."

Tessa's eating oatmeal in the cruel heat of summer and, apparently, is the type of person who wears her name tag around her neck on a lanyard, *before* she's even left the house. Which, frankly, I don't get, since she drives all the way to the hospital by herself.

I'm looking forward to seeing Mrs. G, to the sour lemonade, to the savory nuts and pickled eggs and an eleven o'clock bagel with smoked salmon. I'm glad to not have swim practice—not only because I'm not in the mood to swim all those laps, but because it's an excuse to not see Matt and Zoey together. I still can't believe Zoey checked in with me. Did she wonder if Matt liked me and ask him about it? And what did he say—no?

In spite of everything, I'm a little annoyed and miffed that he moved on from me so quickly.

The morning is quiet as I ride by. It's not yet eight, and there are only a few people out in their gardens, watering before it gets truly hot.

I let myself in as usual, except I don't need to be so hush-hush about it. "Mrs. G?" I call. The sound of opera is booming from the living room, but that's not that unusual, I guess.

I slide out of my shoes, grateful for the air-conditioning hitting my face, but before I even get into the heels, she speaks to me from the living room. "I don't need your help today, Emily," is I think what she says, although I can barely hear it above the sound of the music.

When I step into the living room, she's curled up on the couch.

"Mrs. G?" I say again.

She opens her eyes for a second, but it's like she doesn't really see me. "I don't need you today," she repeats. "So please go."

"Well, what can I do? Should I . . . call anyone?" I picture the emergency contacts list on the fridge. I didn't think I'd ever have to use it, but at least it's there. "Can I get you anything?"

She heaves a big sigh. "Emily," she says. "I'm in emotional pain. Not physical. This happens from time to time. I'm an old woman. There's plenty to mourn in my long life."

Geez.

"Okay, well, I could get you some water. Or tea," I offer. Mom always gives me water when I'm upset, and it does seem to help. I try to think of something that Mrs. G would really like. "What if we go somewhere? We could get our nails done together."

When she opens them again, Mrs. G's eyes are little blue slits. Her mouth is thin and drawn. "There's nothing you can do. I just need to deal with this myself."

Maybe I don't need to worry so much. This is the sort of thing that Matt would say is cathartic, absolutely normal. He's the one who assures Heather she doesn't need a reason to be sad—it's okay to just feel that way, sometimes. Same for me when I'm angry, except I don't cry. I punch my pillow.

I start walking away when I hear Mrs. G say, "I was selfish."

I turn back around again. "What do you mean? What are you talking about?"

"Ed and I could have gotten together sooner, but I didn't

want to leave the city. I knew that marrying Ed Granucci meant no more living in New York. It meant we'd start a family and I wouldn't be a flight attendant anymore."

She shifts on the couch, then pulls herself up.

"So I said no, when he asked me to marry him. The first time he asked me."

Call me hard-hearted, but this doesn't strike me as *that* bad.

"He couldn't understand why I would turn him down, when we were so clearly in love. He was eager to be together for the rest of our lives, start a family. So, for two years, we didn't speak. I was flying all around the world, he was starting his own business."

Mrs. G fidgets with the tassels on the couch cushion. "He started seeing Sheila Mather, my best friend at the time. I dated other people, too. Nothing serious, since no one wanted to date someone who wasn't in the same state half the week."

"That makes sense," I say. "I mean, you both dated other people in high school, didn't you?"

It's like she doesn't hear me at all.

"Then they got engaged. And I let them." Mrs. G has her hands over her face now. "Oh, it was so awful. They had already sent wedding invitations, they had their eye on a house, and then I come home, and I break them up. Dear Ed, the one true love of my life, and dear Sheila, who I also loved so, so much. How could I do that to them? Both of them? Sheila and I never spoke again. Why was I so stupid, Emily? Do you know?"

I feel frozen, standing there in the living room. For a few seconds we just stare at each other. Then I will myself to speak. "You weren't stupid," I say softly. I can't believe I'm in this position, consoling my older employer about something long buried in her past. Then again, a lot of unbelievable things are happening this summer.

"I can tell you this, Emily, because I know you won't judge me. I can confide in you. I feel so comfortable with you."

Well, that doesn't make me feel any better.

She holds out her hand, showing me her ring. The band is yellow gold, and it has a pearl in the center, dazzling white and perfectly spherical, with tiny diamonds surrounding it.

"The day after Ed broke off the engagement, he came over to my place, slipped the ring onto my finger, and said, 'Finally.' It was his grandmother's ring, all the way from Italy. We got married in the courthouse. We didn't want to waste any more time being untrue to ourselves and each other."

I have this feeling like I've been, oh God, hit by a truck or something. Like I need to step away from this. The story feels big and adult, something I'm not supposed to know. It's definitely not the romantic drama I'm used to hearing around South Lake High School.

"I'm going to, um, make you a cup of tea," I say.

In the kitchen, I set a timer for Mrs. G's tea to steep, and then there's a rap at the door.

It's Ezra, with two armfuls of groceries. "Make yourself useful, fellow artist," he says. "Two more bags in the car."

I huff, not sure whether to be pleased or annoyed. But I go

get the groceries, because at least it's *something* I can do for Mrs. G.

When I come back in, Ezra is checking on his aunt. Unlike me, he's right up next to her, squatting down beside her like he's talking to a toddler, speaking softly and soothingly. I can't hear what he's saying, but it seems to be helping, because she's nodding—which is at least more positive than the responses she gave me.

While I tidy up, Ezra unloads everything. Instead of the usual black outfit, he's wearing shorts and a green Trampled by Turtles T-shirt, and it makes him seem more down-to-earth, and okay—cuter. He slides a few boxes of pasta into the pantry, then rearranges some of the other dried goods. I'd usually have more to say, except I'm still shell-shocked by what Mrs. G told me, so I'm grateful Ezra is going on, telling me where things go and wiping down the counters.

"I wish I knew what, precisely, she's so upset about," says Ezra. "I have . . . theories. Well, one theory in particular."

"You don't know what she's upset about?"

"Oh heck no. This just happens from time to time."

Huh. *In-ter-es-ting.* So Mrs. G told *me*, but she hasn't told her great-nephew.

Ezra continues, arranging peaches and nectarines in the fruit bowl. "Have you ever broken up with someone and think you're doing well, but then, a month later, that one song comes on when it's dark and everyone else is asleep and you just, like, crumble?"

I have to wonder if he's speaking from experience. It sounds like he is. But what kind of girl would date Ezra? It would have to be someone as poised as he is. Or would someone a little rougher around the edges be more helpful? Opposites attract, is what I've heard.

I say no, but I don't think he hears me, or maybe that part's not important, because he goes on. "I think that's how it is for her: something triggers a memory, and that memory spills over into grief, and she basically acts like she did during the months after Uncle Eddie died."

Inwardly, I shudder. It's hard to imagine feeling *that* bad for months, but of course I would if, for instance, Mom died.

I still can't believe Mrs. G told me about how her marriage began. It must be her biggest regret. But if she didn't tell Ezra herself, then I certainly shouldn't be the one to let him know. I head into the bathroom to splash cold water on my face and get myself together.

When I'm back in the kitchen, Ezra is sliding the last of the snacks into the pantry. Even I have to give him credit for his meticulous order of operations: the ice cream and other perishables first, then the produce, then the dry goods.

"What are you up to now?" he asks.

"I guess I'll go home."

He raises one eyebrow. "Well, technically, you're still on the job. So let's go for a drive."

I don't mean to, but I make a face. Not because I don't want to, but because who just goes for a drive?

Already, he's got his keys, jangling them on his index finger. "I'm not gonna lie," he says. "Part of the joy of having a car is that you get to shuttle yourself in an air-conditioned vehicle from one air-conditioned place to another. If that's not luxury, I don't know what is."

I consider my options: I'll be struck with boredom at home. The likelihood of running into my parents while in someone else's car is extremely low. And—I *am* still on the job. Talking to Ezra is part of my employment, really.

Yeah. That sounds all right to me.

In the living room, Ezra says bye to Mrs. G and kisses her on the cheek. I feel like, when she looks at me with shared understanding, now we both know something together.

ℓℓℓ

I get into Ezra's car, a dark green Camry. It's not, like, a Lamborghini or anything, but it's not bad, either. Clean, a pretty color. And is it cool that he has a car at all? Yes. Yes, I have to admit, it is. I haven't been in a car driven by a cute boy before just by myself, so it seems like something I should be psyched about. We both put our sunglasses on and settle in.

The minute he turns the car on, the AC is on full blast and the music is, too—some orchestral thing. "What an epic drive," I say over the music.

He nods and holds up a finger, telling me to be quiet. I roll my eyes—I do that a lot around Ezra—as the violins swell and Ezra hums along to it.

Then, out of nowhere, he says, "Don't worry. My aunt will

of course pay you for your time today. It's not like it's your fault she can't accept help today."

I flinch. "I wasn't even thinking about that." Does he think I really need money, or something?

"Sorry," he says. "As someone who wants to be a musician, it's, like, all I think about."

He pauses, adjusts the music just a hair. He fiddles with the volume and then, weirdly, the bass, as if our conversation is just a quick side note but the real event is listening.

"What is this, anyway?" I ask when it finally quiets down some.

"So it's Beethoven's *Eroica* symphony. And what's super cool about it is that it starts with a surprise."

Then he starts the song, er, symphony, over again. It starts with these two blasts, there's a pause, and then the melody begins, in a completely different mood from the opening strings.

Then he starts it over again. And again.

"It's *so* cool, right?" he says. "And okay, maybe you won't appreciate this as much but in the fifth measure, he goes to a C-sharp. Which is totally crazy in the key of E-flat! Or would have been, back when Beethoven was writing it. Still is damn cool now."

Ezra drives fast and, unlike me, has no problem merging onto the highway.

I settle back and listen to the music. Of course I'm not getting it the way Ezra is, but it definitely has the sound of excitement and adventure. If I were going to make it a color, it would be a bunch of burnt oranges and brilliant yellows exploding into the sky.

We get off the freeway somewhere and it occurs to me that I should be careful. That I should maybe even be freaked out. Mom and Dad would call this a stupid decision, getting into a car with a boy I barely know. But a guy who takes care of his great-aunt and goes to private school for classical music really can't be that bad. Can he?

We toddle along on back roads, past farmland and woods and sweet little houses with no neighbors for miles.

"Where are we going?" I ask.

Ezra shrugs. "Nowhere in particular. Driving here is nice. There's hardly any traffic, you can go fast, and the only living creatures around are squirrels and the occasional deer." We coast downhill and wind alongside a lake. I can see why someone would enjoy driving here. For a good while, we just listen to the symphony and watch the summer day. We get to be in all that greenery and sunshine without the heat and sweat.

Though I guess Matt would say that what we're doing isn't great for the environment.

"So how often does Mrs. G get like that?" I ask finally.

"You saw her. She seemed better already, didn't she?"

"Why doesn't she, I don't know, talk about it? See someone about it?"

Ezra guffaws. "Can you imagine her in therapy? She's a traditional Southern lady. And who knows, maybe she talks to friends about it. . . . I don't think she does, though. She's— I mean, she's a tough one, right? She wants things to appear just so, including herself, and she's very private about her pain."

And then—it's weird and it's irrational, I know—but I have

this thought that I wish I could be as close to Mrs. G as Ezra is to her. My own great-aunts and -uncles live so far away, and there's a language barrier. I picture myself at thirty, at forty, with kids of my own, still fumbling around in my mediocre Spanglish, the type of conversational level that makes it impossible to have a meaningful conversation, and I shudder. That was why I studied pretty hard for Spanish at school. Plus, when you have a last name like Chen-Sanchez, you've got to be at the top of Spanish class, or people will talk.

"So," Ezra says, "why pastels? Like, why not clay, or photography, or whatever else there is for you artists to make stuff?"

Okay. I *do* like it that he calls me an artist. It's like he takes my stuff seriously.

"I tried sculpture and photography freshman year and enjoyed them, but pastels are so vivid and rich. I like that they're forgiving—it makes it easier to experiment with them—and I feel like a kid playing with chalk. Of all the mediums I tried, it was the one where I felt like I could just do it for hours and hours. Maybe that's not a good enough reason."

"Of course it is," he says. "That's how I feel if a practice session is going well. The minutes fly by."

"It was cool hearing you play, the other day."

He makes a face. "Eh, I'm still working some things out in that one. Needs a lot of work. Like, the transition into the exposition could be smoother, and my accompanist always seems like she's ahead of me when we get to the key change."

I have no idea what he's talking about, but that's okay. The classical music jargon is . . . kind of hot.

Finally, we head back onto the freeway, and soon enough we're in River's Edge and turning onto Rock Road. When we pull into Mrs. G's, he takes off his sunglasses because we're under some shade now, so I take mine off, too.

Then he asks, "Do you want a ride home? I could put your bike in the back."

I consider this. It's hot as blazes, as Mrs. G would say. But Dad would freak if he saw me getting out of a car driven by a boy he's never met.

"It's cool. I'll ride back. And thanks for the drive."

I'm about to open the door when Ezra reaches out. His hand is huge and warm on my bare arm but it brings goose bumps to the surface. It's a feeling I could get used to.

"I hope— You're okay with not telling anyone about her memory, right? I mean, it's not anything that's causing any trouble, you know. It's just little things. Pretty ordinary things. And I know her, it would really destroy her if people knew. She has a lot of pride."

"Who would I tell?" I say. Because it's true. Not Mom and Dad, not Tessa. The only person I'd like to tell is Matt, but what would he be able to do about it that I couldn't?

Ezra says, "She must really like you. She wouldn't hire just anybody."

I try to suss out if he's being sincere. I'm generally skeptical of smooth-talking Southern boys. He seems to mean it, though. "Thanks," I say.

Then we're looking at each other for a beat too long. I should just get out of the car. Like, right now. Now!

"Thanks for the drive," I say, trying to sound casual as I accidentally lock the door, then unlock it, then finally swing it open.

The whole time I pedal back home I think, *Was that a date?*

CHAPTER 8

THE WEEKEND SLINKS BY. But what's worse than boredom is the abject misery I feel, which I think is due in part to the weight of what Mrs. G told me about her husband, mixed with something like nerves and maybe even elation about riding in Ezra's car and wanting to see him again. I'm dying to talk with Mrs. G about what she told me—or anyone, for that matter— but she doesn't need me on Sunday, either. I start a new drawing: Just the top of Mrs. G's head, those big red-orange curls, and then something I've never done before. Words swirling around in her hair: *Dear Sheila, who I loved.* I take a long time perfecting the typography, outlining the words in a color just a tad darker than her hair, so that you could almost miss it if you didn't look carefully. When it's done, it looks like a vintage movie poster, but it's probably not something I'll use for my art school portfolio. Just a side project to get things off my chest.

Speaking of which, I so need to start finishing drawings, it's not even funny anymore.

After dinner on Monday night (only Monday and I'm already feeling like it's been a *week*), Mom knocks on my bedroom door, then just comes in, because that's how my parents are sometimes.

"What are you doing?" she asks.

"Nothing," I respond. And yes, I know that's the world's most irritating response, but I was having another "time lapse" with my phone. "Your phone is taking years and years off your life and you don't even know it," Matt has said several times. He even keeps his phone grayscale so that it "repulses" him, as he put it. But even that doesn't work for me. You can still read when it's black and white. Food and clothing aren't as attractive, but they *do* look kind of vintage.

This particular time lapse involved searching and searching for the perfect red-orange lipstick, the one that would change my life forever. I have several lipsticks that are the same-ish shade, yet why is there always this search for the holy grail color? I think it's because the perfect beauty product is the one that makes you into the person you *want* to be.

I guess Mrs. Granucci is right: one swipe *can* change your life.

"Well, if you're looking for something to do"—this is one of Mom's signature phrases—"you can come downstairs and unload the dishwasher."

So I do, but not before heaving a heavy sigh.

In the kitchen, I stack the plates waitress-style, really asking for it.

"Emily, please don't do that," Mom says. "We're in no hurry here; you can do a few plates at a time."

"No accidents!" Dad calls from the living room.

As I'm working on the silverware, Mom says, "So, Em, is everything okay? You seem really down."

Well, I mean, you might have cancer, and on top of that I'm bored—which is one of the worst feelings ever. "I'm just sort of preoccupied about something, is all. But it'll be fine."

"You don't want to talk about it?"

Oh come on. I've already told her more than I wanted.

"Well, you know, Mrs. G is older, and, like . . . well, you know. She can be a little cranky sometimes."

Mom knows how that is. I've heard her trying to placate Ama, or hanging up the phone with an exasperated sigh.

"If you don't want to talk about it, that's fine. But just don't let her crankiness get to you. I had to learn that the hard way."

From the living room, Dad calls, "It's just a job! If she's not treating you well, you can always quit! You don't owe her anything!"

"It's okay!" I call back. "Just a one-time situation."

"Just quit," Dad says.

I sigh.

Mom puts her hand on my shoulder. "You know how Dad is. He just wants the best for you, is all. At some point, I would love to meet this Mrs. Granucci. She sounds like quite a character."

"Not me! I don't need to meet her," Dad says, which makes Mom and me laugh. "All she does is make you stressed."

"We've had plenty of good times," I say.

I should be the one comforting Mom—she's the one who might have cancer—but instead she's listening to me go on about this old woman who, I realize, I only met like a month ago. I guess Mom isn't that bad.

‿ℓℓℓ‿

The next day, I'm drying my hair after swim practice when I see my phone light up with a call. There are only a few people who will call me out of the blue—actually, there are only two: Mom and Dad. My friends and other people from school, and even Tessa, know you're supposed to avoid calls at all costs, and if you must call, you should always text first to ask when is a good time. Phone calls make me anxious. And they feel so urgent. You see your phone buzzing and lighting up, the name and number flashing; it's so impatient, like it's got to be some sort of emergency.

I take a look at the incoming emergency: Mrs. G.

Now I really don't want to answer it.

What if she's calling because she wants to tell me more about what happened with Ed? It's probably therapeutic for her to share with me, but I gotta be honest, I really don't want to hear it. Or what if she's calling to tell me not to come over on Friday? It's weird, how I simultaneously don't want to hear more about her dark past but do want to spend the night there. I mean, the pickles are really good. And there's a cute boy there.

I let my phone ring. If she really needs to talk to me, she'll call again.

Several seconds later, I have a voicemail. That's another

thing that no one in my generation does—except for Matt. Why make someone hold the phone to their ear, listening to you go on about what you need for thirty seconds, when they could just read a text?

"Hi, Emily," Mrs. G says into my ear. "Well, I am so sorry for my behavior the other day. I was just having . . . one of those days!" She says that last part a little too brightly. "Well, that's all I really wanted to say, and, of course, I'd love to see you at the usual time, and I'm sure we'll have a nice weekend together."

It's not much of an apology, and she doesn't say a word about everything she told me, nor does she apologize for what kind of feels like an overshare that's kind of killing me right now, but I guess it'll have to do. Is she having what they call a vulnerability hangover? Is she trying to pretend our conversation never happened? I text her.

> Hi, Mrs. G! Thank you so much for the voicemail. Apology accepted. See you Friday!

The exclamation marks make it sound happier than I feel. But it's better than nothing.

ꙮ

That week, we all head to the hospital again for Mom's surgery. We sit around in the waiting room, Dad pacing.

Mom, however, is completely stoic. I don't know how she does it.

When it's time, we all hug and kiss her and whisper our I love yous, and then Mom's wheeled away. To pass the time we head down to the cafeteria, even though none of us are very hungry.

We're the kind of family who orders water if and when we're eating at a restaurant, but today I make a great cocktail with seltzer water, Cherry Coke, fruit punch, and blue Gatorade, then grab a little cup of banana pudding for dessert, because how often are you in the hospital for your mom's surgery? Dad sees this and pays for it without complaint.

"We have to stay positive," Dad says, sawing at a chicken breast with his plastic knife and fork. "It's all in the mind. If we keep our spirits up, then we can fight off anything."

But I know what happens if we keep our spirits up. We'll be crushed when we do receive bad news. That's why I like to keep my expectations low.

Dr. Kim was right: it feels like we've barely had time to down some not-great lunch in the cafeteria when Dad gets a phone call that the surgery is over and we can join Mom in her room.

When we go in, Dr. Kim is standing there in her mint-green scrubs. Damn, I wish I were a doctor. She's so cool and competent.

Mom is lying there, eyes open but barely. She's got something like a tube in her neck and wires everywhere. But she manages a weak smile, which immediately assures me. "At least they got the jumbo olive," she says.

My parents never call family meetings. They don't believe in that type of formality. Heather's family, on the other hand, has meetings once a month, going over everything from sibling rivalries to chores, even deciding where they will eat on the weekends. They always begin and end with prayer: for the family, for each kid, for our town and state and country. Our family isn't so democratic. But today, the day after the surgery, Dad sits us down in the living room and says he and Mom have something to tell us. He takes his glasses off and rubs his temples for a second. That is never a good sign.

"It is thyroid cancer," he says.

Tessa starts crying immediately after that word—even though her own boyfriend has told us that the odds are insanely good—because that's how she is. It's like if she doesn't cry, the big news didn't happen. She cries over everything, though, like once she came home sobbing after she hit a squirrel. Now she dabs at her eyes with a tissue, making sure to be gentle about it so she won't smudge her mascara. Because even when she's coaching herself through premature grief, my sister cares about her Maybelline. I've never been much of a crier. I don't think it accomplishes very much at all.

Matt, of course, would disagree. He says it releases endorphins, and that holding it in only makes things worse ("I'm not holding it in, though," I always have to remind him). The Ziegler family is like that, though. Every week, they go around the room and talk about how they're feeling and why, and they ask for forgiveness from each other—it's pretty much an ideal situation, if you're into that sort of thing. I could see someone like Tessa thriving in the Ziegler house, whereas I would just sit there, not wanting to share how I was feeling, or even feel what I was feeling.

Mom tells Tessa to stop crying. She says, "If you cry over *this*, what are you going to do when something really bad happens?"

That's the kind of thing my mom says. She's tough as shit, my mom. And yet, there can't be news that's much worse than one of your parents having cancer. I'm pretty sure that's at the top of the list of bad things that could happen. It's when Tessa cries from frustration over a school project, or when she starts to tear up over an Amazon Prime commercial, that she's really insufferable.

"We're all in this together," Dad says. "Mom will have another surgery and they'll remove her entire thyroid. They'll follow that up with radioactive iodine therapy. It's called RAI for short. And it should kill off the rest of the cancer cells."

I immediately picture Mom walking onto some planet surrounded by scientists in head-to-toe white protective gear, hands and heads covered, face masks on, about to transmit these neon green radioactive waves into her body.

That's not exactly how it works.

For RAI, Mom has to eat a low-iodine diet for at least two weeks—otherwise, the iodine that already lives in your body (it's fittingly called "resident iodine") will make it harder for the cancer cells to absorb the radioactive stuff. My parents are overachievers, so they're going to do the diet for three weeks. Dad shows us a list, from the hospital, of all the things

Mom needs to abstain from. Do you know how many things you can't eat when you're on a low-iodine diet? You can't have sandwiches, pizza, chocolate, or cake. You can't have grilled shrimp. Fish tacos are out. You can't have ice cream, cheese, milk, or butter. You definitely can't have the crispy golden chicken tenders at Sharky's. And since we're a family, we will all be eating this diet along with her, starting next week. It sounds like a plainer variation of the meat-and-three, except it is more like a meat-and-one.

Then Mom will walk into the basement of the hospital (again, fittingly, that's where the Nuclear Medicine Department is) and take a pill. Afterward, she will need to isolate from us for five days, during which a variety of side effects could appear.

Tessa takes a big deep breath through her nose and then exhales as if blowing air into a flute—doubtless it's a tactic she learned from some podcast about calming yourself. She makes it through two breaths like that, and I'm weirdly proud of her.

Then her face crumples and she starts to cry again anyway.

I'm sorry, but Tessa always looks really funny when she's crying. I have to do my best not to look at her, or I'll crack up.

Now Tessa's hugging Mom, and telling her she loves her so much. And I've never really been into hugs—Tessa's the type of person who will scream "Love you!" at a car full of her girl-friends. I'm more of a "Later bish" type of person.

Mom knows this, and still, she gets up, and she *smothers* me, smashing my face right into her Talbots blouse that she got for 50 percent off at the after-Christmas sale, and I can smell the overpriced dry shampoo that Tessa sprays in her hair on days when she doesn't wash it.

"I just love you girls so much," Mom says. "It's going to be okay."

ᐧℓℓℓᐧ

Matt, I've already texted, and like a champ he says he's going to send me good vibes and bring me the highest-iodine snacks to eat in secret.

Mrs. G has teased me more than once about how maybe my best friends don't exist, and all week long I've been counting down the days till I get to talk with Heather. It'll feel good to just hear her voice, I can't help thinking, in the midst of everything. Early in the evening, my phone buzzes with a WhatsApp video call.

"Hey, Heth," I say, and the words are barely out when she screeches, "Emmmily, my queen!" in this high-pitched voice.

It's after 10:00 p.m. where she is, so I pictured her in pajamas, talking quietly in her room.

I peer at her on the screen. She looks older and different somehow. She's done her makeup all . . . nice, I guess? Her skin is smooth with foundation. I'm not sure if I like it. But okay.

"How *are* you!" she says, and I realize that she's raising her voice because there are other people in the room with her. There's also music coming from somewhere—I can't put my finger on it, but it's one of those girl-power-anthem-type songs, like Katy Perry or someone.

"Good, good," I say. I want to tell her about Mom, about Mrs. G, about Matt and Zoey, but the timing feels off to just lay all that news on her at the very beginning of a conversation. Even with a best friend, you have to ease into things sometimes—especially if one of you is talking in a room full of other people. "How's London?" I put a big smile on my face and try to ask it cheerfully, excitedly.

"*So posh!*" she exclaims in a fake British accent. "Oh man, I love it here, everything has changed since we've last talked, which is why it was so hard to connect earlier—well, that and the time difference. I'm living with three girls and I just love them. We all get along great."

"Oh yeah? No more beotches?"

"What?" she practically yells.

"Never mind," I say.

"Yesterday we saw a play at the Globe, can you imagine?"

Yes, I think, *yes I can, because we freaking built a model of the Globe Theatre in Honors English freshman year.*

"What'd you see?" I ask instead, but she doesn't hear me.

"And tonight, at midnight, Lexi's meeting a guy from Italy at Big Ben."

Someone in the room—I'm guessing it's Lexi—squeals.

"Sounds sketchy to me," I say.

Heather laughs. "I had a feeling you'd say that."

Then she puts the phone really close to her face. "Check this out: Lexi did my makeup."

I can't help feeling like she's not being completely herself on the phone, what with everyone around her—and that makes it hard for me to be *my*self, too.

"Nice," I say.

"And, Em, get this: I've been . . . *drinking*! It's not like I have a lot, or anything, but it's just, like, part of the culture here, you know? *Kids* start drinking with their parents when they're, like, in elementary school."

That part, I'm not sure about. But Heather? Drinking? She didn't even go to parties when she was here. Maybe *that's* why I'm having trouble talking with her.

"Well, just . . . be careful. Drink a bunch of water." I never thought, in our some seven years of friendship, that I would ever sound like the more cautious one between the two of us.

Heather laughs again, even though I'm being completely serious. "Oh yeah, you would know all about drinking water. Speaking of which—"

But I cut her off, because I know where she's headed.

"I'm really digging my new job," I say.

"That's right, the Spanish-house lady. It's going well?" Just a month ago, this would have been really prize information, but now she's in London and why would one of our mysterious neighborhood houses mean anything to her? I tried to explain to her about Mrs. G via our messages, but it was hard to do her justice.

"Mrs. G, yeah. She's fantastic." Uh-oh, there I go again, using one of the three-syllable adjectives that Mrs. G herself would use. "It's hard to explain, but she really gets me."

"Uh-huh?" Heather says, but I can tell she's not really listening—she's preoccupied by something or someone else in the room. And apparently, my news doesn't hold a candle to posh London and meeting boys at the stroke of midnight by Big Ben. Still, I press on.

"Her house is beautiful," I say, "and we spend a lot of time eating treats and . . ." I want to tell her the most important part, about how Mrs. G asked me to remember things about her life, but something about that feels secret, sacred. It's not the kind of thing I can explain over a distracted WhatsApp call. Everything I'm saying sounds boring and somehow too adult to share right now, compared to what she's up to. And trying to tell her about George Harrison would just be plain stupid.

"Sounds fun!" Heather says. "Anyway, what's going on with *Matt*?"

I hear a girl behind her saying, "Ooh, boy trouble?" The other girl tries to stick her face in the screen, but Heather pulls the phone away. "Is he super enjoying dating Zoey Kebabian, or is he still, like, totally in love with you?"

I can't help but feel super irked and turned off. Heather's never said that before, but then again she's never not listened to me so hard before.

"He and Zoey are doing really great," I say. So now what, I'm defending him and Zoey? "He's not *in love* with me. Geez, what is with you?"

Then, even though she's the one being a total jerk right now, I immediately feel bad for snapping at her. I guess she *has* teased me before, saying things like, "You know you're going to just end up together like Anne and Gilbert," and stuff like that, but she hasn't in months.

"Sorry, Em, I'm just teasing. I mean, you know how he kind of hangs on you sometimes—wait, WHAT?" Heather says, and suddenly I'm not looking at her but at her shoes, which are sparkly, pointy things. Matt hasn't "hung on me" for a while. Ever since Zoey came into the picture, really. Heather brings the phone back to her face again. "Sorry, we're just getting ready to leave."

Like a total dork-sauce, I say, "So late at night, though?"

So it's happening: the thing that Matt always predicted, jokingly, because of Heather's über-conservative, sheltered family. We always joked that she would be the one of us to "go wild." But we expected it to happen in college. Not while we were all three still in high school.

"Heeethhiiiee!" someone says. "We're leaving! Get off the phone already!"

Hethie? I think. What an awful nickname. It doesn't knock off any syllables, so what's the point?

Heather laughs. It's a new laugh that I haven't heard before, almost flirtatious. She brings the phone back to her face again. "So sorry, Em, we'll talk more another time! It's just, like, during the day I'm in classes and then volunteering and I can only talk to you when I have Wi-Fi, back here at the dorm, and then after dinner everyone wants to go out, and I don't want to miss anything—"

"I get it," I say. "Go enjoy."

"Oh my god, thank you so much for understanding. You're the best. But everything's good, right? It was great to see you for even a few minutes."

If I don't bring up Mom now, then I won't during this phone call. But the timing, and the atmosphere . . . It's just not right.

"Yeah," I say. "Yeah, it was good to see you, too, Heth."

CHAPTER 9

BY THE TIME I'M back at Mrs. G's place that weekend, it's as if the events of the previous Saturday never happened.

Every time I walk into the Spanish house, it's like I become a different person. I like myself when I'm with Mrs. G. She doesn't know who I am at school, and she thinks I'm so smart and original, when everyone else thinks I'm just . . . weird. The minute I put on those shoes, I don't feel on edge like I do at home. I wish I didn't feel this way, but I do. I don't even reach for my phone like I do at home—so often it's a reflex that I don't even think about, staring into it like technology's going to save me from reality.

Mostly it's the lack of judgment, right? That's got to be what it is. The way Mrs. G seems to unconditionally support everything I do, while my family seems to unconditionally criticize everything I do.

After enjoying Mrs. G's comfy guest room on Friday night, I step into the kitchen on Saturday morning, and she is all activity: holding herbs up to her nose, wiping her hands on her apron.

"Oh!" Mrs. G exclaims when she sees me. "There she is."

When she's positively beaming with pride about me, it's hard to hold a grudge, even with an apology that was more of a sweeping under the rug.

"So, you're doing better?" I ask.

"I am!" she says, hands on her hips, eyes darting around the kitchen to see what needs doing. "And, you know what, Emily, you are a true mensch for handling it so well. You were gracious, and you weren't afraid. I appreciate that very much."

"Sure thing, Mrs. G." The truth is, I was kind of freaked out, but I don't say so. "So you're feeling better about, um." I don't even know what to say. I don't want to bring it up because what if it sends her spiraling again? So I just say, "I'm glad you're feeling better about what you told me."

"Oh Lord," Mrs. G says. She waves her hand as if to wave it away. "Right. About how much I miss Ed! And I still do. Every damn day." She shakes her head. "That's grief for you, isn't it? Sometimes it just all feels fresh as the day it happened."

Something in my stomach twists. Is she just trying to avoid talking about it, acting like our conversation didn't happen?

Or does she not remember what she told me?

"If there's one thing I know," Mrs. G continues, "it's that I could never be one of those people who go to the White Moose in a big group like that. By the busload. I live by myself, and I never, ever want to live in a nursing home. If I'm not doing well, I want to be not doing well with my dignity intact."

I take a deep breath. So she doesn't remember. But I do, and it's like I know a little too much about her past now. I can't say I feel so hot about that.

She cocks her head at me. "You're quiet today, E. What is up with that?" Before I can say anything, she snaps her fingers. "I know what you need," she says while walking. "An iced coffee. And you know I don't do half-caf, like that handsome young friend of yours!"

~ℓℓℓ~

That weekend, I eat all the savory, crispy things that we won't be eating at home. Mrs. G and I spear gherkins with tiny forks, toast onion bagels so brown they're just hardly this side of burnt. We top them with scallion cream cheese and smoked salmon and capers, tiny salt bombs. We smash hot pink pickled eggs on toast and dress them with English mustard that burns the insides of our noses.

"If it doesn't make my mouth pucker," says Mrs. G, "I'm not interested!" Her mother's recipe for pickled vegetables made the air so pungent that, even from the living room, we held our noses for a little bit as the mixture came to a boil.

"My mother thought we should always bring a gift, so these pickles were often the thing we brought. It embarrassed me. I told her once that we were the only people who brought something, and she said, well, if we wanted to be accepted, we had to work a little harder.

"I couldn't understand why we had to care so much about what people thought of our family, but now I do. She was scared. She wanted, maybe needed, people to like her, to accept us. To make sure her kids weren't left out among all these Southerners.

"Ever since she died, I make sure to bring a gift—and you know, I do feel closer to her, doing that."

"I'm so sorry," I say. "When did she die?"

"Oh goodness, I was only thirty. My mother suffered in secret for a good while, maybe months. I had pulled away from her for quite some time, and suddenly I was back and wanting to know her and things were good between us, really good—and that's when—"

Mrs. G takes a breath here.

I put my hand over hers. I've never done that before. She smiles at me gratefully, and it reminds me of the moment when I first knew Heather and I were going to be best friends—when she told me she wasn't allowed to listen to Taylor Swift at home and we looked at each other and both burst into song: "We're happy, free, confused, and lonely at the same time!" I knew then that when we were together, we could be ourselves.

Mrs. G continues. "I still hear her telling me, 'Oh, Leila, that skirt would go better with this shirt, and these linens are the ones you should put on the table when you have company,' and all the little decisions like that." Mrs. G shook her head. "I've never really met anyone else who took such care with every tiny thing."

It doesn't sound like love to me—in fact, it sounds like the kind of thing that certain people are obsessed with on social media, wanting everything to look good. But who am I to say something about Mrs. G's mother?

"She could be so . . ."—Mrs. G sucked her voice in here—"*critical* of me. The only girl in a family of boys! But I see now she—she just wanted me to be okay. She knew how hard it is to be a woman in the world."

I wonder if that's why Mom is so critical of *me*. If it has to do with protecting me, making sure that I do okay. But maybe I'm tougher than she thinks. Maybe, even if people are hard on me, I'm going to be fine. Maybe that's just something she needs to learn.

That's when, unexpectedly, my eyes well up and I turn away. I blink, furiously, and then Mrs. G dips her head toward me and says, in an astonished voice, "Emily! What's wrong?"

"It's . . . ," I say. "It's my mom."

Mrs. Granucci regards me over the top of her glasses. "Your mama is sick?"

The way she says "your mama" almost makes me laugh.

"Why didn't you tell me?" she asks.

I purse my lips together, then decide to tell her the truth. "I didn't want you pitying me. I didn't want extra sympathy or for you to treat me different because of it."

Maybe Mrs. G and I are even more similar than I think. Maybe we're both private about our pain.

"Different*ly*. When have I ever pitied anyone?"

I tell her the details of the diagnosis, and the treatment,

and the odds—which are truly good. "I feel stupid crying about it," I say.

"Stupid? Why?"

"There's such a high chance that she's going to be fine, and besides, crying doesn't do anything."

"Still, it's hard to see someone you love suffer, isn't it? Your body wants you to cry, so let it cry! Hiding your fears makes them even scarier." Then it's Mrs. G's turn to pat my hand. "We'll just have to hope and pray," she says, which isn't that different from what Dad said about it. "That's all we can do, isn't it?"

lll

That night in bed, I go on a Google deep dive about memory loss in people who are Mrs. G's age. It turns out there are a few different types of dementia, but by process of elimination I deduce that Mrs. G has Alzheimer's: not only is it the most common, but the other ones wreak havoc on your body in a way that isn't happening to Mrs. G—and thank goodness for that. Apparently, some of the first to go are the housekeeping abilities, like cooking and grocery shopping, paying bills.

After that, it's the basics: moving around, getting dressed, bathing, eating.

I picture Mrs. G needing someone to feed her, and my stomach bottoms out.

That's when I muster every ounce of self-control in my body (and okay, a little help from opening Instagram) and keep myself from looking for more. Who am I to WebMD Mrs. G? Just because I read it online doesn't mean it's true. You can always find the worst-case scenario if you go looking for it. Not learning more means maybe she's okay. Maybe it's just normal aging stuff. She remembered a ton of stuff about her mom, so is it really that big of a deal that she forgot what we talked about last week?

Yet, even as I scroll through reels of pastel drawings and good-looking food-fluencers making pastries, I know that something is wrong, and I am helpless to fix it.

ꝏ

In the morning, it's eggs Benedict as usual, only it's not as usual.

Mrs. G is making the hollandaise sauce, but it's runny. I'm doing the eggs. Even though I'm following all of her—Julia's— instructions to a T, they're gloppy messes. Ezra's in charge of the English muffins, and they've been in the toaster too long.

I'm realizing, though, that usually Ezra and I are sous-chefs in Mrs. G's kitchen. We take orders from Mrs. G, and this morning, she's not giving much instruction. In fact, she's struggling with her sauce. She whisks and whisks the hollandaise, sighing great big sighs, as if that will thicken it up. But I'm pretty sure she forgot a step. Or two.

"Mrs. G," I say, as gently as I can. "It's totally okay to start this sauce over. That's what you always tell me, remember?"

Ezra meets my eye, and I cringe at my word choice.

"How about you go relax with your coffee," I suggest, "and Ezra and I make you breakfast today?"

Mrs. G's shoulders sag at the suggestion, but she says, "You're right. I've got to eat humble pie sometimes, I guess! And it's just lemon and eggs. Cheapest foods on the planet." She pours the ruined sauce down the sink.

When Ezra and I finish cooking and bring breakfast over to the table, Mrs. G is pleased. I don't have an appetite, though. All I can think about is how—according to my doomscrolling last night—inability to prepare meals is one of the first indicators of cognitive decline. I take my time eating, which makes me feel even more full, which then makes me even more anxious about not being able to finish the food.

"You know," Mrs. G says, "even though I didn't graduate from college, I wasn't just a housewife. I was once a flight attendant."

I know about her flight attendant days already, but I let it go. I'm relieved that she's talking about her flight attendant memories. I once announced I wanted to be one—during our family trip to Panama when I was five—and Dad said that that wasn't a good job. Even now, knowing I most likely won't become a doctor, my parents like to suggest I become an optometrist or a dental hygienist. Steady, useful, respectable jobs. *Good* jobs, is what they call them.

It seems to me that good jobs are super limited.

"The feeling that you could go anywhere, be anyone . . . I love the South—it's my home, but it can be hard to get away from yourself, get away from who people know you to be," says Mrs. G.

I've thought about that a lot. I sometimes think that if I could get away from how my parents and Tessa see me, I'd be a lot better off.

ꮯꮮꮯ

Ezra rinses the dishes off in the sink while Mrs. G takes a shower. I put the breakfast things away.

"So," I begin, "I was doing some googling last night."

Ezra nods. "I've been reading, too. And I wanted to ask you not to tell anyone about her . . . condition."

That makes me pause. "Her condition? So we're on the same page that this is a condition—not just little memory things that we can laugh off."

He nods.

"We have to tell someone." For some reason there's a lump in my throat as I say it.

"You can't!" Ezra whirls around and grabs my arm. "You can*not* tell anyone. Don't you know what that would do to her?"

Seeing my expression, he drops his hand. "Sorry." My arm is soapy from where his hand was, and he grabs a towel and dries it off.

"You're calling it what it is. A condition. Why are we keeping a condition a secret?"

Ezra glances around, making sure that Mrs. G can't hear us.

"It's not a disease like . . . I don't know, Parkinson's is a disease. She can't take anything for it. Resting up won't make it any better. All she can do is live her life the way she wants to, on her own terms, before the condition takes that ability away from her. So can't you just let her do that in peace?"

"She— To some degree she's aware that she's . . . losing her memory, right? Otherwise, why did she hire me to do the simplest things, things she's capable of doing? She's scared. That's why she has me unplug everything." As I'm saying it aloud, I realize I've known this for a while but am just now admitting it. "So, I don't see how keeping it under wraps is going to help her. Or anyone."

Ezra runs a hand through his hair. "Being independent is, like, the *most* important thing in her life. Telling someone accomplishes nothing. Family will freak, and they'll make her go to one of those homes that she hates."

He's right, of course. The last thing she wants is to "live with a bunch of old fogies." She said that as if they aren't her peers. And I guess I do the same thing, about other people my own age.

Now she's having trouble making hollandaise. But later, she'll have trouble with things as simple as going to the bathroom. The image of Mrs. G being that helpless is enough to make me catch my breath.

"What happens . . . ," I ask. "What happens if I do tell someone?"

"It would absolutely ruin her. This"—he waves his hands around the house—"this is her legacy. She doesn't want to have to leave it. And, you know, it's not like she's going to hurt herself. The memory slips, they're minor. So don't— please."

I want to agree with him, but the thing is, the memory slips don't feel so minor anymore. Ezra's got those pleading eyes, those super-pretty hazel eyes that are a little green in a certain light, and I have to admit it was kind of endearing when he dried off my arm earlier. I say, "Okay, okay, I won't tell anyone at all."

Later, it seems like things have calmed down some. It's too hot for a walk, so Mrs. G makes a lemon tart. I dust George and other things in the living room, put a hat on his head just for variety. The afternoon passes slowly. I just keep finding things to do so that I'm not sitting idly. And I'm thinking that for the first time in my life my behavior reminds me of Tessa. I'm switching the laundry over when I think I hear my name from Mrs. G's bedroom.

"Do you need me, Mrs. G?" I call.

Then she appears in the doorway.

"Emily," she says. Her voice is so cold and quiet, I know immediately that something's wrong. And I mean *really* wrong. She usually shouts my name, stretching it—"Emmmmily"—to summon me.

"Yes, ma'am." Already, I know I'm in trouble. Again.

Mrs. G holds up her left hand and stretches all five fingers, then points to her fourth finger. "My ring. Ed's family ring. It's missing."

My heart sinks. Her pearl ring, the one that belonged to Ed's grandmother. Does she remember she told me that story? Even a little bit?

I follow Mrs. G to her bedroom and she points to the little box on her bed. It's empty, a little slit in the velvet where the ring usually sits.

"Where is it, Emily?" She folds her arms across her chest.

"Wait, what?" It's the only way I can think to react, or rather, I can't even think right now. Because how is this happening?

Or maybe she's not accusing me of anything, other than knowing where it could be. I swallow. "I don't know. I can help you look for it, though."

She laughs, but it's not a pleasant sound—it's the sound of both contempt and disbelief. "Where. Is. It," she says again.

How? How is she possibly accusing me of . . . of . . .

As the realization dawns on me, my body feels suddenly hot. I'm sweating, and something like butterflies explodes in my stomach, but not the good kind. "What do you mean? You think that . . ." Except I can't bring myself to say it. *You think I stole from you.*

"Please don't do this to me," she says. She presses her hands to her temples and starts massaging her head, moving her fingers in little circles.

I recognize the feeling inside me now—and it's white-hot anger. Anger that Mrs. G, who has thought only good of me, who has challenged me to be better, who gave me a *key* to her house, and poured her memories and stories into me, thinks I'm stealing from her.

I'm so shocked, I have no words.

"I should have known better than to hire you," she practically spits.

I've read about anger that overwhelms you so much you can't speak, but I've never experienced it. Not even at my parents. I usually yell; everyone in my family knows how to do that, at least. We know how to explode, and throw plates, and stomp our feet, and generally make our feelings known. Mrs. G's style, though, is something I've only seen in movies. And the fact that she's keeping it quiet is making me want to scream. It makes me want to never come back here again. My heart is beating so fast that I have to consciously tell myself to take a breath.

So many responses flutter through my mind. My arms are shaking. I have this impulse to throw something in this room. Maybe one of the bougie silver frames that probably cost more than one hundred dollars at a store like Bergdorf Goodman. Maybe some other piece of jewelry. What I really want to do is run from the room. But what if Mrs. G tries to hurt herself? I can't believe how many different emotions I'm feeling toward her at once.

"I—I invite you here, into my life, so you can help me—and then you—you come in and you take my things! And what's worse," she continues, "is that you come in and start telling me *your* stories. Like it's all about you."

Well, that hurts. I only tell her things because—well, because she asks me about things. Which I trust—trust*ed*—her with. And now she's blaming me for doing the very thing that she pressured me into?

"Oh yeah?" I say. "You wish you'd hired some pretty rich blond girl instead, I bet."

And I bet you wouldn't accuse her *of stealing your jewelry.*

In this strange span of her outburst, though, she's now completely changed. Her eyes widen, and then she's crying. And I mean *really* crying. Worse than the crying she did on that day she told me about Ed, which is stoic by comparison. She's wringing her hands and the tears are streaming down her face, taking her mascara with them. But I get this feeling that she's not crying because she feels sorry for accusing me, although maybe there's a little bit of that—she's crying hard about something else entirely. Maybe about knowing that she's losing control.

She's got her right-hand fingers circling the ring finger on her left hand.

And what am I doing? Am I comforting her, offering a glass of water? Telling her to breathe? No. After what I've witnessed, it's all I can do to be in the same room with her. And yet, after a few seconds, I feel my anger dissipating, replaced by bewilderment and concern and a tight, sad feeling that must be grief. Because a twinge of terror has made its way to my core. Something is really wrong.

"You're going to be okay," I say, trying to sound soothing. Whether she's really going to be okay is another story, but whatever.

I run to the kitchen, fill a glass with water. It occurs to me to pour the afternoon vermouth early, just to help her calm her nerves, but it seems wrong to give alcohol to an unstable person.

Mrs. G takes great, heaving gasps and tries to drink the water. I stroke her arm—but so, so lightly. There's a part of me that's both afraid and angry still.

What do I even say? *I didn't take anything* wouldn't help to find the ring. It wouldn't solve the problem.

And even if I did find the ring, she could still think I took it, couldn't she? And how bad would that appear—not only for me but for my entire family. That the second-born Chen-Sanchez daughter went to work for a rich white lady and stole from her. And word would get around, because it always does in River's Edge, and people wouldn't want to be friends with my parents or Tessa, and Mrs. G would hate me forever, and . . . and . . .

And I can't believe it, it's super weird, but the only person I can think of to call is Tessa. She'll know what to do.

I dial Tessa and face the wall, grateful that Mrs. G's hearing—while not bad—isn't 100 percent, either.

Tessa picks up on the first ring, probably because I call her so rarely that she knows something must be wrong.

Still, she answers her phone with an irritated "What."

My sister.

"She thinks I took her ring," I half whisper. "I think something's wrong. Like, really wrong." I wait a beat. *Please don't say something insensitive,* is what I'm thinking. *And don't blame me for this.*

"Geez," Tessa says. "That is messed up."

"Thank you," I say. "It's so messed up."

Tessa sighs. Somehow, in that sigh are a million little disappointments, recognitions: that she and our parents were right to be skeptical of Mrs. G, that I'd fooled her and everyone else into thinking I had a really good job, that I've been keeping something about Mrs. G from everyone. But Tessa doesn't launch into a lecture, doesn't tell me that it's my fault I accepted a job with such vague duties, or that I should have spoken up the moment I realized that something was off.

She says: "Stay calm. The important thing is to stay calm."

Yes, I'm relieved that she's not freaking. But also: "How! How do I stay calm right now?"

"Breathe with me. One breath in, a super-deep breath. One breath out. This situation is only temporary. The important thing is that you don't escalate it by retaliating."

Whoops. I sort of already did, and then she cried.

I take a few more deep breaths, Tessa guiding me through them on the phone.

Then Tessa says, "You need to get out of there, but you probably also shouldn't leave her alone. If she has another outburst, you might need to even call the police."

My heart jumps. The police! But I couldn't. Not on Mrs. G.

"I can ask someone else to come stay with her," I say.

I call Ezra. He says he'll be here in fifteen.

Then I poke my head into Mrs. G's room. The woman in there now is nothing like the one who was yelling at me earlier.

She's slumped over, defeated. I hand her the tissues and tell her to holler if she needs me. Then I sit on the couch and put on my "Calm Vibes Only" playlist. The first song, "Strawberries & Cigarettes" by Troye Sivan, makes me feel instantly calmer. Still pissed, still shaky, but better.

When Ezra comes in, he's all "Where is she!" and asking his aunt if she's all right.

Back in her room, she's a little ball on the bed.

"Is *she* all right?" I ask, once we're out of earshot. "What about me?"

Then Ezra does something unexpected. He throws his arms around me, so that my face comes right up against his cheek. I can feel his stubble against my face, can smell the too-much-cologne he wears.

If I weren't in such a state, I would actually enjoy this moment. Because yeah, he can be a pill, but he's still a hot guy who plays cello, and call me tacky, but that too-much-cologne haze actually smells really good.

"I totally get it if you don't want to do this job anymore," Ezra says. "If you want to resign, we will miss you, but we would both understand."

Leave it to Ezra to use a word like *resign* for a summer job. Like he's Mrs. G's personal manager or something like that.

"I appreciate it and I'll think it over," I say, trying to match his tone. Really, I haven't even thought that far yet. I'm still recovering from the whole episode. "I think I'm gonna go now," I say.

"Please, do."

Coasting down the hill of her street, all I can think about is flopping down onto my bed, being at *home* instead of at Mrs. G's house. And yeah, home has been sort of sucky this summer, but it's still a place where no one will accuse me of stealing anything, even if they do accuse me of some pretty stupid stuff sometimes.

For once, I'm relieved and grateful to see Tessa standing outside our house, almost as if she's waiting for me. In fact, I'm pretty sure she *is* waiting for me. Well, that's nice. I'm not really a hugger, but she pulls me in for one right away, and this time I'm happy to oblige, though she steps away pretty quick and says: "You stink."

"It's the damn hill," I say, though the hill goes up *getting there.* Shit. If I stink now, then how did I smell when Ezra hugged me?

She sinks down to the front steps, so I do, too.

"You okay?" she says.

"Been better."

She nods. "You did good. I would totally be crying right now if that happened to me."

For once, I don't say something snarky back. "Thank you. For talking me through it when I called, I mean. It really, really helped."

"So, like . . . it's pretty sketchy that you're taking care of someone who is exhibiting signs of dementia."

"It was so minor before, though," I say, sounding like Ezra. "Today was the first really difficult one."

Tessa regards me. "I know you care about her," she says

slowly. "We learned about some of this stuff, you know, at the hospital. When they act out like that, with aggression, even combativeness? Paranoia? It's called sundowning."

"Sundowning," I repeat. It's a surprisingly poetic word for what it is.

Tessa nods. "It happens in the afternoon and evening. And—" She stops, as if thinking of the best way to break the news. "Well, if she's sundowning, then she's definitely not at the beginning stages of the disease."

I take a breath.

"Em," Tessa continues, "she's probably had Alzheimer's for three-ish years by now, maybe more."

I look at the grass, let this news sink in.

We watch a young family make their way down the sidewalk, stroller in front and toddler in hand. Then a boy a little younger than us glides along on a skateboard.

Tessa pats me on the back. What is it with Tessa and touching? "So I guess that's it for your summer job," she says.

"Wait, what?"

She turns to me. "What do you mean, 'wait, what'? You're not seriously thinking of continuing to work for her?"

I think back to the anger, the fear. Tessa's right, and Ezra was, too. It doesn't feel like things can ever be the same for us again, in more ways than one. At the same time, I can't help remembering how Mrs. G looked when she was crying. So helpless, and so desperately sad, like she knows she hurt me, and she also knows she was powerless to stop it. She knows that she lost control of herself for a second.

When I don't say anything, Tessa continues. "She needs help—not that you weren't helping her—but, like, real help. Someone to come live with her. Or better yet, to be put in a place with actual medical staff around twenty-four seven."

To be put in a place. No. I can't imagine Mrs. G living with a bunch of other old people. Nothing against old people. And what she needs isn't just a doctor or a nurse. What she needs is a friend.

"So I guess you're not going back next weekend," says Tessa.

"I'm going to think about it," I say, even though she's probably right. It doesn't make sense at all for me to go back. But I don't say that, because I haven't fully accepted it yet. The rest of the summer without going to Mrs. G's? What would I even do all day?

"You're at least going to tell Mom and Dad, right?" Tessa says.

"How is that going to help anything?" I don't mean to sound so harsh. What they'll do, I'm pretty sure, is freak. That'll only make things worse.

Tessa turns toward me then. "Em. It's going to help because you were in a dangerous situation. They can figure out what to do. You need to give them more credit—they really are trying to change."

"Pfft. They don't *care* about her. They're just going to be super worried about me, and they're going to tell me not to work there anymore, and then—"

Just then, the front door pops open. It's Dad.

"What are you girls doing here? It's so hot. Come inside!"

We follow him in, and then Dad sees my face. "Rillo," he says. "What's wrong? Did something happen?"

"Everything's fine," I say, shooting daggers at Tessa's face. She's never been a good liar, but she says, unconvincingly, "A stressful day on the job."

"But what happened?" Dad just doesn't know when to let things go. He looks from me to Tessa and back again.

"Can't we just keep some things to ourselves?" I blurt out, because I'm not in the mood to lie, at the same time that Tessa says, "Mrs. Granucci accused Emily of stealing."

Dad's face changes, a dark cloud passing over it. He rubs his mustache.

He shakes his head, says, "That woman. I *know* you would never do anything like that, I know I raised you girls right. If she really knew you, she wouldn't have accused you like that."

"Dad . . . ," I begin. I want to tell him about Mrs. G's memory. I want to tell him so badly. But I promised Ezra, and besides, it would feel wrong because Mrs. G herself would hate it. "She just, like, had a moment. Usually she thinks really highly of me! She even offered to write me a college recommendation."

"Well, that won't be happening anymore, because you won't be going over there again."

"What?" I say.

"Is there any question about it? It's over!" When he says "over," it sounds like "ovah." "She doesn't deserve your under-standing, your sympathy. It's like I've been saying all summer,

Rillo. It's not personal, she's not your friend. It's a job. And it was a good experience while you had it, and I respect that—you wanted to work and you did. But it's over now. Don't waste any more of your time there."

Of course, I was already thinking about not going over there—I'm so angry I can hardly even stand to picture Mrs. G's face. But it's one thing to make your own decision about something that happened to you, and another to hear it from one of your parents. In fact, hearing Dad say that, assuming such a final decision, makes me want to go back just to prove him wrong. Just to say *I'll show you*, like when Mom tells me for the fifth time to wear a sweater and it makes me want to stand outside shivering just to show her I'm capable of making decisions myself.

"She had no right to talk to you that way. I want to speak with her. Give me her number."

"Don't you have it already?" It's not very nice of me to say. But he did make me give him all her info before the job interview.

"I don't know where that piece of paper is now. Give me her number."

"No. You're not calling her," I say. "It's just—I know her. It wouldn't do any good."

But Dad doesn't need to get her number from me. She's one of the few people I know that still has a landline, and her home phone number is in the River's Edge directory.

Then what? Then he'll riffle through the directory, even if he can only remember that her name is trisyllabic and starts with a *G*. He'll find it. He'll call, and I'll be too embarrassed to ever face Mrs. G again. She'll feel bad. And sure, there's a part of me that's still angry at her, but there's also a part of me that knows she has got to be feeling horrible right about now, and there's no reason to make her feel worse.

But when Dad wants to do something, he does it. Especially when it's something that has to do with one of his kids getting hurt. Amid everything, I nearly forgot that about my parents, how fiercely loyal they are to me and Tessa, even when they're disappointed in us. They're allowed to be critical of us, but other people aren't.

And Dad does just that: he gets the directory—a laminated floppy stack of papers, spiral-bound (because even though there's one online, he prefers using the hard copy)—and starts flipping through it, saying, "Granary, Granary," under his breath.

He finds her number, I can tell by his face. He looks at the spot on the page for several seconds. But then, instead of dialing, he just closes the directory and puts it right back on the shelf.

"Okay, Rillo. I won't call her. You're getting older now, you know her better than me, and you know what the right thing is to do. But, if you change your mind, I know exactly where the number is, and I will try her." He stops and considers. "It's good of you, taking care of an older neighbor like this. I appreciate that you care so much about her."

I raise my eyebrows. "Thanks, Dad," I say. Maybe Tessa's right, maybe our parents *are* changing.

Or is it me? Am I seeing something in Dad that I didn't before? Am I the one who's changed?

Up in my room, I make a list. Pros and cons of going back to Mrs. G. Among the pros are the beautiful, ice-cold house; Mrs. G herself (when she's in a good mood); less time being bored at home; the food; Ezra. The cons: the tension between us now; Mrs. G herself (when she's in a bad mood).

A list with that many pros is making me rethink things.

CHAPTER 10

THAT NIGHT AND THE next night we prepare for Mom's second surgery. Tessa and I wash our hands all the way up to our elbows ("This is how surgeons do it," she tells me) and change the sheets on Mom and Dad's bed. There's only space for one of us to spend the night at the hospital, and even though I'm taller and it's going to be hell, I volunteer to sleep there. I don't need to be at Mrs. G's and I want to do *some*thing helpful for Mom, for once.

Plus, I've always been a better sleeper than Tessa. I think it's because I'm not as uptight.

The next morning, it's the same drill as Mom's first surgery. Mom goes in for pre-op and we wait. When we see her again, she's on a stretcher in a gray hospital gown. She doesn't look like the mom we know: her skin and lips are pale, her features tired. But her eyes are still resolute: she will not let *not* having a thyroid scare her.

* lll*

We eat in the hospital cafeteria. We buy garishly bright flowers from CVS. Dad paces.

I get a text from Matt: *How many extra steps do you think your dad gets from all the pacing?*

Lol.

Afterward, we meet with Dr. Kim. "She did beautifully, once again," she says. "The scar should heal up very soon. She should eat soft foods and walk regularly. Her voice is going to be a little hoarse for a couple months." Then Dr. Kim shows us before-and-after photographs of where the tumor was, and the thyroid, and in the next pictures, where they aren't. It's weird, seeing the inside of someone, especially if that someone is your mom.

Then Dad and Tessa leave, and I settle in to spend the night with Mom.

"Thank you for being here, Emily," Mom says, with some effort. I think she says it at least twice, if not more. I think she's sort of out of it after the surgery.

I do things like change the channel on the TV. Put a straw in a cup of water and hold it up to her mouth. Tell the nurse what she wants, because Mom's voice is super raspy.

Mostly, though, I binge cat videos and beauty tutorials on Instagram. And mostly, she sleeps.

If you've ever spent the night in a hospital, you know you never really sleep. The nurses come in constantly, and they flick all the lights on, and they take Mom's blood pressure and listen to her heart and check her incision and ask how she's feeling. So I barely get any sleep at all, because whenever I finally do drift off, a nurse is back with yet another task.

But whatever discomfort I'm feeling has got to be so much worse for Mom, and I have to remind myself that it's good I'm here for her, that for once I'm doing something helpful for my family.

$\sim\!\ell\ell\ell\!\sim$

In the morning, I pull my chair close and Mom smooths back my hair. I haven't showered two days in a row (I didn't want to sacrifice sleep before pre-op) and have been sleeping on a bench/couch thing, but if anyone's going to touch your hair when it's gross, it's probably going to be your mom. Even if she does tell you your hair doesn't have a style, and that maybe you should get a haircut.

"I know your father is not always an easy person to get along with," Mom says now. "But his parents were hard on him growing up. He doesn't always know how to express how proud he is of you."

Her voice is a little hoarse, but better than yesterday.

"I guess," I say. Mom has told me this at least a thousand times now. In terms of being proud of me, well, I don't know that there's much to be proud of.

"We never told you this, Emily, but back when Dad was growing up, his family lost everything in a fire."

Leave it to my mom to dump a big family secret right after a major surgery.

"Was anyone hurt?"

"It happened while they were away. But they lost the entire

store, and their little place above it, after it had been going strong for two years. Abuelito could have given up and gotten a corporate job, but he was bent on making the dream of a family business come true. So they rebuilt everything from scratch. You can understand why your father is always so, so careful. And maybe you can have some patience for him, and see that his worry just comes from a place of loving you."

That did explain some things. Why Dad always made us check and double-check. Why he always expected or predicted disaster even when it seemed highly unlikely. It makes me think, too, of Mrs. G. Her fears also come from a place of love, for her home and for her own life.

"Why didn't Dad tell me this?" I ask.

Mom sighs. "He's a proud man, Emily. He's old-school. He feels pressure to not show you his emotions, tell you what really happened. He's not like . . . well, he's not like some of your guy friends, who wear their feelings on their shirts. But he's trying to change."

That part makes me chuckle. Matt definitely wears his heart on his sleeve.

I think of how Dad let me call the shots about Mrs. G. Then I feel bad, because why is it so much easier to have patience and empathy for Mrs. G than it is my own parents?

As if reading my mind, Mom says, "Sometimes, it's harder to love your own family than other people's families."

I snort. "Ain't that the truth."

"But fighting isn't all bad. If you can talk things through, it shows you care about each other, that it's worth being honest with one another." Mom sighs. "Your dad and I, we need to open up to you girls more. We try too hard to be perfect, but that's not fair—to us or to you. Nobody's perfect." Mom sighs again. "I don't know why we try so hard to come across like we are."

～ℓℓℓ～

Back at home, the support comes pouring in. It comes in the form of flowers and plants, prayer cards and greeting cards, visits with casseroles and cookies and forced conversation. It's downright ironic, is what it is—that my family lives in a region of the country where people will give you the coat off their back in the name of Christian charity (real or otherwise), drive you to the hospital, add your name to the church prayer list, and keep showing up, but my parents just want to handle this thing themselves. Honestly, I think they expend more energy explaining that it's not a big deal, it's not fatal, and they don't need emails, than they save by receiving the help.

Steve and his family drop by with a massive flower arrangement and oolong tea and Taiwanese pineapple cake.

After his family leaves, Mom explains, "This Alishan oolong is a very fine tea. It means that his family respects us a lot."

Tessa beams.

"*Somehow,* they respect us," Dad quips, and it's nice that he's joking for once. The surgery went well, and I'm at home and not at Mrs. G's. . . . I can't help thinking he's relaxing just a little.

Then, when it seems like we've had our last unannounced visitors for the day, the bell rings again and Dad groans: Who could possibly be here so close to dinnertime?

"Just don't answer it," Dad says.

We all stay seated for several seconds until curiosity gets the better of me and I open the door.

On the welcome mat is a mason jar of hot pink roses and a bag of salt-and-vinegar potato chips. There's also an aluminum-foil-covered dish and a tiny card that reads *Granucci Bolognese. Skippy and I are around when you need us.*

Sometimes it feels like our neighbors are in competition with each other, trying to see who can show us the most care, bring us the biggest casserole. It's getting to the point where we're running out of room in our freezer. And now it seems like every day there's a Tupperware to return to a neighbor.

The next morning, Thursday, we're sent to drop off the latest right after swim practice. Kelly and Doug live a few blocks away. It's humid as a rainforest outside.

I suggest that we leave it on our porch and text them to come get it, but that doesn't go over very well.

"It's not like anyone's going to see you," I say in Tessa's general direction. I'm standing in the kitchen eating cereal—as usual, I'm starving after practice—and can hear her rummaging in her cosmetics bag in the downstairs bathroom.

"I'm just putting on sunscreen," Tessa calls from the bathroom. "And you really should, too. The sun can get to you even indoors."

When Tessa emerges from the bathroom, she has put on sunscreen and curled her eyelashes and put some pinkish stuff on her lips.

"You're still eating," she says with a huff, as if this is just so completely inconvenient. She checks her watch. "I've got to leave for the hospital at eleven. We're learning how to take blood pressure and collect urine samples today."

"Thrilling," I say.

It's only ten, and the hospital is, what, fifteen minutes away, tops.

I down the rest of my cereal milk like it's soup and set it in the sink. Then I peel a banana.

"You know what, I can just drop it off on my way to work," Tessa says.

"A walk will be good for you," Mom says. "We want you girls to have a little time together."

Tessa comes up and gently puts her arms around Mom for what they dub their "morning hug." "Love you, Mom. We'll be right back."

I wave and say bye to Mom. Of course I love her, I just don't see the need to say it every forty-five minutes.

Outside, Tessa sets off at a good clip. Thankfully, I have long legs so I can move slower through this rainforest weather and still keep up. I don't know what the big hurry is when we're just going a few blocks. I'm behind her for a little bit when she turns around and huffs in my direction.

"Still right here," I say. Because, seriously, a difference of a few feet is not going to change anything. Besides, I'm the one carrying the bowl.

We arrive at the house and Kelly greets us in the front yard by gushing, "There are my *girls*!" She sets her watering can down with a slosh. "Now listen, y'all didn't have to return that at all. I would've picked it up!"

"It was no problem," I say, thinking, *Told you so.*

Kelly reaches out and touches both of us on the (sweaty) arm like she's about to hug us, but then gets the vibe that we'd rather not. "Now tell me," she says, "how is your mama?"

"You know Mom, she's a trouper!" Tessa says, at the same time that I say, "About the same."

Tessa grabs the bowl from me and hands it to Kelly. "Thanks so much," she says. "It was delicious."

"Yeah, thank you," I say. It wasn't delicious and I see no reason to lie about that.

Kelly beams. "I'm *so* glad y'all liked it. I'll text you the recipe! And listen, it's getting hot. Why don't y'all come in for a bit?"

We both know that the minute we step foot through her doorway, we'll lose an hour. At least. So Tessa and I both say versions of "No, thank you, we need to get going."

On this, at least, we are agreed.

"Are you sure? Y'all don't need to be polite. I've got cookies."

We turn those down, too, and then Kelly says, "Well, we're prayin' for her. Let me know if you need anything."

Tessa and I both say thank you, Tessa smiling big enough for both of us, and then we book it, speed-walking the hell away from there.

People offer their prayers in the South the same way the minute you get a dog, everyone wants to pet it. Even people who don't believe in God start saying they'll pray for you.

We walk past several houses without speaking, both of us probably relieved to have it over with. Maybe Tessa's thinking about her internship presentation. Or maybe she's thinking about college. I won't bring it up.

"Remember the last time we went in there?" says Tessa. "She was showing us videos of their dog . . . while he was right there."

"Oh my gosh. It's like, we're already playing with your dog IRL, so why do you need to show us his Instagram account?"

Tessa actually laughs. "I totally forgot about that. I wonder how many followers he has."

It's too bad that the only time Tessa and I are talking about something fun is at the expense of one of our neighbors, but hey. At least it's something.

Then Tessa asks, "How are things going with your art, by the way?"

The question, coming from Tessa, feels weirdly polite. She's speaking to me like someone she's getting to know at school, the way all the student council members do, like they've been trained in the art of small talk.

"Oh, geez. I don't even know what I'm doing most of the time. Sometimes it's like I don't know what it'll be until I sketch it—and then it's completely different from the idea I initially had."

I'm expecting Tessa to not get this at all. But she nods and says, "It's slow going with my presentation and I think it's because I'm waffling. One minute I'm sure I'll research diagnosis and treatment, but the next, I'm interested in occupancy and wait time, efficiency issues like that." She shakes her head. "Either way it's a lot of research because I have to explain the problem and then suggest ways to improve the system." Honestly, none of it sounds that interesting to me, but it's cool— I had no idea Tessa struggled that way. I always thought she got ideas and then just sat down and did the work.

I guess I should know better than to assume my sister is a robot.

Just then, a huge gray Jeep turns the corner and honks a couple of times in a friendly way. Then several voices call, "Hey, Emily!" It's the Zieglers, all five of them, plus Zoey. And I know what's happening: their annual summer trip to Maine. A long weekend, the only time Matt ever misses swim practice.

And wow. Zoey's going with them. I say hi back, and we talk a little about how things are going, how Mom is, how they missed me at practice earlier in the week, how the River Rangers are doing this season.

"Will we see you at the swim team retreat at our place?" Mrs. Ziegler asks me.

"It's going to be loads of fun!" Mr. Ziegler says.

"Oh . . . I don't know," I say. "Maybe! I'll just have to check, um, my schedule."

We exchange some quick pleasantries about having a good trip, and how they had hoped to leave two hours ago, but *you know how it is!*

"Can you believe Zoey has never tried s'mores with Reese's Cups?" Matt says, and Zoey slings an arm around him and says, "Can't wait!"

What the hell? Matt never made *me* a s'more with a Reese's Cup. Honestly, it sounds like overkill. You don't need peanut butter on top of all the other flavors. Then they're saying bye and zipping around the corner, and I feel a lump in my stomach. Like this summer couldn't get any worse. How come Matt never invited *me* to Maine? I guess our family isn't really the camping type because, as Dad puts it, why would we travel and bring a bunch of gear to sleep on the ground, when we came to this country to not have to sleep on the ground anymore? But still.

"Okay," says Tessa. "Is everything okay between you two?"

Between Matt and me, she means. "Not that you even care," I snap.

Oof. It's my sore spot. I'm immediately sorry. There was no reason to be a jerk to her then, but it's such an ingrained pattern now. It takes real effort to not be so mean.

And God bless Tessa. I mean, she just takes one of her deep yoga belly breaths and then walks ahead of me by about three feet.

We walk like that nearly all the way to our street, and it's kind of funny, how she's basically speed-walking, but I'm taking about half the number of steps and am not that far behind.

Finally, when we're almost at our house, she stops completely and turns around to face me.

"Thanks for waiting," I say.

She just sighs.

Then the side of her mouth turns up in a smile. "So you have to double-check your schedule for the swim team retreat, huh?"

I roll my eyes. "I'm not going to that. I'd rather hang with Mrs. G."

Tessa's face changes, like she's reconsidering me—I must not be so bad if I actually *enjoy* hanging out with an elderly woman. "That's sweet," she says. "You're probably learning a lot. Like patience, and how to get along with older folks, especially considering the most recent episode."

I don't correct her, because just once I want Tessa to think of me as being on her level, just another teenager, instead of her annoying little sister. When I'm not mad at her, that is, that's what I want most: for us to be able to talk just like two normal people who could possibly be friends.

"Sorry about earlier," I mumble. And earlier and earlier and earlier.

"Yeah," she says. "Me too."

This temporary truce, I know, will last only until we get to our house, and then things will go back to normal—which, for us, is tense. But for now, we take the last steps to the front door together, remembering how our parents often tell us that when they're gone, we'll only have each other.

ℓℓℓ

The next day is Friday, but I don't go to Mrs. G's, and she doesn't reach out when I'm not there on Saturday morning. She doesn't leave me a dozen voicemails, like Matt did.

So I don't check in, either, although I think of her throughout the week, when swimming laps and drawing and doing what I can to help out while Mom recovers from surgery.

It turns out Mrs. G is as stubborn as me.

Then, the following Friday, my phone buzzes right after lunch.

It's Mrs. G.

I peer at the screen for a second. It's a photo of her that I uploaded what feels like forever ago, and for a moment I'm struck with sympathy for her, all alone in that big house. I forget, just for a few glorious seconds, about the ring incident. And everything I know about that ring.

I hold the phone, feeling it vibrate in my hand. Then I hit decline and send her to voicemail. Sure enough, in about a minute, the little red circle appears.

In my room, I waste time staring at myself in the mirror and trying to figure out how I can do my eye makeup more similar to Dr. Jessica Kim's. Then I figure it's not even worth it.

I flop onto my bed. Do I want to listen to Mrs. G's voicemail right now? No. No I do not. But I do anyway.

"Hi, Emily!" Her voice is all bright and cheery. "Emily," she repeats, and now her voice is more serious. She pauses, as if we're in the same room together and she's making sure she has my attention. "I owe you an apology. I found the ring yesterday. It was in the pocket of my apron. Oh, what a relief! I'm so, so sorry. I really screwed up. Well, who am I kidding. I wasn't in my right mind. I really f-u-c-k-e-d up, Emily."

She stops, then says, "It's better to talk about this in person, but while I have you—I would be honored if you continued to work for me, but I'd understand completely if you chose not to."

She sighs deeply, and then it sounds like Ezra is telling her to hurry it up.

"I'll let you go now. Please do feel free to text or call. I really didn't mean to frighten you, Emily, and I don't even remember what hurtful things I may have said. I'm so, so sorry, again. I hope you can forgive me."

Was she in her "right mind" when she confided about Ed? I stare at my phone for a long time, then I bury it under a pillow. Out of sight, out of mind. That's what Matt does when he's trying to study.

Then I sit at my desk, in front of my sketch pad. I'm not in the mood for colors right now, I know that much. With my pencil I start sketching what I see, just for something to do, to take my mind off things. I draw my desk lamp; I draw the little Taylor Swift bobblehead Heather got me thinking it was hilarious. But it's not working. I know it's not rational, but whatever, it's what I'm feeling—that Zoey gets to spend all that time with the Zieglers when Matt knows I'd love to get away. And Mrs. G, well. What does she think, I'm just an empty vessel for her memories? I push so hard my pencil breaks.

I don't want to text or call her, at least not right now.

Right now, I want to go for a swim.

∼ℓℓℓ∼

At the pool, the water's as warm as a bath, and most of the pool is taken up by hordes of kids in bright-colored suits, with their floaties and noodles and pool toys, except for the single lane that is already occupied by . . . Matt.

"Getting your laps in so you can go faster than me at practice?" I say. It's not the best opening line, but, whatever.

He doesn't hear me. He's practicing his breaststroke and using all his concentration to swim.

When he's at the opposite end of the pool, I dive in, and for a minute, we share a lane. Then we end up meeting in the middle, literally—we both stop in the center.

"It's weird," he says, catching his breath. "I recognized you by your kick just now."

"That is weird," I say. I don't mention that that means he was looking at my legs.

We're both talking to each other with our goggles on, and somehow it's easier to talk to him when we can't see each other's eyes.

"By the way, I didn't get to thank you," I say. "Thank you so, so much. I ate all the chips in one sitting. And my mom loves the roses. She was so flattered you would give her so many of your prized flowers."

"Oh, there's plenty more where they came from. Roses are like . . . well, they're like your mom. They're pretty on the outside, but they have thorns—and they actually grow better the more I cut them back."

"What an analogy," I say. Also, I had no idea he thought my mom was pretty.

"So," says Matt, "you're at the pool, but we don't have practice. What's wrong? Did Tessa do something that's going to make us hate her more, like get into Vanderbilt? Or join Doctors Without Borders?"

I frown. For once, it's not about Tessa.

I plunge back into the water just in time to hear Matt say, "No, Em, no, wait, get back here!"

I swim a lap, and then another, flip-turning at the ends of the lane. It's a pity Coach isn't here to see this, because even though my form is probably off the wall, I'm swimming like I mean it. I've never had this much endurance. I hold my breath longer than usual and I go at a consistent pace, and I don't stop to take a break. My lungs are burning, but it's a good kind of burn. All I can think about is Mrs. G's cold, calm voice accusing me of taking her ring and how she's starting to lose it and I'm just wishing wishing wishing that none of this had ever happened at all. That somehow I could go back to being fifteen. Before Mom got sick and before I ever got a C plus and ended up at Mrs. G's.

Then I'm crying underwater and I don't even realize it

until I'm super short of breath and it's not just from the swimming. I'm hearing her voice again, and I'm seeing that stupid ring, that huge pearl that represents her marriage but also the weight of her regret. A secret that she doesn't even remember telling me.

Matt, I suppose resigned to the fact that I'm going to swim until I'm good and ready to stop, is sitting in a chair, watching me. The pool's so crowded that he just plants himself next to a family, with all the snacks and sunscreen and pool toys around them. Matt is sitting there slathering sunscreen all over himself. The boy will bake if he doesn't reapply. I've seen his skin peel and it's not pretty.

When I'm truly too exhausted to keep going, I get out and plop down next to him, weirdly hiccuping from both the crying and being out of breath.

"Hey, hey, hey," he says, and slips an arm around me. Not in a making-a-pass-at-me way but in a we've-been-friends-forever kind of way, and both of us have damp skin and it's terribly hot, but it feels nice anyway. "Your mom's gonna be okay, right? I mean, the surgery went well and everything. I feel like maybe the worst is over."

I swipe a hand under my nose and a string of snot comes away with it. "It's not about that."

That makes me feel guilty. too—like I should be crying about Mom instead of about Mrs. G.

I grab Matt's towel and use it to dab at my eyes—carefully, because I need to make sure I don't get sunscreen in them.

Heather was the one who told me that sunscreen isn't just for white people. Well, her and Tessa.

"Well, shit," he says. Matt never swears. He's more likely to spell out a swear than to actually say it. Then again, I never cry.

So I tell him: about the accusation, and about what she said about inviting me into her life, and how she said she should have known better than to hire me. He even offers to listen to the voicemail she left me.

What he says is: "She screwed up big-time, but she only screwed up once, and her apology does sound genuine. And yeah, she could do it again, but does the good outweigh the bad? The fun chats and the lemonade and the George Harrison and the just basically not being your house?"

That makes me laugh. "I guess," I say. "But you know, I don't have such a need to leave the house anymore. Things at home aren't as bad." It's true. Something has shifted after Mom's surgery. We're all a little nicer to each other.

"But wait, isn't there that guy, Esau or whatever—"

I laugh. "Ezra!"

"Whoops, wrong Old Testament name. Aren't you guys in love or something?"

"I never said that—"

"But it's obvious in how you talk about him. And I'm pretty sure you only like him because he plays cello," Matt says.

Yeah, Ezra is . . . I mean, how could I not find that boy attractive? But even though we've been around each other all summer, he doesn't *know* me like Matt does.

"Oh, like you're much better?" I say. "You only like Zoey because of her hair!"

"Hey, her hair reflects her personality."

I take a risk and ask, "How are things going with her?"

"Good!" he says, almost too enthusiastically. "Yeah. We have a lot in common. But I mean, it's new, right? We're still getting to know one another."

"Well, you had the camping trip to get to know each other." I try to keep the bitterness out of my voice when I say it.

Matt chuckles. "Oh, yeah. Well, my parents have been wanting me to bring a girl to that for, like, ever. They went there as college sweethearts, you know." We both just face the pool for a while. We've talked each other through crushes, but neither of us has had a serious relationship before. Until now.

"So, okay," Matt says suddenly. "You told me your issue and I'm going to tell you what I think—but I know you won't like it."

"My issue?"

"About Mrs. G. You can't force her to go to the doctor. She sounds stubborn as all get-out. She hasn't even really admitted that she has a problem. You could tell her family, sure, but that'll make her super mad and who's to say if that'll actually change anything?

"I think the safest thing for *her* is for you to go back. If you can deal, you know, with possibly more of the same. Can you read a bunch about it and be emotionally prepared if something similar happens?"

Matt's the one who has told me before that, deep down, I really love Tessa. It's this whole cycle: resent her, then feel remorse because of that resentment, then recognize that I wouldn't spend so much time and energy disliking someone if I truly didn't care about them. In that case, I just wouldn't think about them at all. But the fact that I spend so much time thinking about Tessa, Matt says, means that I really love her.

And well, I've spent a whole heck of a lot of time thinking about Mrs. G—in all kinds of ways: worrying about her, delighting in her, feeling seen by her. Which means I must really care about Mrs. G. And she needs me. Besides, who else is going to comb George's hair?

CHAPTER 11

THAT NIGHT, I READ about the different stages of dementia. About denial of symptoms, and moodiness, and trouble with routine tasks. I read about the precautions we can take, and about a village in the Netherlands designed for dementia patients. How they still get to live their lives: they garden, and they go to dinner, and they meet up with each other. The roads are built in a circle, designed to keep them safe, and happy, and creative. And more importantly, not living in isolation. Maybe Ezra and I can create that circle for Mrs. G.

Later on, I work on my birds pastel again. I've done away with the cage and now just have us-as-birds in our backyard. It worked better for colors and atmosphere that way. The three of them in a tree. Damn, it took forever to make that tree; I used pastel pencils to add definition to the leaves. Now I'm working on blending and choosing the colors of the birds.

There's a knock on my door—even though I've told my family never to interrupt me while I'm drawing. I hate to be this high maintenance about it, but really, it's one of the few things I ask.

"Can it wait?" I say, carefully shading in a darker blue for my bird-self's wings.

"Not really, because I'm headed out after this."

I'm surprised to hear not one of my parents' voices but Tessa's. Before I can say anything else, she lets herself in, then softly closes the door behind her.

I haven't talked to Tessa with the door closed in God knows how long. Maybe not since we were in elementary school, when we'd sleep over in each other's rooms, giggling until Dad appeared in the doorway and grumpily told us we'd woken him up.

Or, I'll admit it, when I read the second Harry Potter book before bed and was too scared to sleep by myself.

I spin around in the chair to face her. She's wearing a silk—or more likely it's polyester masquerading as silk—cream-colored button-down shirt, and dark straight-leg jeans. She eases herself onto my bed, which is unmade and where I absently tossed the old fashion magazines that Mrs. G let me borrow. Tessa, on the other hand, is very neat and put-together, like a Parisian.

That, or like a super-stylish waiter.

"You're going out?" I ask.

She smiles. "Yeah, Natalie and Sarah-Bradley want to see a movie."

Sarah-Bradley is one of Tessa's double-barreled-first-name friends. We do live in the South, after all.

"Oh! Good. I'm glad." And I am, because now that I think

about it, Tessa hasn't been *out*-out all summer. She's usually a social butterfly. I have a feeling that Mom being done with her surgery has now given her the permission she needs. She peers over my shoulder, but instinctively I put my hand over my drawing to cover it, like a child hiding a surprise letter. "I'm not done yet!" I squeal, surprising myself.

Tessa smiles. "Does that mean I can see it when you *are* done?"

I feel my mouth drop open a little. What is up with this new Tessa? "Sure," I say, because I'm pleased she would even want to.

"Anyway," she says quietly. "What are you going to do about your job?"

I take a deep breath. "You're not going to like it."

She drops her head into her hands. Tessa can sure be dramatic when she feels like it. "No, please say you're not going back there."

"I wish I could."

"Why?"

"I'm sorry. How about . . . I'll quit at the end of the summer. It basically is almost the end."

Tessa furrows her eyebrows. "What good is that going to do? What if it's too late by then?"

"I'll—I'll quit once something super serious has happened."

"Em, this *was* super serious."

"You don't know her like I do! She's completely independent. She just had, like, an episode." Even saying this, though, I know I'm being in denial just as Ezra is—and just as Mrs. G herself is. But it's what I'd like to believe.

But Tessa is shaking her head. "It's only going to get worse, Em. I'm so, so sorry to tell you this. But I know you already know it."

I can feel my eyes start to fill, and I breathe deep and will them to stop, because as I've mentioned before, I don't think crying does diddly-squat. Tessa is looking at me, all sympathetic with her big doe eyes, and that's the thing that makes me chuckle.

It's weird: Back at Mrs. G's house, I was seriously considering leaving the job. But the more that Tessa says I need to leave, the more I feel myself wanting to stay. The Mrs. G in my mind—the one with the big laugh and three-syllable adjectives—can do no wrong. And let's face it: besides my family, she's the person I've spent the most time with this summer.

Anyway, Tessa is upset and annoyed and worried, and she has every right to be.

So it sucks that I have to ask her what I ask next.

"I have to ask you a favor," I say. "Can you cover for me?"

Tessa buries her face in her hands again.

"Please? Tess, please. You *know* they would otherwise be unreasonable about it."

"What am I supposed to say to them?"

"You don't have to say that much. *I'll* tell them I'm going on the swim team retreat. At the Zieglers."

I used to go on the swim team retreats, which the Zieglers host in their massive basement, and Mom and Dad were surprisingly fine with it. In fact, they even encouraged me to go, in the name of team spirit and neighborhood bonding.

"In fact," I add. "It'll be easy. You're going out anyway, so you won't have to say anything unless they ask questions."

Without looking at me, Tessa says, "Okay."

ꙅꙙꙙ

I know, I know. It's so cliché of me, like a high school movie, but here's why the "sleeping at your best friend's house over the weekend with a bunch of other people" works: He lives super close by, so if anything were to happen—say, there was some family emergency and my parents needed me home—I could ride my bike back home super fast. Secondly, the swim team retreats are heavily chaperoned, highly structured events with the coaches and a bunch of volunteer parents, so how rowdy can they really get? Thirdly, the Zieglers don't have a landline. So if my parents needed to get in touch with me, they'd just text or call my cell anyway, and it wouldn't be hard to tell them what was up. No communication with Matt or his family necessary.

So that's what I tell them. I feel terrible about it, because even though my parents can be insufferable sometimes, they (1) like Matt overall and are really good to my friends and (2) just want to be around me. Case in point: they start asking if I want to ask a few friends to spend the night at our place instead ("It's not the same! Plus, it's too late to change plans now," I say). Then Dad says to have a good time, and call him if I need anything, and they'll see me Saturday for dinner. So I'm off on my bike and hoping for the best.

Do I feel guilty as hell? Yes. Do I almost cave? Yes, multiple times. Especially when Mom, reading on the couch, says, "Oh, Emily, I feel so much better that you're not going to that woman's house anymore. I was starting to get worried about you. And you know, it's so nice that you girls are going out. I felt bad that you were both homebound because of me."

Grabbing her purse, Tessa says, under her breath, "Well, *one* of us was more homebound than the other."

And I look Mom in the eye and say, "Thanks, Mom. Me too."

I text Mrs. G to let her know she can expect me in the morning, and she texts back *Thank you so much, Emily.* I've already rehearsed it a bunch of times, what I'm going to say to her when we see each other; I've basically written out the kind of script that I write for phone conversations. Well, I'll let Mrs. G speak first, probably. Because she sounded really, really upset on the phone and I figure it'll calm me down— I guess?—to hear from her first.

What I'm planning to say is that, yes, I understand that she wasn't in her right mind, but I still need to let her know how it made me feel. But do I? What good will it do? She already apologized. Am I needing her to apologize even more? I'm not sure.

_லe_

That night, at Mrs. G's, I let myself in as usual and go to my room. But it's not the same. I'm not carefree like before. Part of me even wonders if I should lock the door to my room. What if she tries to do something weird at night? But I'm thinking too much like Dad. She's sound asleep—she always sleeps well because of her meds.

Her meds. Yet another thing Ezra and I should check on.

In the morning, I hear her get up, but I lie there, wondering if another big episode could happen the minute we talk, wondering how I'm going to react. Playing through the incident in my mind and telling myself I can do this. I am capable of staying calm in a crisis.

Then, things are awkward. It's not anything she's doing, it's what she's *not* doing. She's not humming to herself as the coffee maker percolates. She's not grinning wildly when I emerge from the bedroom, asking me how I slept. She's not sliding an English muffin onto my plate and nearly shouting, "Eat up!"

It's oddly quiet.

"What can I make for you, Mrs. G?" I ask. "The usual?"

"I'm just going to have cereal," she says. So I pour Cheerios into the blue ceramic bowls, one for me and one for her.

She sits at the kitchen island, but I sink into the cool leather couch with my bowl. The timing and the mood just don't feel right for me to launch into any big scripted speech. Minutes pass; it's been so long that after a while I forget that I'm trying to avoid talking to her and am really just into the clickbait I've landed on somehow about why everyone loves Paco the endangered lizard. Turns out it has something to do with his alert, beady eyes.

So I'm startled when Mrs. G says, not even loudly, "Today

will be a light day. Take care of George, and water the plants, and can you please throw out anything old in the fridge? Ezra will be over later. Other than that, you're free to enjoy the house."

"Yes, ma'am," I say automatically.

She folds her hands and places them in front of her. "I so appreciate you coming back, Emily. You have no idea what that means to your senile employer." She smiles ever so slightly, but it's a sad smile. "I'm afraid that something like that will happen again."

Her eyes mist over, sadder than I've ever seen them—even sadder than the Ring Accusation Day.

"I am so, so sorry about what I said to you," she says.

I put my hand over hers. "We're going to do our best," I say. "Both of us." That's all that I can promise her.

"How's your mama doing?" she asks, and I'm glad to be able to give her good-ish news.

lll

Ezra and I decide to make a list: ways to make Mrs. G's life as safe as possible.

We add things like signs around the house, labels on drawers to help her remember where things are, a pad of paper by the phone listing things she might need to tell someone. Thankfully, she isn't so far gone and wandering around the neighborhood or forgetting who we are.

Just the thought of that makes me feel awful.

It hits me then, that I'm spending more time and energy

trying to help Mrs. G stay above water than I am helping my mom with anything.

Ezra must see my face change, because he says, "What's wrong?"

"Nothing," I say quickly. Then I say, "It just feels, you know, strange, making this list."

He nods, and then keeps going. Matt would have pressed me on that, would have insisted something was up and I'd feel better if I talked about it, but I can't expect Ezra to do that. It's already nice that he asked at all.

We make a note to keep an eye on the car. That we'll pump gas for her. And that, eventually, we're going to have to put our foot down (feet down?) about her driving at all. That, I'm putting off until as long as humanly possible, because good Lord, does she love it so much. It would be a shame to take away one of the things she loves most in life.

After breakfast, I find Ezra in the laundry room, sorting Mrs. G's super-expensive organic-cotton summer tops and dresses into whites and bright patterns. The guy loves to do laundry, I've discovered. Which is just as well because I'd just as soon not. It's like he's showing off one of the skills he learned at boarding school.

"How long do we hide this for?" I ask him.

He takes a lavender-scented dryer sheet and holds it up to my nose. "Breathe that in. Lavender is calming."

Then he tosses it in.

How long are we going to live like this? is what I'm wondering. And how is it, too, that I've entrusted this information to a guy around my age, who I met only a couple of months ago, and sworn to him not to tell a soul about Mrs. G's health condition—a lady who I also just met a couple of months ago? How did this go from being the easy dream job that was like a vacation in my own neighborhood to being the most high-stakes and dreaded part of my week? I'm shocked when the thought pops into my head: I wish it was Mom or Dad, not Ezra, who was standing here in Mrs. G's laundry room with me. At least they could handle this thing when I feel like I just can't. Not anymore.

Ezra thumps the dryer closed, turns the knob to the lowest heat, and breathes a great big heavy sigh. "I don't know."

"Because you know what?" I continue. I don't think the dryer sheet helped much. "This is getting ridiculous. It's getting unsafe and out of hand." I look him in the eye after I say that, trying to show him how serious I am.

"There's actually not much that's dangerous if someone's in the house with her all the time."

"That's a great big *if*."

On our phones in the laundry room, we read up on what there is to be done, exchanging information with each other. We talk about doing crossword puzzles and staying active, studies that show that vitamin E is helpful (Ezra adds spinach and almonds and sunflower seeds to the grocery list). We're not flirting and we haven't talked about art in a while, but we *are* doing this very intense caretaking thing together. That's not nothing.

Then Ezra says, "It would be completely understandable if you quit. I mean, I'm family, I have an obligation here. You— I mean I get that you dig her and stuff, but you have no obligation, really. You're doing so, so much for her and— I don't know. That's pretty great. Thank you, for everything. Obviously she thinks you're awesome, and so do I."

Then he runs a hand through his hair, and it leaves that one stray curl hanging over his brow like he's a freaking Disney prince, and I kind of want to hug him. Or more.

Then I just say the dumbest thing ever, which is, "You're welcome."

And then Ezra puts one hand on my shoulder and leans in and kisses me. It's a long, soft kiss, way longer than Matt's attempt, as if he's had practice. His other hand goes into my hair. His lips are dry and I don't know what I was expecting, but his mouth tastes like jam and coffee. Which isn't the worst taste in the world.

I never pictured my first kiss in a laundry room, but it's better than a corn maze. I'll be honest, though: It's not a life-changing kiss. I expected to feel more. My heart's not hammering, I don't feel any closer to Ezra, and I still have this pit in my stomach from not knowing what to do about Mrs. G. When Ezra pulls away, he smiles at me, so I smile back: a reflex. And then he goes back to folding laundry, and I head to Mrs. G's office. First (real) kiss: check.

I start cleaning out Mrs. G's filing cabinets and desk drawer, recycling things like receipts and old ticket stubs, still thinking about the kiss. If anyone had been watching, it would have *looked* like a movie kiss, like he really knew what he was doing. But that doesn't mean it was a good one. I can't help comparing it to the only other kiss I've had. When Matt held my hands, it was kind of . . . nice. Yes, it was weird, but things can be nice and weird at the same time. And if I felt butterflies—or bees or whatever—during Matt's kiss, then I'd expect to feel even more of that with this classically hot guy.

Except I didn't.

Mrs. G said I can open anything and make my own call about what to keep and what to throw out, so I do. It feels good to declutter. It especially feels good when it's not your stuff and you don't have a personal attachment to everything. That's when I find an envelope, stuffed and unsealed, all these little yellow papers sticking out of it. I'm about to toss the whole thing straight into recycling, but figure I should at least see what it is, so I open it.

They're tickets. Driving tickets. A couple are for speeding and a couple are for running red lights, and one is for not having her license with her in the car.

No wonder she's so afraid.

The thing is, I'm also terrified. What happens on the day when I let myself into her house and she doesn't know who I am, or worse, thinks I'm an intruder, assumes I'm part of some awful scheme that's taking advantage of this old woman, letting myself into her house after dark on a Friday night? What am I supposed to do then? Or what if, on a day when neither Ezra nor I am around, she leaves the house and forgets why? And nobody has any idea where she's gone?

And there's no telling when that will happen, but it will probably be soon. What Tessa explained the other day is that Mrs. G is in a phase of abrupt decline. She could plateau sometime soon—that means she would be relatively stable—but we don't know when that would be. It could be so, so soon, or it could take months, years, even—that's how this works. Every evening I breathe a sigh of relief that that hasn't happened yet.

Today, other than breakfast, Mrs. G has barely left her room. I don't get it. I don't get how, just a month ago, she was so in denial about losing her memory that all she did was leave her room, leave her house. It was as if, by leaving, she could delay its progression. And I think, in some ways, she succeeded. But now it's as if she's not only accepted it, but succumbed to its force. She's been awake since at least seven, that much I'm aware of, because I heard her shuffling around, opening and closing drawers, then the squeak of the mattress springs as she crawled back into that old bed.

I approach Mrs. G's bedroom, trying to step loudly so that she's not startled when she hears me at the door. Sometimes I'm even worried that she'll forget we're here.

Then I knock, in a way that I hope sounds gentle and inviting. A question, not an intrusion.

"Mrs. G?" I ask.

"Not right now, Emily," she says.

"Oh . . . I just wanted to make sure you're okay? Do you want some lunch?"

"I said not now."

I take a deep breath to steady myself. I'm on the verge of apologizing—not because I owe her one, but because I want to smooth things over—but I stop myself. I'm trying to *help* her, for crying out loud.

And, honestly? Right now she sounds like what Matt would call an absolute B.

"Okay," I say, "I'm going to make you an iced coffee and you can get it whenever you're ready."

There's no reply. I roll my eyes. She can't see me doing that, and I know it's mean. But it makes me feel worse, not better. In the kitchen, I make the coffees, and then I do all the little things that she's told me to: water the fig plant in the living room, take out the trash and recycling, throw away some expired things in the fridge. Later I'll check the mail, but it turns out there's not a whole lot to do in the morning if Mrs. G doesn't want to do anything. Her house is a well-oiled machine.

The fig tree is doing wonderfully, so tall. It makes the living room less stuffy. I snap a photo and send it to Matt.

In seconds, he texts back, *Willy.* Then, *No, that's Stewart. Definitely Stewart.*

Knowing Matt is around makes me feel a little better, but I don't want to leave Mrs. G's. I call home and say the Zieglers are inviting me to stay over one more night, which is feasible. Dad sounds a little annoyed, but he says to be back in time for lunch, and I say I will.

After dinner that night, we watch *Bye Bye Birdie*, which Mrs. G loves. It's fun, I'll give it that, but there's a little something weird about high schoolers singing about how they're going to meet "older men." Still, I'm happy to watch it because it's one of her favorite movies, and she seems in a relatively good mood during it. We get to the part where they go dancing at a club, and Conrad Birdie and Kim McAfee and the high schoolers around them are dancing and singing about how they've "got a lot of livin' to do."

That's when Mrs. G says, "I remember when he came to our town."

I think she's joking, so I say, "Oh yeah, totally. I remember how he moved his hips and all the girls screamed so loud."

Mrs. G says, "But you wouldn't have been born then." She sounds utterly serious, and I realize: she is serious.

"Conrad Birdie . . . ," I say slowly, "came to your town?"

Mrs. G nods. "And he was handsome as ever. Even more handsome than he looks in the movie."

My body feels cold all of a sudden. Ezra laughs nervously. "Aunt Lydia, do you mean Elvis?"

"Why is this funny?" Her face is genuinely confused.

"*Bye Bye Birdie* is a movie," I say. "None of that actually happened."

Then Mrs. G's face flares with recognition. "Of course. I know that." Then, with embarrassment, she smiles again, her face relaxing. "I was just having a good time. A temporary . . . what do you kids call it? Brain fart."

She gets up off the couch and fetches the vanilla ice cream from the freezer, then she sprinkles cinnamon on top and brings back three spoons. Okay. So this is the Mrs. G that we know. Maybe all is well. Maybe she *was* just having a tempo-rary "brain fart."

Mrs. G says something then, only I can't hear it over the sounds of the movie.

"What?" I say.

Mrs. G grabs the remote and lowers the volume. "You made fun of me," she says.

"I'm sorry," I say, because it seems like the best thing to say under the circumstances. "I shouldn't have said that."

"You young people."

I stiffen. Mrs. G never says that—never calls us young in that tone, as if we're beneath her.

"You think you know everything. And you think one little apology can make up for a complete lack of disrespect."

Well, I have nothing to say to that. I stare face forward, feeling like if I even move a muscle, she'll just interpret it the wrong way. What else am I supposed to say, besides sorry?

"Auntie Leila," Ezra says, "I don't think Emily meant—"

"I know damn well what she meant," says Mrs. G. "And don't you go defending her. She's not family, you know."

Of course I'm not family, but all this time she's certainly treated me like I am.

Suddenly the TV goes black. "It's late," Mrs. G says, and it comes out as a growl. She's holding the remote. "We should all get to bed."

lll

Only I don't sleep. I'm on eggshells, as it were. I just replay the conversation over and over again in my head, against my will. If I had only kept my mouth shut. I hurt her feelings, she thought I was making fun of her, it's all my fault.

But then I think of what she said later. *She's not family.* So basically saying that I'm not one of them. And then I'm angry all over again. *If I'm not family,* I picture myself saying to her, *then why entrust me with so much?*

That's a wrong move, though. On my phone, what I read about dementia is that you shouldn't argue with the person.

But it's not like Mrs. G to stay upset overnight. It's not like her to get upset, period. So I keep telling myself that everything will be okay in the morning. I tell myself that, but it doesn't make sleeping any easier.

◦ℓℓℓ◦

It's nearly three in the morning when my phone buzzes with a text. And then another, and another. I could turn off the vibrate setting at night, but what if I miss something important? Matt has pointed out to me before that the likelihood of some emergency happening while I'm sleeping and my ability to do anything about it at that hour is roughly one in a thousand, but I guess a girl can dream.

I can't sleep anyway, so I take a look. They're not texts after all; they're WhatsApp messages. All from my best friend in a time zone five hours from mine, which means she's probably sending these soon after waking up.

Em

I'm so so sorry about your mom

Why didn't you tell me???

I guess timing wasn't great, which is my bad

Matt told me about it

How are you doing, friend? Sending so much love and light. I'm always here if you need me

I figure, she's up, I'm up, and we're both obviously free at the moment, so why not? I give her a call, audio-only this time. I tell her everything—about Mom, Mrs. G, Matt and Zoey. I face the wall farthest from Mrs. G's room, speaking so low it's a near-whisper, and it's almost like Heth and I are talking to each other in side-by-side sleeping bags in the dark, keeping our voices low so we don't wake our parents, like we did all the time in elementary school. We talk for over an hour, and her voice, her listening ear, her full attention on the other end, is a balm.

CHAPTER 12

IN THE MORNING, WE have breakfast, and Mrs. G doesn't say anything about the night before, so I don't, either. We talk about nothing in particular, like how we both slept and what we're eating.

Maybe she doesn't even remember what she said last night. It's not the past that she has trouble remembering. It's the present.

When we're done eating, she stands at the front-hall mirror and ties a scarf around her hair.

"Going to Michaels," Mrs. G announces.

It's one of the few rainy days we've had in a while, gray and drizzly, still eighty degrees, and so humid the air feels thick. Rain where we live usually means a break from the heat, and I guess it is nice that it's eighty-five degrees out instead of ninety-five.

"What do you need? I could get it for you and just stick it in my backpack."

It wouldn't be the most comfortable—the roads around River's Edge aren't made for bikes or pedestrians—but it's definitely possible, and I've done it before.

"All the way to the craft store? In the rain? That sounds dangerous and not to mention uncomfortable." Then Mrs. G cocks her head, like she's onto me. "I'm perfectly capable of driving," she says.

Then she puts her hands on her hips. "If I could only find my keys, as usual!" She looks and looks. I also look, but I'm pretending. If I find them, I won't tell her—and that way she won't be able to leave.

Then I hear the jangle of the keys from the kitchen, Mrs. G's voice, triumphant: "Found 'em!"

I try, quickly, to think through my options. Could I grab the keys from her, tell her, "No, you're not leaving"? Which would then risk making her very upset, and possibly she would just walk out in the rain? Or should I call someone—someone with some authority—to tell her what to do? What's worse: physically restraining her, calling the police, or just letting her do what she wants while I'm supervising?

I think of all those tickets. How many tickets until she's not supposed to be driving at all? She still has her driver's license, though.

I can't help thinking it's ironic that for the first time in my life *I'm* going to be supervising someone else's driving.

In the car, I take care to put the directions into her phone, with the sound on, even though she knows how to get there. Then I load up her favorite playlist, "Classical Bangers."

"Emily, that's not what I want to listen to right now."

"Okay," I say as calmly as possible. "Tell me what you want and I'll plug it in."

The drive goes smoothly. If anything, Mrs. G is overly cautious—never exceeding the speed limit even by a mile, coming to a complete stop at stop signs. She's driving like someone who's taking their driver's license test.

Well, someone who's not me.

Mrs. G parks far from other cars, as usual, so we can "get our steps in" is what she says, but I'm wondering if it's to avoid a fender bender.

Once we're inside, the air-conditioning and lack of mugginess helps a lot with both of our moods. As do the frames, mini chalkboards, fake flowers, and jewelry-making kits. We leave with two bags full of craft supplies, and I'm so relieved Mrs. G is in such a good mood that I don't even worry about putting on my "Calm Vibes Only" playlist on the way back.

When we get to a light that turns yellow, Mrs. G slows way down and then comes to a complete stop as the light turns red. As, of course, she should.

To our left, cars are lined up, waiting for their own light to turn green.

But then Mrs. G looks right, and looks left, and decides to step on the gas. As if it's a stop sign and not a red light. Right as another car comes through the intersection.

"Brake!" I scream, but it's too late.

The other car lays on the horn, but everything happens so

fast. It comes careening into the driver's side door—Mrs. G's door.

Both of us scream, more from fear and shock than anything painful—at least that's how I experience it.

"Lord Jesus Almighty!" Mrs. G says.

I can almost feel the anger from the other car as it pulls over in a huff, tires squealing on the side of the road.

Everything's fresh in my mind from driver's ed: pull over as soon as possible, don't discuss what happened with the other driver, call the police.

And I'm trying to say these things to Mrs. G, glove compartment already open with insurance information. But two things are different here compared to how they were outlined in class: One is that, without a doubt, *we* are the ones at fault here. Secondly, things aren't going according to plan with how you're supposed to stay in the car until the police come. How you're not supposed to start talking with the other driver about who's at fault, and you're certainly not supposed to leave your car and put your hands on your hips and start screaming incoherently at the other driver, which is exactly what Mrs. G is doing. It turns out, he is a beefy Southern gentleman with a penchant for salty language.

"Lady!" he says. "What the hell were you *thinking*?"

"Don't you dare speak to me like that!" Mrs. G says. "I could be your *grandmother*."

"Well, that much is clear, and my grandma sure doesn't drive anymore for that very reason. She's too old to! I wouldn't let her get behind the wheel."

My hands are shaking as I dial the police, trying to remember all the steps we went over in driver's ed. In Dad's car, which is the one I've been practicing on, all the instructions for a possible car accident are written on a piece of paper in the glove compartment. He can be super annoying sometimes, but I have to hand it to him, the man is prepared for all situations of life.

"We've been in a car accident," I say to the emergency responder. "We're—" I crane my neck out the window. I should have looked this up on Google Maps before calling. "We're on Meacham Road? Across from the Publix."

Beefy Southern Guy goes over to the front of his car. "Headlight's busted, and I'm going to need a new hood, probably."

Then Mrs. G takes a good look at the side of her car. In all the commotion, she was so intent on giving the guy a piece of her mind that she didn't think to check on her car (or herself). The door is badly dented, and there's some sort of bar in the middle that's protruding a bit. But all things considered, it's not that bad.

"Are you okay?" I ask Mrs. G.

She blinks at me. "What have I done, what have I done?" she says, wringing her hands. "Are you okay, Emily?"

I look Mrs. G over the best I can. Thankfully, there was no major impact for either of us. Not even bruising or anything like that. As far as accidents go, it could have been worse, a lot worse. In fact, the car almost looks like it was just in a fender bender, really.

Still, no way are we getting back in the car, no way are either of us driving.

A handful of people rush through my mind to come pick us up: Ezra, Matt, or even Coach.

I try Ezra, but he doesn't pick up.

Coach would be at church. Matt, too.

The only family that wouldn't be in church right now is my own. The Christmas-and-Easter-only Catholics.

Maybe I get some sort of free pass because I've just survived a minor car accident. Or maybe I'll get yelled at. I deserve it, for sure.

I could text Tessa, tell her to come get us. There's no way, though, that I can count on her loyalty after asking her to cover for me.

The police come and we give insurance information.

For a few minutes, it's a veritable he said, she said. It's so clear that Mrs. G was in the wrong, but she keeps insisting that the light was green for her. Finally I just tell the officer that Mrs. G ran the red light. He raises his eyebrows at us. "Are you okay to be driving?"

"You're darn right I am!" Mrs. G says.

The officer sighs and looks at me, like I'm the one in charge. "You might want to talk to her doctor," he says, which makes Mrs. G even angrier.

Since it's raining, we both get back in the car to wait. I call Dad. He picks up before the first ring has even finished.

"Dad?" I say, and my voice comes out all wobbly.

"What's wrong?" I can hear the panic in his voice. Tessa's the crier, not me. "Rillo, what's wrong?"

"Everything's fine," I begin (except that it isn't). Then I

force myself to keep my voice calm. "We were in a small car accident just now. Me and . . . Mrs. G."

He pauses for a second, and I know it's because I've said Mrs. G's name. Then he says, "Send me your location. I'm coming."

He doesn't say anything about how I'm not supposed to be with Mrs. G right now, and for that I'm grateful, although I know I'm really going to get it later.

Mrs. G sits there, her head in her hands, her elbows on her knees.

Every time I hear a car behind us, I get this feeling that's simultaneously hopeful and full of dread.

Then Dad's gray Honda Accord comes slowly down the street and pulls over right behind us. I've never been more relieved to see his car.

When I get out, his face is stony, but he opens his arms and hugs me tight and makes sure I'm okay.

Then he sees Mrs. G, and I can see the surprise on Dad's face—she's not what he imagined, with her bright red bob and big earrings made from recycled materials.

He introduces himself to Mrs. G, who normally would be the picture of Southern hospitality, all warmth and questions, but is too shaken to say much except "nice to meet you" and "thank you." I see his eyes take in Mrs. G's outfit, her designer handbag, the pearls at her throat. He looks from the Lexus to me and back again. Then he says Tessa can take Mrs. G's car back to her place when she gets back from her internship, and he'll drive Mrs. G and me back. In the car, all three of us are completely silent.

Dad parks on the long steep driveway and helps Mrs. G into the house. Inside, I see Dad's eyes float over the foyer, then the living room, the artwork and the expensive rug, and George. He leads Mrs. G over to the couch—with her leaning on his arm, it reminds me a lot of how he treats Abuelita—and waits until she's settled onto it, then tells me to boil water, which I do. It's a trick of Mom's—boil water the minute you come home, because you'll inevitably need it for something: to make pasta or tea, or to clean something.

Then I realize I'm still wearing the heels. I slip out of them, but not before Dad has a chance to register them as well.

During all this, his gestures are strong and caring, but his face is impassive as ever.

"Mr. Sanchez—" Mrs. G says. She's sitting there with her hands folded on her lap.

"Jorge," Dad says.

"Mr. Jorge, I can't thank you enough."

"Of course," Dad says. "So you have someone coming to take care of you?"

"My nephew should be here any minute. Can I get you anything? Water, coffee, tea?"

"No, thank you. I need to take my daughter home."

Mrs. G was livid mere minutes ago, but now she looks crumpled and defeated. If Dad weren't here, I'm sure she would be curled up on the couch. "I'm so, so sorry," says Mrs. G. "Really, the whole thing was my fault. On a day like today, I should have just stayed home." She tries to laugh it off, which makes me cringe.

"More importantly, it looks like you didn't have any injuries," says Dad. "Let's hope so. Now you just rest."

The water comes to a boil, and I don't hear the rest of their conversation. I pour a cup of peppermint tea for Mrs. G and bring it into the living room on a saucer.

"Rillo," Dad says. "We're going home."

"I can ride home," I say. I'm being ridiculous—I'm already in so much trouble—but can I really leave her here after what happened? Waiting for Ezra?

"Now," Dad says.

I go into the guest room and gather up my stuff.

Then, in the living room, I bend down and hug Mrs. G, which I've never done before.

"Emily," she says, and pats me on the arm. Her eyes are wet. "I'm so sorry."

"It's going to be okay. Call me if you need anything," I tell her.

Dad lifts my bike like it weighs nothing and sticks it onto the rack on the back of the car. As we ride home, I keep going over and over it in my head: I saw Mrs. G look both ways— why didn't I catch then that she was about to continue on? Or, once she stepped on the gas, was there anything I could have done—if I'd been thinking faster, I could've grabbed the steering wheel, swerved us out of the way, maybe. Really, though, the best thing I could have done was made her stay home. If I really cared about her, I would have been okay with fighting her, with maybe even physically restraining her from getting into the car.

"Why?" Dad says, breaking my train of thought. "Why did you have to get a job like that?" He's speaking to me, but facing forward. "How do you think it looks? You, coming over here to clean this rich old white lady's house?"

The words land in my gut, shock me into silence.

But only for a second. "That's not what I was doing over there," I say. "I was her companion—"

"Don't treat me like I'm stupid, Emilia."

How can I explain it, though? How can I tell Dad that my main task, my most important task, is to remember Mrs. G's memories, stories, habits? The things that make her who she is?

My next thought passes over me like a dark cloud. That, if I don't remember her memories, if I don't take notes, and record them on my phone, and talk about them with Ezra, and make the stories a part of me, does Mrs. G even exist anymore?

"And on top of that, you disobeyed me, and you lied, *and* you were away right after Mom had surgery! As if you think this woman is more important! On top of that, you could have gotten seriously hurt!"

He's so pissed that he even takes a hand off the steering wheel to count the number of my transgressions.

Unexpectedly, my eyes fill. The tears stream down my face and I can't stop them.

Dad looks over, a little alarmed because I'm not an easy

crier. When Tessa cries, we all know what she needs. She wants to be hugged, to have someone rub her back. Me, no one has any idea what I want. Plus, Dad's driving, and he's not sure whether to reach over to console me or what. And I don't even know what I want.

Or rather, what I want is to crawl into a hole and never come back out again.

One hand on the steering wheel, he reaches back, hands me a box of tissues.

"You don't have to cry," he grumbles. "We can talk through this."

"It's not that," I say. "She's losing her memory, Dad."

He takes a deep breath, and I can see him turning everything over in his head: the hours spent at her house, the way I was so vague about everything I was doing there. "That's very serious. Who else knows?"

I shake my head. "Her nephew knows. She wanted us to keep it a secret."

His face changes, then hardens. "She shouldn't have asked you to do that. For many reasons, but one of them being that it's too much for you. And you're not even family! That's not fair. That was incredibly unfair to you."

I nod. Maybe it was unfair, but it didn't seem like it at the same time. What seems more unfair is that it's happening at all. How some old people live to do everything just fine until they die: driving and playing tennis and even dating new people. But Mrs. G—although she did everything right in terms of challenging herself and playing memory games and reading the news and exercising, doing everything she could to stay healthy—she's the one who's stuck with this condition that's only going to get worse and worse.

Dad pulls the car over. "Should we go back?"

"I don't know. She should be fine." But what I want to say is, you're the adult. Tell *me* what to do. This is the one time I want you to do that.

"You're right," he says. "And she has that boy there—"

"Ezra."

"Ezra. So she's safe."

When we get home, Tessa rushes at me and throws her arms around me, then checks me all over for injuries. Mom hugs me, too, and then she pours me a cup of ginseng tea. I don't even like it very much, and it's hot outside besides, but it's the action that's soothing—seeing the water poured from the teapot spout, and drinking it from a mug that I can't remember us not having. We drank British-style tea at Mrs. G's—with milk and sugar and saucers—and this feels so simple and cleansing after all of that.

I sip it to the last bitter drop, letting Mom rub my knee, and feeling bad that she's the one taking care of *me* in this instance.

"I'm really, really sorry," I say. "I . . . I screwed up big-time. I shouldn't have lied, and—" I look at Mom, at the scarf she's still wearing from after her surgery, her face all pale and sad. My voice is barely a whisper. "I really should have been here for you, Mom."

Mom rubs my shoulder. "What matters is you're okay. And you're here now, right?"

Dad just looks at me, his mouth a grim line.

Fair, I think.

Later, in my room, I put my headphones on and crank them all the way up. My favorite song these days is "Your Best American Girl" by Mitski and I listen to it twice through before I see Dad's face in the doorway. He must have knocked and I didn't hear it.

I slide my headphones off, sit up. He joins me on the bed.

"Listen, Rillo. About what you told me in the car. How bad is it?"

"It's— The worst is when she thinks I've done something that I haven't. Then it's really bad. It's like . . . it's like she becomes another person."

"Why did she ask you to keep it a secret? And for how long?"

"I guess earlier in the summer, but I didn't realize. When we first met—it was weird, she—"

"She what?"

"She asked me to remember what she told me about her life. But at that point, I don't know, I didn't know what she wanted from me. I didn't know she was even starting to lose her memory then. And for a while she denied it, right, like I would be so surprised when she let something slip, but if I brought it up, she stubbornly refused to believe it."

Dad nods, like he understands this, has seen it before.

"So, she put you in an unfair situation. I'll give you that. But I don't understand why you felt the need to be with her so badly. Why did it have to be your responsibility to keep it a secret? And moreover, what really hurts me is that you felt the need to lie to us about where you were going." He shakes his head. "That is what's *really, really* disappointing."

"Why would I tell you about Mrs. G when all you do is predict disaster? If I had told you, what good would it have done? You wouldn't have let me go over anyway."

"The thing is, Rillo, I can see you care about her, and I'm sure she cares about you, too—to some degree."

My heart does a little somersault, and not the good kind. "To some degree?" I say.

"This is a job, Rillo. And she's taking advantage of you, I feel. She sees you care about her and, well, she's also older, and rich—she knows the power she can have over you."

Now it's my turn to be confused, and a little disgusted, even. "That's not true. You don't even know her! Why do you always have to think people are taking advantage of you?"

"I'm more experienced, Rillo," Dad says, his voice calm and even. "Once you've been around for as long as I have, you'll know. The world isn't all sunshine and roses."

"I *know*," I say, practically growling, my voice is so low. "I don't think that. I've *never* thought that. Tessa might think that, but that's before I came along."

Dad looks at me. "What do you mean?"

"Everything's so easy for her," I practically spit. "And it's because you and Mom—you give her so much attention! The world is sunshine and roses for *her*. All you can talk about is Tessa this and Tessa that. But what about *me*? It's like you love her more." Even as I say it, I can tell how much of a brat I sound like, but since we're having it out, I might as well say how I really feel, and it's the first time I'm admitting this.

I can hear that Tessa's in her room, right next door, but thankfully she has the good sense to stay in there.

"How can you say that?" Dad says. His face is genuinely shocked. "You know we love you both equally. It's just that it's hard for us—"

"Well, if you guys weren't such helicopter parents, I wouldn't have felt the need to hide it from you! And Tessa wouldn't have to cover for me, either! For once, I want to be able to decide something for myself."

As soon as I say this, I'm thinking, *Rewind, rewind, rewind. How—how is it that I'm clearly very much I-screwed-up-majorly in the wrong, and yet I'm still running my mouth blaming my parents?* At the same time, I can't help thinking that I do have a point. Matt would say, *You tell them, Em.*

Then, of course, Dad gets up and stands in Tessa's doorway, and I follow him.

"Tessa, you knew about this? You knew that Rillo was still going to that woman's house? And you lied to us?" He looks from me to her and back again. "I'm very disappointed in both of you girls."

"It was my fault, Dad," I say. For a brief moment, I have this hopeful inkling of a feeling that maybe everyone will forgive each other because I'm at least owning up to what I did wrong. "Please don't get mad at Tessa."

Tessa's just sitting at her computer, dumbfounded. I catch a glimpse of pie charts on a PowerPoint slide.

"You're the older sister," he says to her, ignoring me. "You should have told us."

"Really," says Tessa. "You're mad at *me* for this? For something that *Emily* was doing wrong? Everyone in this family expects me to do nothing wrong and to just be perfect. You have different standards for us and it's so stupid!"

Then she turns to me. "And you," she says. "You think the world revolves around you! You're never *here*! You're so selfish!"

Then she slams the door in our faces, and I can't help thinking, that's supposed to be my act.

CHAPTER 13

WELL, THE VERY FIRST thing I need to do is apologize to Tessa, because she did something nice for me and then got completely screwed. And because maybe she's right—I am selfish. But when I wake up early the next morning, she's already out for a run. And when she comes home, she goes straight for the shower, then to her internship and Sarah-Bradley's house for dinner, and she's gone all day.

I get it when someone's avoiding me.

Ezra texts me, asking me to give him a play-by-play of the accident, and asks me if I'm okay. Then—unlike anyone else our age—he updates me in one big block of text, divided up into actual paragraphs. He tells me how Mrs. G is doing now and everything she's done since I left the house. She's a bit shaken, he says, and she has napped, eaten lunch, and beaten herself up a few times, head in hands. And, she has asked him to please pick up more gallon Ziploc bags because she just ran out. Again. Even though Ezra has seen at least twelve boxes of Ziploc bags in her kitchen.

He says he'll keep me posted and asks me to do the same.

At home, I try to treat Mom extra nice to make up for my transgressions: I bring her tea, and I sit with her and watch her favorite British shows, and I take a super-short, super-slow walk with her around the block. For dinner, we have an easy-on-the-throat meal of congee. It's been a while since I've eaten with only my parents. Dad is still a little mad at me, I can tell, and we're all just sort of polite and delicate with one another. I could apologize one more time—God knows it wouldn't be uncalled for—but then Dad finishes eating quickly and puts his bowl in the sink, and the moment passes.

ele

That evening, I ride my bike over to Matt's house because he's the only person who will understand any of this. At least, that's what I'm hoping. I'm also hoping I can catch just him, and not him and Zoey.

He's in the yard, of course.

"I thought you weren't supposed to garden in the evening," I say, dismounting.

He stands up. "There are certain things that are good before bed. Like watering—it helps the soil stay moist for longer."

"I cannot believe you just used that word."

"Believe it," Matt says. "So, what brings you here, you know, finally, after avoiding me all summer?"

"I have a long story to tell you."

"That works well, because I've got a lot of weeds to pull."

So I sit, on the same stoop where, when we were in

elementary school, we'd sit and eat Popsicles and, in middle school, wait for the bus. I tell him the entire thing, starting with the *Bye Bye Birdie* mix-up and ending with the car accident, and about Mrs. G being as sad as I've ever seen her. He pulls and yanks and prunes and waters, and sprays his homemade weed killer, calling the plants things like "big guy" and "little buddy" and "sweet girlie" under his breath.

After I've told him everything, Matt takes a deep breath and surveys his handiwork. "You could've offered to help, you know."

I look at the pile of weeds he's dug up. "Would Zoey?" I say.

Shoot. Mom's right. I have absolutely no filter.

"Well," he says, "yeah. She's into plants."

I sigh. Of course she is. Because she's into everything Matt's into, it seems.

"Speaking of whom, we usually talk at seven, so I'll have to answer if she calls."

Ugh. Of course Zoey would schedule phone calls.

"What do I do now?" I ask. And why is it that, when I most need advice, it's not an adult who I end up asking, but my insanely nerdy, data-obsessed friend?

He bites his lip, looks down at the pansies. And then all I can do is picture him in this exact same position with Zoey. Her perfect pink manicured fingernails like little strawberry hard candies, pulling up weeds, laughing at his jokes. She'd wear gardening gloves, though. I look down at my own nails. At least half of them are stained with pastels.

"Well, you tell me," he says. "I think you know what your options are."

"Well," I say.

I think of Mrs. G alone in the house, all the possible things that could happen. "Things are getting, well, honestly, things are getting dangerous for her. So I could . . . I mean, I could tell someone. But I really don't want to."

"You slip a note to her doc, or—"

I'm already shaking my head. "No way. If I do that, she'll never forgive me."

"Or maybe the best thing is to call her family. Or tell what's-his-face—the pretentious dude—to tell her family."

But Ezra wouldn't, would he? He was the one who made me swear to secrecy.

"She won't speak to me anymore if I tell," I say.

"Well," he says, "after this summer, you'll be back in school, and I hate to break it to you, but you won't even be speaking to her much then anyway. You think you will because right now you're in the honeymoon phase of your friendship, but it's like high school in the movies. Those couples are not gonna last after graduation."

"I'm pretty sure we've moved past the honeymoon stage." And then, before I can stop myself, I blurt: "Oh, so you're not gonna keep dating Zoey when you're off to Yale or wherever?"

He ignores my question by stepping a few feet away to turn on the hose. How come we can talk about everything except this?

"*Yale?* Come on, Em. Yale's, like, the Slytherin of the Ivy League." He brings the hose over and generously douses the flowers in the barrels that line the driveway.

"Anyway," he continues. "What's worse, Mrs. G not speaking to you, or hurting herself badly?"

I nod. It's a horrible feeling, isn't it, when there's something you know you really have to do, but you find yourself making every excuse to not do it?

We sit for a while, and then I help drag the bags over to the compost pile. I never help Mom and Dad with yard work unless they tell me to, but I can see why Matt likes it. It's calming, and the dirt smells good, and everything's so lush and green in the summer.

Matt used to do all kinds of gardening—a patch with ghost peppers and other vegetables that I'd never heard of, little lemon trees, even pumpkins—but what he loves most, he told me, is flowers, because they bring beauty into the world. Have you ever met anyone more earnest? At least I'm not lying to myself anymore: I'm in love with my best friend and should have acted sooner. But, like Mrs. G, I have waited too long.

Inadvertently, I find myself again thinking of Zoey. How he probably makes bouquets for her and she probably loves them. And the thing is, for once, I'm sort of happy for the both of them. They deserve each other. Matt deserves someone sweet and lively, someone who supports his every nerdy endeavor, who will go down the sheepshearing rabbit holes with him, who actually understands when he explains about magnets and polar opposites and hydrogen bonds. And Zoey—she's always been so nice and so smart, and she definitely deserves a guy who's not a jerk. And so few high school boys are not jerks. The realization that I'm happy for them is mixed with something else, something that hurts. But maybe, also like Mrs. G, it's better late than never.

"Matt," I begin. "Have you ever thought, like—"

But just then, Matt's phone rings. He peels off his gardening gloves in a hurry but then waits a beat. "Yeah?" he says.

"Nothing," I say.

You know how people say you can hear someone smile through the line? He says "hey" in this sweet familiar way that can only mean it's her.

Then he covers the receiver and says that he'll see me soon, and to text me if I want to talk more about my Mrs. G sitch.

I pedal away and my heart twists itself into a knot. I've spent the summer telling myself that it feels that way because I'm annoyed that I don't get to have Matt's undivided attention, or that I wish our friendship could go back to how it was before Zoey showed up.

But now I know it's because I have for sure lost out on a good thing.

I'm getting ready for bed that night when Dad comes into my room.

He takes a look around: at the little piles of laundry, the opened and unopened mail from colleges, the money plant surrounded by trinkets and beauty products. For once, he doesn't say anything about the mess. Dad is meticulous and precise, clean and tidy; I'm not. It's one of our many key differences.

"I thought about it some more, Rillo. I'm still not pleased at what you did, but I can see why you did it—and why she asked you to. Stories and memories—they are what make us who we are, right? And, you know, it couldn't have been easy for you. I didn't take your job seriously, but I'm seeing now how hard it was. It takes resilience, and forgiveness, to go back to someone like that."

"I guess," I say. "Thanks, Dad." But I can't help still feeling ashamed, like I've failed on so many levels this summer, and that the one person who seemed to like my company a whole lot—I'm seriously considering doing something that will make her never speak to me again.

"Have you heard anything from Mrs. G?" he asks.

I shake my head. "Hopefully no news is good news."

"If I'm being honest, I think what was hurtful is that you seemed to want to spend more time with her than with us." He smiles a sad smile. "But I guess that's to be expected. You're a teenager. I forget that sometimes. And what you said about how we treat Tessa differently—"

"Dad," I interrupt, "can we just, like, not talk about that right now?"

Don't get me wrong, I super appreciate it when my parents start baring their souls to me, but sometimes, it's too much at once.

He looks surprised, but he shouldn't, after knowing me

for sixteen years. I put my palms up. "I know I screwed up, majorly, on so many levels. But maybe we can talk about the other ones later."

He purses his lips. "I guess there's no rush."

Then I get an idea. "I'm about to have a difficult conversation, and you have those all the time with your work. Can I ask you for some advice?"

"Of course."

So I tell him about how I'm thinking of talking to someone in Mrs. G's family—her son, probably. But what if Robbie gets super mad? Or what if he doesn't believe me? Or worse, what if he blames me for not telling him earlier?

Dad listens, then says, "You know what I admire about you, Rillo? You're not afraid. And you don't always need to be in control." He chuckles and gestures around the room. "This place proves that for sure. I think it's very brave of you to tell somebody. That's exactly what I would advise you to do."

"I *am* afraid; I guess I just don't express it the same way you do."

"In this situation, with Robbie, you can only control what you can control—which is yourself. I think what you need is a rehearsal."

ℓℓℓ

Dad has me practice. He pretends to be Robbie, and he reacts in a myriad of spectacular, over-the-top ways. In one of them, he yells, in another, he breaks down into sobs. In another, he says he doesn't want to speak with me.

By the time we're done, I'm half laughing about Dad's latent theatrical side and half terrified.

"It's a very brave thing, what you're doing," Dad says. "Brave and noble. You don't owe them anything, but you're doing it anyway."

I write up a script on my computer.

> Hi, Robbie? This is Emily Chen-Sanchez, your mom's companion.
>
> I'm calling because I need to tell you something about her health.
>
> Don't worry—she's doing well and there's no reason to panic— it's just that—

Except that she's not doing well. Why do I feel the need to comfort him before I say what I need to say? No one's comforting *me* about her.

I delete that and then write:

> When would be a good time to talk?

If he gets mad at me for keeping it a secret this whole time, well. That's not my fault.

lll

Robbie doesn't pick up, and I guess that makes sense, since he doesn't recognize my number. I end up texting him, telling him who I am and asking when we can talk, and giving him some available times, like Dad suggested. Robbie chooses one and sends me a Zoom link, and I feel very adult.

Then the day arrives and Dad coaches me through it—how to stay calm as I'm giving Robbie the bad news. Reminding me I'm doing the right thing, and that he'll be nearby while I'm doing it.

Then I'm face-to-face with Robbie Granucci. He's got a kind but tired face, salt-and-pepper hair. Even when all he does is say hello to me, I can tell he's calmer and quieter than Mrs. G—he must take after his dad. He's looking at me with this open expression on his face, though, like he's curious about what I have to say, and like he wants to make this conversation easier for me—which I appreciate a lot.

"Mom told me about you," he says, and it's kind of weird thinking of Mrs. G as somebody's mom—but of course she is. "She's very fond of you, and it sounds like you're doing a great job."

I can't help but smile at that.

"So," he says, "what's up?"

For a second, I wonder if I should pad it somehow by starting with good things: That on the best days, she wants to go somewhere fabulous for breakfast. That she makes up the most ridiculous conversations between wax George Harrison and me. That, in some ways, even though there have been times she's infuriated me, she's also been one of the best listeners I've had all summer. I figure it's better to just rip the Band-Aid off, so I tell him that I think she's having serious memory issues. And then I tell him everything I can, starting with the smaller things—the things that just seemed like minor forgetfulness—and ending with the mood swings.

"To be honest," he says, "I'm not completely surprised. She sometimes will call me a few times in a day—it's like she forgets we just spoke. But it was also easy for her to cover up—she'd just tell me she dialed me by accident." He sighs. "I don't want to embarrass her, because then she gets even more defensive. And I get how difficult this must have been for you," he says. "She's a stubborn old bird, my mom."

Robbie rubs his temples with both hands.

"So," he says. "How bad is it?"

"She accused me of stealing her jewelry, once," I say. "And—she's fine, physically, but she did get into a minor car accident last week. I was in the car."

He drops his head into his hands. "Christ," he says.

"She . . . I knew she wanted me to keep it a secret," I say. That part doesn't surprise him. He knows his mother, after all.

And on some level, I get it, I do. There are so many reasons. There's the beautiful Spanish house that he grew up in and that she's essentially made as lovely as an art gallery; it should be featured in a magazine about interior decorating. She doesn't want to leave that and she doesn't want "just any damn fool" to be a live-in companion. There's all the volunteering she does. There are trips to the White Moose. She loves her Lexus, and she loves to drive.

She doesn't want to lose her freedom.

"What are you going to do?" I say.

"I don't know. At the moment, I just don't know." He smiles at me. "She doesn't spend her time with just anyone, you know. You must be special. It takes an awful lot of courage to defy her wishes, and you've done just that. Thank you for telling me."

"She'll be pissed, I guess. But won't she get that I did it because I—" I almost say *because I love her,* but stop myself just in time. "Because I care about her?"

That sad smile again, he regards me with his palms up. "I'd certainly hope so," he says. "We Granuccis can be a hard-headed bunch, though. Rest assured that you did the right thing. You really should take comfort in that. It shows character."

Afterward, I feel simultaneously relieved and sad. I imagine it's the sort of thing some people feel when they break up with someone who isn't great for them. I go downstairs to get myself a snack.

"So?" Dad says. "How did it go?"

"Well, I told him. And he didn't, like, get mad or anything. Just super sad. But he was glad I told him. He thanked me."

Dad smiles so big, I can only describe him as beaming. "And he should! What you did was . . . it was excellent, Rillo. I am very, very proud of you."

Dad takes me in for a hug, and I realize it's been a while, a long while, since we've hugged like this. He smells nice and fresh, the familiar deodorant he's been using since I was a little kid. Still, it's rare for us to hug. Because every time my parents try to touch me, I find myself scrunching up. Why is that? I wonder. Why do I have such a hard time letting them show me they love me in the way that they want to?

"I know this hasn't been an easy summer, for any of us," he says quietly. "You did the right thing and I am so, so proud of you."

Then why do I feel so shitty?

"I told on Mrs. G," I say. "I'm like a first-rate tattletale who ruins everything."

"That's not true. I'm very proud of you, Rillo. You did something that takes a lot of courage. It's not easy, you know, to tell the truth, to do something that ends up affecting your friendship but in the end is so much better for the other person." He rubs my back again. "I'm proud of you."

And now *I'm* beaming, and it's all I can do to just say, "Thank you," and make sure that I etch this moment into my memory forever.

I can't help thinking that I'd do it all over again—the ring-stealing accusation and the car accident and all the mess of this summer—just to have this moment.

⎯⎯⎯

Then, a few days later, I get an email from Mrs. G.

Dear Emily,

Please thank your father again for his help the other day. I am doing fine, physically, and I hope you are, too. Thank you for the many messages checking on me.

I wish you had not told Robbie. You must have had your reasons. But I do feel that you have betrayed me. I held your confidence in high regard. I, of course, want to hang on to the house and stay here until I croak (and maybe even after—they can bury me in the yard). We are still trying to decide what is to be done. In the meantime, I'm not allowed to drive, or go for walks by myself, or even cook without someone around, and that has taken a toll on my health, both physical and mental. On top of that, Robbie has hired an aide to spend the entire week with me—not just the loneliest parts of it, as you did, which makes me a real grouch. Primarily, I suppose I'm writing to tell you I no longer need your services. It's ironic, isn't it, that you telling Robbie the one thing I didn't want you to reveal has now led to, essentially, my letting you go. I suppose in the end he would have found out anyway.

I hope the rest of your summer has gone well and that your mama is doing better.

Mrs. G

Dear Mrs. G,

I'm so sorry to hear that you're not allowed to do the things you love. How are you doing now? At least a little better, I hope. I want you to know that it was not an easy decision for me to make. I know you trusted me, and I'm so sorry that I broke that trust. At the same time, I was afraid for you, and I hope you can understand that I was in a difficult spot. I really did not want to see you get hurt again.

Although now you have a new companion, I'd love to see you maybe for lunch or tea sometime. I'll have my license soon (fingers crossed) and can take you somewhere fabulous. Or I am happy to come over like old times and make us both egg Bennys for brunch. Please let me know if there's a time when I can come over before school starts.

Mom has radiation treatment coming up. We are all hoping for the best.

How is Ezra? And George?

My best,
Emily

I write back to her, and then crickets. A day passes, then two. And at three, I have to wonder if she'll ever write me again, that this is her way of saying it's over between us.

Days later, my phone rings, and it's Ezra. I take a deep breath, then say, "Hey."

"What were you thinking?" he says.

I picture him pacing, trying to wrap his head around it— even though it was the right thing to do, of course it was the right thing to do. I start to apologize, and then something else occurs to me. It starts in my gut and then makes its way up my throat.

"What was *I* thinking?" I say. "The real question is, What were *we* thinking? How could we keep something this huge, this dangerous, a secret? How could you do that to me?" *I'm not even family,* I'm about to say, but then that's not completely true, either. I'd tried to make a new family of these seemingly perfect people in this perfect house, and now they weren't even going to speak to me anymore.

Ezra ignores what I said, saying, "We had a deal. We had an understanding. I just—I wish you hadn't told. But okay, now that you have, I think I can forgive you."

"You think *you* can forgive *me*?"

Then there's a pause, and his voice changes. "Listen, I know we'll be in different circles soon, but we won't be far from each other. Do you want to meet up sometime?"

Ugh. What is *up* with these boarding school boys?

"No," I say, and then hang up, my heart pounding in spite of it all.

What I'll miss most isn't even getting out of the house, although that was what I loved at the beginning. We became friends, she and I. What I'll miss most is her.

CHAPTER 14

EVEN THOUGH THINGS HAVE gotten so much better with Dad the past several days, that doesn't change things with Tessa. My family is good at talking to one another until someone gets hurt. Then we act like nothing happened at all and wait for it to blow over.

I haven't seen her all weekend. The minute I wake up on Monday—and for once we've both woken up around the same time—and make a beeline for the bathroom, I can tell even then that she's decided not to speak to me.

She did this once before, and I guess I deserved it, but it still didn't fail to shock me. It's one of the things I *don't* admire or envy about Tessa. Yeah, maybe she's more mature than me in many ways, but at least I don't run away from conflict. At least I have the decency to say how I feel, as uncomfortable as it may be.

Honestly, it made me lose respect for her for a few days. She knows she's the older sister; she *knows* how much I admire her (though I'm loath to admit it) and so badly want her approval.

Yes, it's true. Underneath it all, I really want her to think I'm cool.

On the way to the bathroom I say, "Morning," and then, "You go ahead"—because I figure, well, for once I'll be somewhat nice to her.

She acts like I'm not even there. Just faces forward and walks in and closes the door behind her.

God, it's so infuriating.

And as Mrs. G says, anger is only hurt's younger cousin.

It's like this all through breakfast. Tessa talks with Mom and Dad easily and then she doesn't look my way. And I'm too prideful to try to break the ice. I've overheard both Mom and Dad asking her to please work things out with me, but there's only so much they can do.

You know what's worse than fighting with your older sister?

Not fighting.

ele

The next few days feel long and dull. Mrs. G hasn't called or written or texted, so I know she's still mad. Our house feels so quiet, and I do what I can to pass the time without becoming addicted to my phone. I go to swim practice in the mornings, grateful for the constant structure of it.

Then I go up to my room and draw.

Usually drawings take me forever, months at least. And

that's maybe because I'm a master procrastinator, and I waffle about what I'm actually doing pretty much every time. But for this one, I just go for it. The idea came to me earlier, while swimming. I guess it's a landscape, but also sort of a still life? I pull up a photo from last summer: Matt standing proudly beside his rosebush, in full bloom in July. They're hot pink tea roses, and he let them grow wildly, so many they were poking into the driveway and brushing the side of his Jeep when he pulled in. With my pencil, I sketch the bush. I let it take up most of the page, and unlike the photo, I capture the bush even later in the season, when most of the roses have fully flowered, and some petals have fallen to the ground, and still others are yet to open up. Once I get a few sketches done, the remaining flowers fly by. The last part is what takes me forever: a pair of gardening gloves, dropped at the side of the bush after a day's hard work is done, the fingers caked in dirt.

Then it's time for color: The roses are mostly vibrant pink, but a few have petals that are tinged brown, dried at the edges, clearly on their way to the ground. I render the sky a heart-breaking pale blue, no clouds. The gardening gloves are dark green, and it takes me a while to find the perfect shade.

When I'm done, it's well past midnight, and I feel both mentally and physically exhausted, but also satisfied—I would call it finished. I've never truly finished a drawing in one sitting like that. I spray the whole thing with hair spray, making sure to do it quickly and not concentrate it in any one area; that'll set the colors so there's no smudging. Then I prop it against the wall and do something I so rarely do with any of my work: look at it and enjoy.

After the blowout with Dad and Tessa, I'm better about chores, trying to do my part after Tessa accused me of never being around. I unload the dishwasher without being told, I fold Mom's laundry and bring it up to her room. It's boring as hell, but sometimes that's life for you. And in a way, it's nice—talking to Dad with some new understanding between us, listening to music, Mom doing better and better after her surgery, and not having a constant worry in the back of my head about Mrs. G having a mood swing.

Although now, the worry is different. The worry is, is she going to be okay? What is the plan after this temporary one? Is she horribly lonely? The other worry is, are we ever going to speak again?

<hr>

I've never gone this long with Tessa's silent treatment before. Last night I heard Mom outside Tessa's door, saying, "Come on, make up, can you two please make up? Forgive each other? For me?"

It's funny when parents ask you to make up for them. As if it's like, okay, I won't do this for myself, but sure, I'll do it for *you*.

I couldn't hear what Tessa said, her voice was so low, but I imagine it was something along the lines of no.

We went to bed without saying good night.

When we were in elementary school, we made up a code

using knocks, since our bedrooms share a thin wall. Three knocks in a row meant "Are you awake?" A slap plus a knock plus a tap of the thumb (I know, we were very sophisticated) meant "Good night!" We haven't done it in years, but sometimes I think about it. About how close we were.

But I've learned a thing or two this summer, and I'm done with keeping quiet, with secret-keeping. Just because that's how Mrs. G handles things doesn't mean I need to do it that way. So that night I tell myself that if Tessa doesn't make a move tomorrow, I'm going to be the one to do it, no matter how damn uncomfortable it is.

At least that'll make one less person who's not speaking to me.

I've got a little script in my head. About how much it hurts when she doesn't speak to me. About how it's a disgusting power play since she's the older sister, and it's so immature, like it's the 1960s and we're a husband and wife who secretly hate each other. About how I know I'm insufferable, but come on, I'm working on it.

Can I somehow, please, convince her that I can change? That, in some ways, I already have?

ℓℓℓ

The next morning, it's the same routine. Tessa goes into the bathroom, and stares straight ahead when she comes out, pretending I'm not there. At breakfast, she makes conversation with Dad and completely ignores me. He looks concerned, but thankfully he doesn't say anything. Then Tessa goes up to her room.

Here's my chance. I bound up the stairs.

"Hey," I say, standing in her doorway, just blurting it before I can second-guess myself. "Can we talk?"

She's at her laptop, perfecting her slides for the presentation, and she doesn't even flinch. But I'm not giving up. I stand there, and I keep standing there, watching her typing, for what feels like a full minute.

Then she heaves a big sigh and looks straight at me. "You ask a lot from me, you know."

"I ask a lot from *you*?"

She looks at me like she has all summer. Like I'm the idiot, and she has to slowly, condescendingly, explain things to me.

"First, to cover for you. And it's not like I'm good at lying."

"What's that supposed to mean?"

She narrows her eyes at me. Okay. Fair.

"Second, what's been going on all summer. You, leaving the house, and me, keeping everything together. When I'm the one with a *real* job, and a boyfriend, and college applications—"

"My job *was* real! And I've been making dinner!" I say, already knowing that it's not the right thing to say. That fights are never about what you're actually saying.

"You made like two meals!" Tessa says.

"You don't even want me around, though! When I *am* here, all anyone does is criticize me."

"Because you're hardly here. When you *are* here, you don't *do* anything—"

"Every time I try to help, it's like I'm doing it wrong anyway. Isn't that what you always say?"

"If you were around more, you could learn. But that's the thing: You're never here! I'm the one who has to see Mom suffering every day, and *without* my sister around to help share the work. I'm the one who puts up with Dad's anxiety. I'm the one who does all the housework, while you get to go to someone else's clean, nice home and . . . eat cookies! Or whatever it is you do there all day! And after all of that, you have the audacity to ask me to *cover* for you? And *then* I get blamed for doing *that*? Grow *up*, Emily."

I didn't even know Tessa had it in her to be this angry. Her eyes are flashing, like she absolutely despises me.

"I'm really sorry, Tess. I really am. You . . . you don't even know what happened this summer, though. Mrs. G—"

"Mrs. G this and Mrs. G that! Do you think I even care? How can *you* care so much about her when there's so much going on with your own family?"

"You seem to have it all under control! It's not like you leave anything for me to do anyway! And . . . and"—this last part is something I've barely articulated even to myself, but I realize as the thought forms that it's true—"and maybe I needed to leave the house because it sucked so much to be here. To have to see Mom in pain, with her hoarse voice, and Dad constantly watching her like a hawk. I don't even know how you can stand it."

At that, Tessa's face softens—but only a bit.

"It does suck. But at least if you were here, we could be in it together."

She turns around then, back to her computer, with a defiant spin, so that I'm looking at her stubby ponytail and not her face.

"Wait," I say. "We're not done talking yet."

Then she turns to me with a face that says, *Are you seriously going to push me on this?* She purses her lips and looks resolutely at her screen. "We are done. I can't do this anymore."

So it's not going to be like the movies. We aren't going to make up and become some great team. Even after being vulnerable with each other. And it's not like talking has helped very much, either.

~elle~

At swim practice that Monday, Coach says, "We only have seven more of these together before the season's over. So make this one count. Okay, people, let's go!"

It didn't hit me earlier that it's the end of July. When school let out at the end of May, and I stood at the top of the stairs watching Dad hold my report card like it was a dirty sock, the summer seemed like it would never end. The swim practices all blended together, one after the next. But now I find I'm going to miss them: that first plunge into the too-cold water, and then your body growing used to it. How when you're in there, all you can do is think about moving forward.

The warm-up is two 100s of our choice, focusing on technique and turns. I dive into the cool water and give it my all, freestyle. But I don't focus on technique or turns. I make a splashy big fuss with my kicks, I throw my arms into the water and pull them back in fast scoops, as if getting water out of my way. I don't even practice regular breathing. I give it everything I have, and soon I'm passing the swimmers in the other lanes. This is stupid and I know it is, a waste of energy before practice has really started, but today I want nothing more than to exhaust myself—my limbs and my brain and my lungs—so that there isn't room to think about anything else. Not Matt or Tessa, not Mom or Mrs. G.

When I turn my head to breathe, I can hear Coach yelling something, but I'm not exactly sure what. It's not easy to hear when your ears are covered by a cap *and* they're underwater. So I just keep swimming, wildly. If you could even call what I'm doing swimming.

When I finally stand up at the wall, Coach says, "Where was that energy at the last meet? Your technique's gone to shit, by the way."

"Sorry," I say to Coach. "I'll clean up my technique in the next set."

"You okay? Do you need to come take a lap with me?"

When Coach says "take a lap" like that, it means go for a walk to the far side of the pool, where no one can hear you. It means she's going to try to ask about my feelings, about Mom, about what is going on inside my head that has caused me to swim so badly.

"No thanks," I say. "I'm good."

Meghan Morehart, in the next lane, lifts her eyebrows

at me. *Mind your own business,* I think, and it must come through in my face, because she faces front and calls, "Let's go, Zoey!" and claps her hands, even though we don't usually cheer for each other at practice.

Then practice is over and everyone's heading to their bikes, or their cars if they're lucky. My arms and legs feel like Jell-O. I sink onto one of the plastic pool chairs.

Coach reminds me to drink water, says that if I clean up my technique next time, I won't feel so spent. "Use your energy effectively," she says. She leans forward and pats me on the back. "Hang in there."

Then she squats down next to me, shielding her eyes.

"Look, I was going to tell you next week, when I give everyone their assignments, but I knew you'd put up a fight so I'm going to tell you now. And I don't want to hear it."

"Geez," I say, "am I really so bad?"

She smiles. "You know what you want and you speak up for it. But sometimes, Emily, you do need to put your head down and respect authority. Anyway, I'm going to put you in the 50 fly."

"What!" I begin. I *hate* butterfly with a passion. Everyone knows that, including Coach. Maybe especially Coach.

But she's making the zipping-her-mouth-shut motion and saying, "Zilch, nope, I don't want to hear it. Sometimes you need to do hard things. I know you hate it, I know it's your worst event. And you know what, that's why I'm putting you on it."

If this had happened at the beginning of the summer, I

would've put up a fight. But I've learned a bit about picking your battles, and just maybe a little something about how time works. How, in the grand scheme of things, it's only one swim meet. A tiny humiliation in the midst of a summer when your mom has cancer and your employer/friend is losing her memory and your best friend who you're kind of maybe in love with is dating another girl, is really nothing at all.

"Okay," I say, "I'll do it."

I see Matt and Zoey heading toward the bike rack. They're not holding hands or talking or anything, which, even though it's stupid, makes me feel a tiny bit good, kind of like seeing that you've gotten one more like on your Instagram post. Then Matt turns around, and even from this distance, I can see he's giving me a concerned look: *Everything okay?*

Then Zoey turns around, too, smiles and waves.

I paste a smile on my face and give them both a thumbs-up.

♾

After that, I do something stupid. I ride my bike back over to Mrs. G's street. I'm curious about my replacement. But there's nothing to see, just the house, the garden carefully manicured as usual, the weeping willows, the white lace curtains in the window. I imagine her seeing me, and then, what, exactly? There's a part of me that hopes she'll come outside with a big smile, saying she's sorry and won't I come in for a coffee?

Nothing at all happens. No one looks out the window or steps onto the porch.

I don't know what I was expecting, but I feel like a creep.

That week, Mom goes to the hospital for RAI. But we can't go with her, because the radiation is that powerful.

When she's back, we talk to her over FaceTime. "It was like a sci-fi movie," she tells us. "The radiologist showed up wearing a mask and a lead apron and gloves. Then he gave me a pill to take." She shrugs. "Right now, I feel about the same."

Mom settles into her room, and I take her dinner tray carefully up the stairs. Outside my parents' bedroom, I squat, grateful for the million squats we have to do at swim practice sometimes, and set the tray down on the floor. I knock. "Mom?"

I can hear her easing off the bed, the squeak of the springs, and then the door cracks open and she takes the tray inside. "This is beautiful! Thank you, sweetie."

It always sounds really off when Mom and Dad use terms of endearment like that. You don't hear non-white people using them—I'm sorry, but you just don't. Unless they're in another language. But she's trying, so okay, I'll take it.

"You're welcome, uh, sweetie," I say.

I can hear her chuckle, faintly.

"Bon appétit," I say, then turn around to eat my own frozen pizza (DiGiorno Rising Crust), which I plan to devour in front of the TV.

"Wait," Mom says from inside. "Stay and eat with me."

"What? I thought we weren't supposed to."

"You can't come in, but you could sit outside the door. If you don't mind."

I rush back downstairs and then back up, then plop down crisscross applesauce on the carpet right outside her door.

"It's kind of lonely in here," Mom admits.

"I can imagine," I say, but really I'm thinking, *Why didn't I think of that before?* and *Tessa would have thought of it.*

"I turned on one of those British detective shows I like."

With the door between us, it's easier to talk. It's almost as if we're talking on the phone.

"Oh yeah?" I say. "Which one?"

"They're all kind of the same, I guess, but I don't mind. They're something to distract me from my anxieties."

"That's not exactly my idea of soothing, Mom." Also, I hadn't thought before about how anxious she would be. But of course she would be—it's just that Dad tends to show it more. I guess that's how self-absorbed I've been this summer.

Mom chuckles. "They're so extreme that there's something weirdly calming about them. Like our real lives can hardly compare. There's a kidnapping in this one, and of course the two detectives involved are starting to fall in love."

"Of course."

I take my first bite of pizza. Damn. Pepperoni is heaven after three weeks of low iodine.

We sit in silence for a while, and from behind the door, I can hear the sounds of Mom eating: the fork and knife tapping against each other, the glass with ice cubes being set back down on the nightstand. It's nice. Even though we can't see each other, we're still eating together.

Then Mom says, "So I take it you haven't made up with your sister yet."

I sigh. "I've tried."

"You know, Aunt Sue and I fought all the time, too. Life just seemed so much easier for her! Ama and Lǎo Yé weren't as hard on her. Maybe they figured she would just do her own thing anyway. She was always the more independent one."

"But now you guys get along great."

"Well, things are different once you leave your parents' home. Some siblings grow apart—we grew closer together. It's unique, having a sister. No one else knows you quite like she does; no one else shares the same childhood."

It's true. There are rare times when we're in a group—hanging out with our extended family or people from school—and Tessa and I will make eye contact and laugh at some inside joke, something that only we can get because we share the same parents and home. That hasn't happened in a while, though.

Mom says, "Dad told me, you know. About what you said about how we love Tessa more."

"Oh, no, Mom, I didn't mean that—"

"We love you so much, Emily. I know we're hard on you. It's not easy, being the second child. Tessa's always been an overachiever in the very conventional sense, and as a kid she was very compliant. And then you came along, and you were just so *loud*, you wanted to do your own thing. But little girls are always being told to be quiet, aren't they? You say what's on your mind, and you always have. That's not a bad thing.

Dad and I shouldn't compare you to Tessa. We're wrong to do that. And we're going to try to stop."

I lean forward and rest my forehead against the bedroom door.

"I love you, Mom," I say.

"Oh, Emily."

"I'm sorry," I say.

"What for?" she says. "What are you apologizing for? We've already been over your grades, and you've already betrayed your employer, so what else do you have to be sorry for?"

Wow. Leave it to my mom to list everything I've done wrong, even when I'm already apologizing.

"For not being there for you this summer. For not being as good as Tessa."

"You're very strong, Emily. You're my strong girl. You've been there for me in a different kind of way. You've given me hope and you've inspired me—with your art, and your resilience, and how you've handled Mrs. Granucci."

"My art? Really?" I say.

She nods. "I was dusting in your room and saw the one of the rosebush. It's beautiful."

Why is it that my mom is the one who's sick, and yet she's comforting *me*? Also, why oh why am I fishing for compliments.

I sink lower on the carpet and wipe my eyes. I feel like I've failed at everything, like I'm right back where I started from at the beginning of the summer, if not worse off. Matt is still with Zoey. Heather and I haven't talked in a while. Tessa hates my guts. Mrs. G isn't speaking to me; it's as if we never met.

"Are you crying?" Mom says. "Don't cry, Emily. If you cry about this, you won't have tears left for the really sad things."

That's my mother, still thinking this isn't that bad.

"I feel like a failure," I say. "Tessa with her perfect grades and her perfect hair. Me with my bad grade . . ."

"And your wild hair," Mom says. We both laugh, though I still have tears running down my cheeks.

"You don't need to feel that way, Emily," Mom says. "It was very, very disappointing that you got that grade. Of course it was. And this isn't about Tessa—this is about you. It was disappointing because we know you're so much better than that. You're so bright. It embarrassed us—didn't we always raise you to do your very best work, always?—but the main thing that made us so angry is that the grade doesn't reflect what you're capable of. It's as if you just—you just gave up. And this family is not the type of family that gives up."

I sniff, wipe my nose with my napkin.

"But the grade doesn't change that you're our Emily," says Mom. "And the important thing to remember is that it doesn't change your self-worth. The grade doesn't make you less of a person, and it doesn't define who you are. Even if it feels that way now."

I have this overwhelming ache to hug her. I pull my knees up to my chest, the tears really coming now, coursing down my cheeks and onto my arms. I swipe my fingers across my nose and come away with a string of snot.

I'm disgusting.

"I love you too, Emily," says Mom. "Very, very much."

Sometimes Mom really isn't that bad. Sometimes both my parents surprise me.

ele

That Friday is the last swim meet of the season—the big championship where teams from six different neighborhoods compete. Mom can't come, of course, Dad doesn't want to leave Mom alone in the house, and Tessa has her work. And I'm fine with it, I really am. I'm not one of those high school athletes who are actually serious about what they do. It's just a swim meet, and it's not even for school.

At the meet, we all stick one foot into this little kiddie pool, the water dirty from our feet walking all over the grass. It's uncouth, is what it is, but it's part of tradition, and I figure this might well be the last summer I do this, so I do it. The air smells like chlorine and sweat, sunscreen and candy.

Matt and I eat Airheads, watermelon for him, blue raspberry for me. Coach says it's best not to eat sugar before meets, but what the heck, it's just what we do at the last meet of the season. We stick our tongues out at each other and I know mine is blue. It's one of the few times Zoey isn't with him, and I'm wondering if he asked her if he and I could hang out, just the two of us.

Or maybe she doesn't eat sugar.

Car after car pulls into the lot, with _River's Edge Rangers_ and *We're on the edge* and *Eat my bubbles* written in blue and silver marker on the windows.

People sit in circles in their team suits, a big mass of tanned bodies in teal. Coach walks around with a clipboard that's guaranteed to be soaking wet by the end of the hour. The announcer, one of my teammate's dads, bellows through a megaphone that the 100 breaststroke is starting. That's the event I would have liked to swim, but whatever.

We've already sat through all the eleven- and twelve-year-old events, which have taken up most of the morning. That's part of why swim meets are so damn exhausting. Not only do you sit around making small talk in your damp suit between events, trying to keep your energy up without eating too much, but you have to be there early for warm-up and then wait around for hours while the littles swim. And sure, you could leave to go home, but no one ever does. That's not team spirit.

Then Coach comes around and tells me to get ready because my event is coming up. She puts a hand on my shoulder. "You got this. I know it's not your favorite event, and I appreciate you doing it—for the team. Just enjoy yourself. I saw you swim with passion at our last practice. Do it for you."

Sure enough, the announcer calls out that my heat is coming up. Matt high-fives me for good luck and then I'm sitting on the bench right behind the swimmers for the current event. I've told myself all week that I don't really care about this meet at all, but now that it's happening, my body is responding in its usual way: stomach churning, heart beating faster. It's a full event; there are five other swimmers, and they all look more intense than me. They're stretching, taking deep breaths, swim caps covering their ears as they prepare (one of them, clearly a butterfly champion, has everyone on the other team screaming her name), so it's clear that they're good.

Meghan Morehart and Alison Brieland are the other two on our team, and of course they're bound to do well.

I remind myself it's okay to come in sixth place and get a pink ribbon. What counts is that I'm here. I only need to compete against myself.

Then the previous event (the 50 backstroke) is over and those swimmers emerge, panting and dripping, and then it's our turn to climb up onto the blocks. I lower my goggles around my eyes. The block is metal with a grippy covering, and I feel the rubber surface under my feet.

"On your marks," the announcer says. "Get set," he continues, and we all crouch forward in unison. Then the starting beep resounds from the speaker, and I push off my block and into the water, and I'm not thinking about anything at all. The crowd is screaming. And I'm remembering what Coach said about efficiency and beauty. It's silly, but I imagine myself as an actual butterfly, skimming close to the surface of the water. I've seen truly elegant butterfly strokes, and I aim for that: my whole body undulating in an elegant wavelike motion, my head leading and hips following. I finish each stroke by dragging my thumbs along my thighs. When I come up for air, I only lift my head as much as I need to, my chin still in the water. And instead of kicking hard—causing splashing—

I think more about kicking with power. Then I'm at the end of the pool and I take a deep breath and do an open turn, pushing myself off the wall with both legs. That's when it happens. My goggles fill with water. My eyes are stinging. Should I stop and adjust? I can't, though, I'll be disqualified, and it'll waste even more time. I just go. I just go even though everything's blurry. But I'm efficient, at least. And the delay has made me mad. So mad. I put the anger to good use: I swim so hard, I ignore the ache in my lungs and the chlorine in my eyes. I am *all* swimmer. When I come up for air, I hear Matt; he must have positioned himself right by the edge of the pool, because it's his voice that I hear yelling, ever so clearly, because he knows it'll matter to me: "Fourth, Em!"

Fourth isn't bad. It's not fifth and it's not sixth, and it's pretty damn close to third. I am all technique now. I'm not even checking on who's in front of me or behind me, which Coach says I waste valuable energy doing. Then I slap the wall and it's over and I heave myself out of the pool, my eyes stinging.

I yank the goggles off and water gushes down my face.

My teammates are cheering for me like they never have before. Coach is yelling things and I can barely understand what she's saying.

I came in third.

"Yeah, Chen-'chez! Yeah, Chen-'chez!" Coach is screaming. "For once you did exactly as I said to, and it paid off!"

Matt comes over to me and hugs me, and it's such a familiar and wonderful feeling. "That was awesome-sauce *and* awesome-nuggets!" he yells.

I only wish Mom could see this. She's the one who always made me swim because she wanted her girls to be strong.

Then I hear a familiar voice behind me saying, "Emmmmm! Get over here, girl!"

It's Heather. She throws her arms around me, in my wet suit and all, even though she's wearing quite possibly the most stylin' outfit Green Valley will ever see.

"You were amazing!" she says.

We regard each other. She looks like she's had an entire makeover—she has blunt bangs and her hair is cropped to her chin, and she's got her makeup on all nice—but she's still the same old Heth.

I hug her back. The sight of her, and the way she's looking at me: It's true what they say about treating yourself the way a friend would. She's clearly so damn happy to see me that I wish I could look at myself that way every time I look in the mirror.

The minute Heather breathes in I know she's about to say something, address the awkwardness that's been blooming between us all summer.

"I was really stupid," she says.

"No," I say. "I should have just interrupted you and said what I needed to. You're my best friend."

Then we're laughing and we're sort of crying and we're hugging. Matt joins us, too, and for a good several minutes, it's just like last summer, and the summers before that.

We all dry off and change out of our suits, then get overpriced pizza from the middle schooler selling it at the clubhouse. Proceeds benefit the swim team, and Matt asks if it's okay to pay a little less, since, you know, we *are* the swim team, and the kid looks confused, and Matt says sorry and ends up giving him a tip of sorts because he feels bad for even bringing it up.

Heather and I talk about everything: her time in London, how it wasn't until she got on the plane that she realized those girls weren't really her friends, and they're probably not going to stay in touch forever like they said they would. How drinking isn't as fun as she thought.

So I guess now we're in an even better place than we were before she left.

And I update her about everything: about Mom, about Tessa, and everything that happened with Mrs. G—or I try to, anyway. It's not easy conveying everything to her about this woman she's never met.

But it's Heather, and that in itself is a comfort. There aren't that many people I can be truly myself with. If something or someone is important to me, then that something or someone is important to Heather. And you can't say that about many people, can you? She listens, and I mean really listens, and it occurs to me that, amazingly, a lot of people have been listening to me very well in the past week. I only hope I'm returning the favor.

Then Heather is off, needing to help her parents with some last-effort vacation Bible school type thing, and now it's just Matt, with three sixth-place ribbons and two fifth-place ribbons, because he is the type of person to swim as many events as he's asked.

"So, Em, I guess you did it," he says.

"I did it, but I'm never doing that event again."

He laughs. "Well, you did more than that, right? Like you basically proved to yourself that you can do well in something you hate. And you did something for the team. You're not the selfish jerk Tessa thinks you are after all."

I look at him. His eyes are so blue, bluer than they've ever been. And he's got this look on his face, so content. He's always been like that, I realize, happy with just the littlest things. The guy gets excited about a new leaf on my money plant, about the way Cheez-Its taste better when they've been left in the sun ("like they're fresh baked!"), about how quickly clouds move and change before a storm.

For a second I picture what it would be like to kiss him, and even the thought sends a zing down my spine.

"Where's Zoey?"

Matt takes a long time to answer, looking down at our paper plates speckled with pizza grease. Then he says, "We're kind of, um. We're taking a break."

My heart flip-flops in my chest. I want to ask him so many questions, like who broke up with who, and are they going to talk again to figure out if it's a break for good, or what.

But I say, "Sorry to hear it," because that's the thing to say.

"Thanks," he says. Without fully looking at me, he adds, "I'll always like her, as a person. Just, I think maybe we're too similar."

I nod. "I can see that."

Then he looks at me, and it's almost like he's trying to figure me out. "Anyway," he says, "we don't need to talk about that anymore."

"Okay," I say. We both just look out at the pool, at the team parents picking things up after the meet and the last stragglers packing their gym bags. And then I turn to Matt and ask, "Can I get a ride?"

CHAPTER 15

IT TAKES TEN MINUTES to drive from the pool to the hospital. Matt takes fourteen. He doesn't speed while I sit there saying, "Hurry hurry hurry." Nor when I turn up the music and yell over it that the whole point of having a Jeep is driving around with the top down and the wind in your hair, and that I can hardly call this wind.

I make it just on time, or rather, I make it just as they've finished introducing Tessa, rattling off from the list of accomplishments that I've already heard about all my life, so I haven't missed much.

Steve has a front-row seat, a big bouquet wrapped in cellophane on his lap. Which I'm pretty sure is bad for the environment, and besides, this isn't, like, a ballet recital or something. I've come empty-handed, but at least I'm here.

As we're sitting there, I wonder what it'd be like to sit there with Matt as my boyfriend and not just as my friend. In some ways it doesn't feel that different. It feels like it's always felt:

like I'm sitting with someone who knows me, who sees me, who I can depend on for basically anything. That, plus a little something more.

Tessa walks up to the front, all megawatt lip-glossed smile, black blazer, perfect hair. Then her eyes land on mine and get all big. For a split second I'm wondering if I made a mistake by coming here without a heads-up. Then her face eases back into its composed, professional, I-am-a-badass expression. Her first slide goes up: "Fast, Not Furious: Improving the Patient Experience in Emergency Rooms." She begins. When she speaks, she has complete command over the room, like she's been preparing for this all her life. We learn about what hospitals can do to provide basic needs for those in waiting rooms, since it's not like those patients were prepared to be there. We learn about several methods for shortening wait times and the overall visits, for improving admission rates and crowding.

Matt and I sit through the other presentations, which are pretty good but not nearly as poised. Afterward, we go up front to congratulate Tessa.

"You killed it!" I say. "Seriously. You were amazing."

Tessa looks from me to Matt, unsure what to make of not only me being there, but Matt, too.

Steve is all, "What's up, Ziegler?"

"Want to go to Sharky's?" says Tessa.

As Matt and Steve both say yes, Tessa says, "I was talking to Emily."

It's been a while since just Tessa and I hung out together, doing something that our parents didn't force on us. At Sharky's, we get chicken tenders with honey mustard and share a plate of fries, and it's almost like we're friends, sitting with the junk food and ketchup between us.

Then she sits back, and I talk, about everything. I've got all the bullet points in my Notes app: How it must not have been easy for her this summer, taking everything on by herself. How I really didn't mean to hurt her, how I was quite possibly a coward for running away. And I'm sure it's hard for Tessa to understand, being the golden child and all, but it's not like everyone at home has been particularly encouraging to me this summer. She has to be able to see that.

"I guess, mostly I was pissed that you weren't around as much. Or if you were, it didn't feel like we were in it together. We could've talked more, helped each other," she says.

I didn't see it before. I just figured Tessa wanted to handle everything by herself, and I guess she assumed I wanted no part of it. But she's right. We didn't have to deal with it alone.

"But maybe part of that was I wasn't asking for your help," Tessa continues. "You're capable of more than I thought—you took care of Mrs. G all summer long."

"Until I nearly got us killed by letting her drive," I say.

"Now, don't go beating yourself up about that."

There's one more chicken tender left, and Tessa cuts it in half, then lets me choose the half I want—which is what our parents used to have us do when we were little.

"Sometimes I wish I could be more like you," she says. And

when I snort, she says, "I'm serious! You really don't give a shit what people think."

"I do, though!" I say. "I just don't obsess over it. And what about you—you're so confident and poised. I mean, geez, running for student council, doing all that public speaking?"

"But I actually have to work really hard to raise my hand in class. You don't see me beforehand, shaking like a leaf, jotting down what I want to say before I say it."

It sounds a lot like what I do to get ready for phone calls. Maybe Tessa and I aren't as different as I think.

Tessa takes a sip of her Coke, then says, "Em, I have to tell you something."

"Shoot," I say, dipping a fry in ketchup.

"I'm not going to be a doctor."

"Wait, what? But it's been your dream, for, like, ever."

"I thought . . . I don't know, I thought I was cut out for this. But then I saw the . . ." She pauses. "It was so awful. I always thought it didn't bother me when I saw blood, and I mean, you know, I'm always so quick . . . but that godawful *smell*." She shudders. "I'm *dying* just thinking about it."

"The smell of . . . ? Or, no, don't tell me." I shove another fry into my mouth. "You can learn to get over that, though, right? I mean, it's been your dream for so long."

She shakes her head. "It was just unbearable. I haven't told anyone this—it was just too embarrassing—but I actually threw up. I had to run to the bathroom in the middle of the lesson! So I was no help at all. And that was just one time. There are going to be other gross things that I can't handle."

She squirts more ketchup on her fries. Tessa's a drizzler; I'm a dipper. "And to be honest, I don't think medical work is really my forte. Like, sure, I can do it—but you know me. I cry at the drop of a hat."

"What do you want to do, then?"

"That's the thing. I just don't know. And it's scary," she says. "The not knowing. The past few years, I just *knew* I was going to go into medicine."

"It *is* scary. But it's like . . . you can either freak out and try to control things, or you can accept that, at the end of the day, things are still going to go how they go, and you can't control everything."

She smiles. "When did you get so wise?"

"I guess I was sort of a glorified housekeeper, but still, I learned a whole lot from my summer gig."

"You really cared about Mrs."—she makes air quotes—"Granary."

"I did."

"So what are you going to do about it?"

The fact that she doesn't say, "So reach out to her," or otherwise tell me what to do, is so refreshing.

I sigh, shove another fry into my mouth. Damn, even mediocre fries are good fries. Is there such a thing as bad fries?

"I don't know," I say. "I guess if I call her, the worst that happens is she has a total meltdown and yells at me, and I guess I've already been through that." I shudder. "I kind of don't want to again, though."

Tessa smiles. "Or you could just show up when she least

expects you to, like you did for me. It's hard to stay mad at someone who does that."

ello

Mom's days of isolation come to an end, and the following Monday the four of us head to the hospital for a meeting with Dr. Kim. She has us follow her into her office instead of just talking to us in an examination room like usual, and for a second I'm worried. Why go into her office if the news is good?

Mom goes in first, head held high. Dad's face is sober and drawn. Tessa files in after him, then me.

"The RAI treatment went well," says Dr. Kim in her quiet, competent way.

Dad says, "Oh," and I see him visibly relax: his shoulders drop and his face unclenches. "Thank God, thank God."

Dr. Kim puts a hand on Dad's arm. "So you can all rest easy now."

"Can she . . . ," Dad begins, and his voice is all shaky and quiet. "Can she eat anything . . . she wants to . . . now?" He's taking his time in between words, and his voice comes out high and strange.

"Oh yes," Dr. Kim says, forcing a laugh. I can tell that she's trying to help Dad feel at ease. "She can eat whatever she wants, although for a little while she might not want to eat anything too hard or crunchy. More importantly, you can all eat together. It's looking very, very good."

After Dr. Kim updates us about medicine and more

appointments and then leaves, Dad looks at the three of us and his face does this weird thing where it tightens up and crumples. Then he just starts sobbing. I've never seen him cry before. I'm not sure how to comfort him or if he even wants that. I reach over and pat his arm. Then he opens his arms to all three of us: Mom and me and Tessa. His hands are all wet from his tears. We get in there, one big snot-fest. Even Mom knows better than to tell us not to cry.

"Let's celebrate," Dad says, after he recovers. "Where should we eat?"

The man has been hungry all summer, is what I think. He ought to get fattened up. He's just as skinny as Mom these days.

We treat ourselves to sandwiches and lemonade and waffle fries from Chick-fil-A right next door. Between that and Sharky's, I've been eating a lot of fried chicken recently, but this *is* the South.

For once, we're not talking about Mom's illness, or Tessa's internship, or my incompetence. We're all eating the same thing and enjoying it, and something about that is so helpful. I haven't seen Dad eat so much and I am relieved to see it. He takes waffle fry after waffle fry until they're all gone.

llo

At the White Moose, I pick the best stationery I can find. It's the classiest and it's also the Mrs. G-est: thick, cream-colored paper with a big looping navy *E* at the top, so Southern it almost makes me roll my eyes, except that it really is classy.

With my favorite black gel pen, trying to make my messy handwriting as neat as possible, I write:

Dear Mrs. G,

Well, first of all, I miss you.

I try to remember Mrs. G's rules for writing a card. This wouldn't be a thank-you card, although I could have a bit of that. . . . I guess it's more of a checking-in card.

How are you doing? I write.

Mrs. G said you should always ask how the other person is doing right away. She would appreciate it.

I know how early-summer-Mrs. G would have responded: "I'm old, Emily, how do you think I'm doing!" but with a smile. Later-summer-Mrs. G might have been sarcastic about it, or chosen not to respond at all.

My memories of our time together are sweet.
I never meant to betray you. You have to know that I felt gutted. I wanted to help—but then it seemed to get to the point where keeping it a secret was no longer helping you. After the car accident, I was afraid. You said that fears are meant to be exposed, not hidden—that hiding them makes them scarier. Well, maybe I should have told you then how afraid I was. Maybe then you would understand.
I hope that you're doing okay. I'm writing to say I'm sorry, and to ask for your forgiveness. Even though

I still stand by my decision, maybe it could have been done in a smoother way.

I start to write *Love* but I don't want her to think I'm trying to emotionally manipulate her in any way. So I sign off with *Sincerely.* On the back, I draw a picture of two tall glasses of lemonade with perfectly square ice cubes.

I mail it to her, because even though I could drop it off, she was always like a kid getting the mail. Waiting takes forever. A few days pass, long enough certainly that she would have received the letter. Then even more days pass—so long that, even if she hasn't had time yet to craft a reply, she would have texted to at least confirm receipt. Then another day passes and I still haven't heard anything.

A week passes.

Why did I think that Mrs. G, who didn't respond to my email, would respond to a handwritten letter? There are many reasons. Technology wasn't her strong suit, so maybe she never even saw my email. Email, you can ignore, but *mail*-mail feels serious. You can't just ignore a piece of paper that someone wrote on with their bare hand.

Am I desperate? Is it absolutely embarrassing that I've written to my former employer, received no response, and now feel the need to show up on her doorstep?

Probably.

But I'm going to do it anyway.

Riding my bike up Rock Road, I'm reminded of the first time I went to her house. How I'd been expecting someone fragile, someone who would need me physically. It ended up being the other way around: I needed her, and her house became the place I looked forward to every week.

I'm not expecting an apology. I'm not expecting much at all. She may even snap at me, or yell. But this time, I've decided, I won't freak out if she does. I'll be the bigger person.

The first time I came here, and every time afterward, I paid careful attention to what I wore, how I presented myself, because those were things that mattered to Mrs. G. This time is no different. I'm wearing a jumpsuit with nice sandals, and I've thrown my damp hair up into a bun on the top of my head. I always try to convince myself that having wet hair outside helps to keep me somewhat cool. I walk my bike up to the front of the house, see the familiar weeping willows, the little fairy house key safe.

I stand there on the front step, and it feels like it's been ages since I've rung the bell. I've only rung it once before, after all. I'm simultaneously dreading seeing her and waiting in anticipation for the rush of cool air that I know is coming.

Then the door opens, but it's not Mrs. G who answers it. It's a young woman, older than me, but not by much, and the first thing I notice is that she has hot pink streaks in her shoulder-length hair. It's cool. The second thing is that she's wearing cleaning gloves. The third thing I notice is that she looks exhausted.

"Hi," I say. "Is, uh . . . sorry to bug you—is Mrs. G, I mean

Mrs. Granucci, around? I'm Emily. I was her companion? Over the summer?"

Saying it like that, I realize how weird it is that I want to see her so badly. We've only known each other a single summer. And I was *paid* to hang out with her. But when you've only lived sixteen years, a summer can be a very long time.

Something in the girl's eyes changes. "Oh yeah, I know who you are. I'm Mara. One of her granddaughters. She told us all about you, but I thought she would've said goodbye."

"Goodbye?"

Mara nods. "Mom took her on the plane yesterday. Dad and I are just here cleaning up. Dad went to the store to get more cleaning supplies, but he should be back any minute."

My face must still be registering confusion, because then she says, "She's moving to California?"

"California?" I repeat. I sound dumb, or like a robot, or both, only capable of repeating the last words of her sentences back to her. But of course. California is where Robbie lives.

"Things are kind of crazy right now, as you can see," Mara says. Behind her are stacks of moving boxes, and some of Mrs. G's pieces of art, encased in Bubble Wrap.

I want to ask her if Mrs. G got my letter, and if she'll ever be back to visit, and if she'll be living with family or in some sort of assisted living, and what the doctor said. But Mara is so completely wiped that I'm hesitant to take more of her time. I look past her and into the house. The hardwood has been cleaned so much it gleams, and without the grand blue-and-red Oriental rug, it looks especially bare.

The curtains have been taken down and George is nowhere in sight.

"It must look pretty different from when you used to come," Mara says.

It's weird hearing about it in the past tense already, as if it were ages ago that I worked here. When really it was as recent as a few weeks ago.

When I don't say anything, she says, "Do you want to come in?"

I shake my head. I'd rather not see it in its current state. "Thanks. I'll get going." Saying it, though, I feel like my heart is folding in on itself. All I can think is that she left without saying goodbye. Was she so upset with me that she couldn't even do that?

Mara says, "You have her cell, right? She's still using that same phone. And she's moving in with us, so it's not like she'll be at some sterile depressing place for old fogies."

Old fogies. At that, I feel my eyes fill. For someone who's generally opposed to crying, I sure have been doing a lot of it recently.

"Hey," says Mara. "We're really grateful to you, for, you know, telling us about it. And maybe she's not acting like she is right now, but I bet she really is, too."

⁓ееҩ⁓

Back at home, I'm about to go up to my room when Dad calls from the kitchen. "Rillo? A couple things came for you in the mail."

The first one is a loud, psychedelic postcard: a gray-striped cat with a speech bubble that reads *Purrrr-ty time is meow! Be there or be square!* It's for Jayson Applebee's end-of-summer party, which is tonight. He's already gotten the word out on Instagram, but must have sent these to try to hype everyone up. I wonder if Heather will want to go, or if she's had enough partying this summer.

The second one is a big package, although I haven't ordered anything online—that I can remember, at least. Then I see that the label on the envelope has a bouquet of lavender in the corner and my name is written in her elegant, sloping hand: *Miss Emily Chen-Sanchez.* Mrs. G would take any opportunity to call a teenager "Miss." The return address is California, Mrs. Leila Granucci.

Tessa always opens things carefully, even Amazon packages, keeping the envelope intact, tearing only on the perforated line. But usually I rip straight into things, not minding if the envelope gets all shredded up. This, though, I open slowly, with reverence.

There are two cloth bags inside, with drawstrings.

Dad is looking at them with curiosity. "Shoes?" he says.

"Shoes," I say.

And then, because Dad and I have come a long way, but I still know he'd be miffed at secondhand shoes, I run upstairs before he can ask any more. I want my own private moment with these.

Up in my room, I close the door, then take each shoe from the bag, feeling the soft leather under my fingers. They're exactly as I remembered. I take them out and slide my feet into them. They look and feel wonderful. I walk around my room, and suddenly I'm back in her house: the marble kitchen island, the cello music, the air as cool as a grocery store. Mrs. G laughing with her head thrown back, asking if I want any more buttered toast with smoked salmon.

Then I slide my hand back into the package. I'm not expecting anything—the shoes are more than enough—but still, I'm hopeful. And sure enough, there's a note, her writing all crammed onto the back and front of cream-colored card stock with a big block *G* at the top. It's like she didn't think she was going to write so much—the small, slanted cursive letters get even smaller toward the end.

Dear E,

Well, first things first: I hope your mama is doing well, and that you are, too. I received your absolutely fabulous, classy letter. Things changed so quickly that I didn't have the time to fashion a reply that would do it justice. But I have found the time now.

As you know, your glamorous (ex) employer is not only senile, but also very stubborn. During and after the five-hour flight (during which I imbibed, quite cheerfully given the circumstances, I think, a Negroni), I had quite a bit of time to mull over things. Oh, sure, I brought a book along, and even the iPad (that dreaded rectangular device) with movies pre-downloaded by the other E in my life (you know him as Ezra). But it's tough to concentrate when your whole life is changing, when things are out of control. And I know, you're in high school and pretty soon your life will change as well, when you go to college, but even you must understand that things are different when you're my age (going on thirty-five) and my condition (still sharp as a tack, when I'm in my right mind).

So I spent the trip thinking and mulling. I want to use the old brain while I still can.

I owe you an apology. We Granuccis are passionate people—you know that—and yet, that's no excuse for my asking of you what I did. So in that vein, I'd like to apologize for asking too much of you, for putting so much weight on you. It was not your job to deceive people. I think of you as my friend, very much so; at the same time, you were my young employee and I your employer, so what I asked of you was beyond reproach. Worse, was how I reacted afterward. I was hurt, I was stressed, I was afraid. Please forgive me for not only asking that of you, but for how I treated you afterward. You did not betray me—you were trying to help me. I see that now.

I can't promise anything about the future. But you know that already.

You asked, Emily, how I was feeling about it all. The answer is: I am afraid. And I am ready.

And so are you. I have you to thank for an absolutely incredible summer. An incredible summer, truly.

I want you to know this about yourself: you are strong. When it comes time to apply for college, ask me for that letter!

Mrs. G

In our living room, I stick my feet up on the coffee table, and Mom flinches, but then I see her decide not to say anything. She smiles at me instead, puts her arm on my shoulder.

And then I smile, grateful that she didn't say anything, and take my feet down. It won't always be like this, I know, but still, it's a start.

"Well, I better get going," I say.

"Are you wearing that to the party?" Mom asks, and before I can answer, she says, "It's very cool."

I look down at my paint-splattered jeans, my old T-shirt, and laugh.

Then I run upstairs to change into a floral dress, and put on some lipstick. It's my favorite shade these days, one that Heather helped me find: a bright pink that works so well with both of our complexions. I remember how Mrs. G used to say that lipstick could change your life. I hope it does mine.

I put on my sneakers—I don't want to seem like I'm trying *too* hard—and get on my bike and ride to Matt's.

⌒ℓℓℓ⌒

He's in no shape for a party. He's watering the flower baskets wearing a black-and-yellow-striped shirt that I've told him before resembles a bumblebee, to which he's responded, "Great. Bumblebees are cute."

There's dirt all over the bottom of his jeans and some on his arms. He's wearing his Great Smoky Mountains National Park cap, and he's sweating through it. There's even a tuft of grass sticking out from a hole in his sneakers. So he's no dreamboat—he's definitely not a polished classical musician—but he's Matt, which is even better.

When he sees me, he drops the hose.

"Hi," I say. "I came to take you to the party."

He raises his eyebrows at me, and then he smiles. "Wait up," he says. "You, Emily Chen-'chez, are inviting *me*, Matt Ziegler, to a party?"

I take a deep breath. I've written so many scripts this summer: to Mrs. G, to Robbie, to Tessa. But with Matt all I need to do is show up and say what's on my mind. That's all I've ever needed to do. It all comes spilling out.

"Look," I say. "I . . . I can't tell you what to do. And obviously you don't have to listen to me. But you've been listening to me all summer, and you give damn good advice, so maybe—maybe I can try giving you advice for once."

He's listening, all right. He's got those eyes fixed on me, partly curious, partly amused.

"I don't know if I'm . . . girlfriend material, or whatever. Actually, whatever, I know that I'm not. I know that, like, Zoey's sweet, and she likes everything you like, and when it comes to gardening I'm no help at all, and I hardly understand any of the stuff you do with molecules and . . . whatever else you do—but I sure as hell want to give it a try. And I know I'm always getting lost in my phone instead of really giving you all my attention. But if you could give me another chance, I know we could be good for each other. I've been a complete idiot this summer."

Matt takes his cap off and dabs at his forehead with his wrist, leaving a dash of dirt there. "So what you're saying is, you want to go to this party with me," he says.

"Unless . . . you have a date already?"

He reaches toward me and takes my hands in his. And for once, I don't need to say anything at all.

ACKNOWLEDGMENTS

A whole swimming pool of thanks to my editor, Phoebe Yeh, who had faith in this project since the beginning. Thank you for pushing me off the diving board. To my agents, Chad Luibl and Roma Panganiban: Thank you for your insightful questions and suggestions, for teaching me to write a love triangle, and for finding Emily laugh-out-loud funny.

I am grateful to these friends, whose expertise in their fields was invaluable: Amanda Bird, for her wealth of knowledge about dementia; Kate Henricks, whose precise language made swim practices feel real; and Lauren Maxam, for fact-checking the medical procedures. Many thanks also to Heather Carey—who makes gorgeous pastel drawings—for educating me as I drafted Emily's art scenes.

Thank you, Mom and Dad, for reading the Mandarin and Spanish in this book, respectively. While she didn't get a chance to read this, I think Mom knew that all the mothers I write are inspired by her—especially this one. To El, my best friend, I'm grateful that we have a better relationship than Emily and Tessa. Lastly, I am grateful to Pete and Libby, who help me so much by being my sounding boards, and by simply being themselves.

READY FOR YOUR NEXT READ?

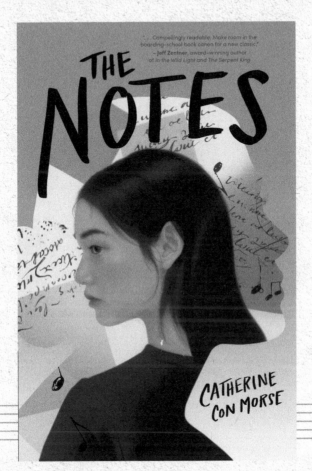

Catherine Con Morse delivers a moving coming-of-age story about ambition, first love, and self-discovery amid the adolescent and academic pressures at a performing arts boarding school. And then there are those mysterious notes. . . .

WE SAW DR. LI BEFORE WE MET HER. IN THE DINING HALL, she wore knee-high black leather boots and sunglasses so large they practically rested on her cheekbones. It was early September in Green Valley, South Carolina, but even our winters didn't call for boots like that. Jenny and I watched as she nudged a tray along with just the tips of her fingers, as if wanting to touch it as little as possible. She stood on the colored tiles in front of the green beans spotted with bacon, the mashed potatoes and their vat of gravy, the dripping kernels of sweet corn. In her black sheath dress, a black leather tote on her shoulder, she looked out of place, her outfit more fit for an office than a school. Somehow, already, we could sense her disappointment. Maybe it was the way she had walked into the room, the sigh when she entered, the pause in front of the trays before resigning herself to take one and approach the counter. *Well, if this is what I have to work with,* she seemed to be saying, *so be it.*

"Whatchoo want, baby?" said Barbara, the dining hall manager. She wore plum-colored lipstick and spoke to Dr. Li in the same way she did us, her *whatchoo* like a sneeze, then a dip into the long, low *want,* ending in a high, soft *baby* that nearly sounded like *babe.*

Dr. Li did not seem the least bit taken aback about being called *baby.* She said, "I'll have some of this, please," and pointed to the wet, dark green mass that we knew to be canned spinach. Her voice was cool and quiet. When she spoke, it was nearly accentless, unlike my mother, who spoke English fluently but not without some remnant of her native Mandarin.

The spinach was slapped onto the plate. "What else?" said Barbara.

"That's it," said Dr. Li.

"That be all?"

"Yes, thank you."

The plate, a bright orange plastic disk, was passed over, and Dr. Li set it on her tray. One hip cocked, one black boot pointed toward the tables, she carried her tray to the salad bar, her shoes clicking on the tile. She stood over the soup and lifted the ladle, inspecting the contents of the tureen. Chicken noodle.

At a table by the windows, Dr. Li sat down and took her sunglasses off. I saw that her eyes were dark and her skin pale and smooth. Her long hair, set loose to the humidity, had begun to curl just the slightest bit at the ends. She ate the spinach quickly but neatly, as if wanting to get it over with. Of course, it hardly needed chewing and, in fact, was a weekly offering we all avoided. It would be reheated and re-salted for a casserole on Saturday, when the dining staff took the leftovers from the week and baked them twice between sheets of flour. Dr. Li didn't know yet that meals were never this calm at Greenwood, but today—three days before the fall semester—was an exception. When school was in session, dinners were frenzied affairs, lunches worse. We simultaneously needed to eat everything and say everything. Now it was well past lunchtime, nearly two-thirty. The dining hall was empty.

Just then, Jenny waved a hand in front of my face. "Earth to Claire," she said. She adjusted her glasses and bent her head toward mine—our faces so close that her light brown ponytail brushed my shoulder—and looked where I was looking.

"I wonder if the Asian Student Society will ask her to sponsor them," said Jenny.

"They don't already have a sponsor?" I asked.

"Somehow, they function without one, since there are no Asian teachers. Well, there *were* none, anyway."

"Where did you hear that?" I asked.

"Everyone knows. Where have you been? Living under a *Rachmaninoff*?"

I groaned.

It annoyed me that even Jenny knew more about the Asian Student Society than I did, given that I was Asian and she wasn't. I had applied to the Society last spring and been rejected. I was pretty sure I knew exactly why, could trace my failure back to first-year Halloween. I'd dressed up as Holly Golightly from *Breakfast at Tiffany's*, a movie that I later found out was on the Society's list of boycotted films. Of course it was: Mr. Yunioshi was a bucktoothed, bumbling Japanese caricature played by a white actor. I cringed at the memory of my elbow-length gloves and fake cigarette holder.

"If you know so much," I asked Jenny now, "tell me this. Why was Dr. Li wearing sunglasses inside?"

Jenny considered, then said, "She's either drunk or stoned. All the really good ones have to get stoned because of stress."

When Jenny said things like that, I wanted to be more like her. She always sounded like she knew exactly what she was talking about, even when she didn't—maybe even more so when she didn't—and I envied that.

Dr. Li headed back to the counter. She didn't look stoned to me. "Excuse me," we heard her say. "Do you have any bread?"

"There you go, babe," said Barbara, and held out a dinner roll with her tongs. "You'll love it here," she continued. "These students are like my own kids. Pretty soon you be feeling that way, too."

"That's lovely," said Dr. Li. But it sounded like she thought the opposite was true.

♩♫

Every fall, we attended the Annual Faculty-Student Assembly in Elizabeth D. Halpern Recital Hall. This year's was my third. Dr. Hamilton, who presided over the assembly, had studied musicology at Penn decades ago. He had been making "introductory remarks" for what felt like half an hour. "And that is why, young artists," he was saying, "you must stay the course, despite how often we artists are marginalized."